MOTHER

Family Values Trilogy

Book 1

Patrick Logan

Books by Patrick Logan

The Haunted Series

Book 1: Shallow Graves
Book 2: The Seventh Ward
Book 3: Seaforth Prison
Book 4: Scarsdale Crematorium
Book 5: Sacred Heart Orphanage

Insatiable Series

Book 1: Skin
Book 2: Crackers
Book 3: Flesh
Book 4: Parasite
Book 5: Stitches

Family Values Trilogy

Witch (Prequel Novella)
Mother
Father
Daughter

Sign-up to my no spam newsletter at www.PTLBooks.com to stay up to date and receive *FREE* books!

Prologue (Conception)

The girl stared at her reflection in the mirror as the steam from the shower billowed about her soft, pale skin.

She brought a hand to her chest and gently lifted her right breast, assessing the weight of it before allowing gravity to bring it back to its resting place.

It seemed bigger today.

No, not bigger—bigger is the wrong word for it. More full. Definitely more full.

Her nipples, hard despite the moist, warm air that engulfed her body, looked a little darker than usual as well, but she chalked this up to her imagination.

This can't be happening… not yet.

She felt like crying.

While most girls her age might have confused what was happening to her body as part of the transition into adulthood, she knew that *this* was not *that*. Her first blood had come and gone many months earlier—young for her age—and she was smart enough to know that the changes her body was undergoing were happening far too quickly to be puberty-related.

No, *this* was something else entirely.

A deep frown, one that wrinkled the smooth skin around the corners of her lips and caused a rash of unsightly dimples to riddle her round chin, made its way onto her face. The desire to cry, to simply drop to her knees and sob, was nearly overwhelming, and it took all of her willpower to resist.

This, too—controlling her emotions—would become more difficult as her body underwent even further changes. Hormonal changes.

The girl turned sideways, her brow furrowing as she scrutinized her profile in the foggy mirror.

It can't be. Please, don't let it be true.

Her hands moved from her breasts to the spot just below her navel, to the slight but perceptible pouch of skin perfectly situated above the muscles that descended into a '*v*' between her legs.

It couldn't be—but it *was*.

No.

If it hadn't been for her breath catching in her throat, the word would have escaped her lips in a moan. And that would have had disastrous consequences.

As she watched, her reflection began to blur, the edges becoming hazy like headlights cutting through thick fog. It was the condensation from the shower that gave her outline an ethereal quality, which was only fitting as her situation was anything *but* real.

A sound from just outside the bathroom door startled her, and she paused.

"Sweets?"

A split-second hesitation was all it took; such a small, seemingly inconsequential act, but it carried with it severe repercussions. The girl swiveled on her bare heels, spinning so quickly toward the half-open bathroom door that she narrowly avoided pirouetting into the corner of the bone-white vanity. Yet despite her spin, she had acted too slowly.

The neatly folded load of laundry that lay artfully across her mother's arms—a pile of colorful socks, graphic t-shirts, and a couple pairs of jeans—fell to the ground in what seemed like slow motion.

The girl slammed her palm against the bathroom door, closing it with a loud bang.

"Mother!" she shouted, hoping that the anger in her voice usurped the fear—the embarrassment. "Mother! Privacy, please!"

After wiping the tears from her eyes, the girl pressed both hands against the back of the door as if she were preparing for her own 'Here's Johnny' moment.

Or maybe she was waiting for that dreaded knock, or the sound of her mother's patronizing voice.

But there was no sound from her room, which, in a way, was worse.

Say something!

The girl pressed her ear against the door between her hands. Had Mother not seen? She fought the urge to look down at herself.

Is it not that noticeable?

She had slammed the door closed so quickly that she hadn't seen her mother's eyes... instead, she had been distracted by the falling laundry, the striped candy cane socks that had done a little dance as they tumbled to the carpeted bedroom floor.

Could she have been distracted by the laundry as well?

Her mind raced.

Say something! Anything!

Her hopes were dashed when she finally heard her mother's voice, her words coming out low and slow, the universal pitch that mothers used to let their children know that they were serious, that they meant *business*.

Oh, the woman had seen alright—she missed nothing.

"Open the door," her mother ordered.

The girl pressed her forehead against the back of the door and squeezed her eyes shut.

Fuck! How could I have been so stupid?

Tears somehow managed to leak from between her closed lids and made wet tracks down both of her round cheeks. The liquid felt oddly cool on her skin, cutting through the steam that had coated the mirror and saturated the air in what felt like a thick paste. The humid air had begun to settle on all surfaces— including herself.

Hot, sticky, uncomfortable air.

Her heart rate soared.

Please—just leave.

"Open the door."

Please.

When her mother spoke a third time, her voice was different. It wasn't calm and demanding, but tight, bordering on hysterical. The sudden change in pitch shocked the girl into opening her eyes.

"You can't have it! You need to get it out!"

'You need to get it out.' She could barely believe that her mother had uttered those words. *It. Get* it *out.*

The girl felt as if her soul had been crushed, as if all of her bones had suddenly been turned to dust and she was but a pile of skin lying on the wet bathroom floor.

"It's not—"

—what you think, was what she wanted to say, but her mother cut her off.

"You're pregnant," the woman hissed.

Hearing those words out loud, even though she'd known them to be true long before her mother had come into her room carrying her stupid fucking striped socks, somehow made it all real.

I'm just bloated, Mom, she wanted to say. *It's just my stupid period, Mom.*

But the only words that she could manage were, "I'm sorry."

And with the utterance of those two words, so very benign on their own, but when combined carried so much weight, tears began to fall in a deluge.

How did this happen?

Her body hitched against the back of the door.

I'm too young for this! Please, I don't want this!

There was a shuffling sound on the other side of the door, and somewhere in the dark recesses of her mind, she realized that her mother was no longer waiting on the other side.

A baby—I can't have a baby.

The idea was so foreign, so *fucking* bizarre, that despite her sobs, the notion of being pregnant, of having a living, breathing—*was it breathing yet?*—being inside of her was nearly incomprehensible.

And that was all it was: an idea.

A scraping sound, like nails on a chalkboard, brought her back into reality. The girl pulled her forehead away from the door and aggressively wiped the tears away from her eyes with the blade of her hand.

The mixture of emotions roiling inside of her, accelerated by hormonal changes like kerosene fueling flames, came crashing down at once.

And this time, so did her body.

The girl collapsed to the damp floor, her legs crumpling uselessly beneath her.

Her final resting place was just a few inches from the wire coat hanger that her mother had forced through the small opening beneath the door.

"No!" the girl cried.

Not this. This can't be the way.

But despite her pleas, her mother was having none of it.

"Hurry! *He* can't know about this!"

The next word that came out of the girl's mouth was tortured by mucous, rendering it barely intelligible.

"Please!"

But despite the desperation in her voice, Mother was having none of it.

"Hurry!"

*   *   *

There was blood in the bathtub. Not as much as she would have thought, but enough to tinge the water a pale pink.

The girl was still crying.

"Hush now, we did what was necessary," her mother whispered, her voice oddly detached.

The woman raised the coral sponge and squeezed it on the back of her neck, allowing the water to spill down her back and over her breasts.

The girl watched the water for a moment, her eyes following the lazy rivers of pink fluid as they traced ravines over her naked body.

My blood. I'm being bathed in my blood, she thought briefly, but then instinctively shook her head. *Not my blood—my* baby's *blood. I'm being bathed in my baby's blood.*

The thought drove a shudder up her spine. Mother took this as a cue to turn her head, and their eyes met.

The girl expected sympathy in the woman's dark green eyes, or in the very least a comforting expression. Instead, she saw neither; her mother's eyes, as well as the rest of her heavily lined face, were a hardened mask that lacked any emotion.

"You did the right thing," her mother informed her, much like a teacher instructing a student that they had come up with the correct answer to a math problem.

'Necessary' had become 'right,' and 'we' had become 'you.' These subtleties were not lost on the girl.

After a short pause, her mother unexpectedly reached out and laid a hand on her cheek. The girl, mistaking this as a comforting gesture, instinctively leaned her head into the cupped hand, wanting—*needing*—some sort of justification, some proof that *she* had indeed done the *right* thing, something beyond her mother's empty words.

But the woman's grip tightened, and the gentle caress became a forceful pinch. The girl in the tub sat up, wincing.

"But you must never forget."

The woman's dark green eyes were focused and unblinking.

"A life for a life, sweets."

Mother paused as silent tears began to pour down the girl's face. When these clear streams eventually met the bathwater, they too took on a tainted pink hue.

Despite her daughter's obvious pain, the woman's grip did not lessen.

"A life for a life. You must never forget."

*   *   *

The texture beneath the girl's feet slowly transitioned from soft and wet to hard as the ground changed from mud to asphalt.

Head down, she put one foot in front of the other, moving slowly, methodically, traveling in a straight line to nowhere.

One foot, then the next. One foot, and then the next, as dawn slowly began to creep around her.

At some point during her walk she heard a car approach, only to come to an abrupt stop somewhere off to her right.

Onward she walked.

Then there was a second car, and then a voice.

"Hey! Hey, are you okay?"

Another voice now.

"Look! She's bleeding!"

Something was gently draped over her shoulders—something thick like a blanket, and at long last her legs stopped moving.

"Call the police! Quick, someone call the police!"

The girl curled into the blanket, her broken mind only barely registering the fact that someone had finally picked up her frail body.

Part I – Sow the Seed

Chapter 1

Arielle Reigns stared the goofy-looking doctor straight in the face.

You think you know everything.

The doctor's smile grew even larger, as if mind-reading were one of the many skills listed on the diplomas wrapped in fancy gold frames and hung around the office.

You think *you know everything, but you don't—you don't know about* this.

Arielle glanced over at her husband for support and was surprised to see that he was staring at her, his light brown eyebrows high on his forehead. He had his typical, *'Well, Arielle?'* expression plastered on his handsome face.

She looked away before anger overcame her, and her gaze fell to her hands tucked in her lap. After a deep breath in through her nose, she looked back at the doctor.

"No," she said bluntly. "I will not undergo any tests."

The smile on the doctor's face slid off like ice warming on a windshield. What replaced it was a look somewhere between concern and frustration.

Dr. Barnes reached up and scratched at the stubble on the back of his head. While some men shaved their heads because they liked the way it looked, or maybe because the style required less work, Dr. Barnes shaved his head because most of it had fallen out naturally. And if nature is guiding you in a direction, why fight it? Why *bother* fighting it?

You can't fight nature.

Just try shooting a hurricane or smothering a tsunami.

"Well," the doctor said at last. The jovial lilt that had been in his voice only moments before had vanished like his smile.

Arielle stared expectantly, but the man just continued to scratch. His long, thin fingers and short nails kept moving up and down the back of his head, making a sound like someone repeatedly doing and then undoing Velcro shoes.

The sound irritated her.

Everything about the man irritated her.

"Well, what?"

Out of the corner of her eye, she saw her husband reach out to her, but she preemptively pulled away, all the while keeping her gaze trained on Dr. Barnes.

"Not now, Martin," she said. Then to the doctor, she continued, "Well, Dr. Barnes, can you help us or not?"

For the second time in less than a minute, the doctor seemed at a loss for words, which annoyed Arielle even further. The man had been all talk five minutes ago, asking personal questions—*How long have you been trying? How are your periods? Regular? Are you having sex when you are ovulating?*—but when she put *him* to the question, the man could only stand there gaping… and scratching his balding fucking head, of course.

"Well?"

Dr. Barnes cleared his throat and brought his hands to his lap. Leaning forward, he finally spoke.

"We need to do some tests first before I—"

Arielle shook her head quickly, her shoulder-length blond hair whipping back and forth. Forced to pull strands away from her face, she wished that she had put it up in a ponytail.

"No," she stated firmly. "No tests."

The doctor turned his dark, beady eyes to Martin.

"No," Arielle interrupted, wagging her finger back and forth in front of her. "No, don't do that. Don't look at him. It's not up to him."

The doctor raised a hand defensively.

"Mrs. Reigns, I didn't mean to—"

"Can you help us or not?"

Dr. Barnes shook his head.

"Without performing tests, there isn't much I can do, I'm afraid. I mean, if you wanted to undergo just a *few* tests, we can consider going the in vitro route."

The man was speaking slowly, and it was obvious to both Arielle and Martin that he was choosing his words very carefully.

"No, not in vitro. It's not natural."

The doctor's expression remained neutral.

"Well, I'm going to be frank with you, Mrs. Reigns, at forty-one years of age—"

"Thirty-nine," Arielle corrected him.

The man stared at her for another moment before interlacing his long fingers and continuing.

"At your age, it's going to be difficult to conceive. I can prescribe some iron pills and something else to try to make sure that you are ovulating. But, without doing some tests—which are completely harmless and minimally invasive—my hands are tied."

"No tests," Arielle reiterated.

Martin reached for her again, and this time she let his hand rest on the back of her arm.

"Sweetie, why don't we get some tests done? I'll have my sperm analyzed and you can—"

She pulled away and turned to face him.

"No tests! I said no tests! What's wrong with you?"

The words had come out more forcefully than she had expected, and Martin recoiled. When his shock faded, it was replaced by a sad and confused look.

He doesn't deserve this.

Arielle took another deep breath in through her nose. She had been scared that something like this might happen, that she would lose her cool.

Her thoughts turned briefly to how well Martin had treated her over the past seven years, ever since the day her maternal instincts had switched on, and from then on out, there had been no way to shut them off.

'It's okay, baby,' Martin had told her countless times. 'You are more than enough for me.'

He would always smirk when he said this, letting her know that he was only partly kidding—joking around to try to lighten the tension... the tension that seemed to constrict around her throat like a noose.

No, Martin definitely didn't deserve her outburst. The doctor, on the other hand...

Arielle was about to apologize to Martin—the words were on the tip of her tongue—when Dr. Barnes suddenly chimed in.

"Mrs. Reigns, if you think you would be more comfortable with a female doctor, I have a colleague—"

Arielle turned back to the doctor, her eyes narrowing.

"What the fuck is wrong with you? I said no tests!"

"Woah!" Martin exclaimed, once again reaching for her.

Arielle stood and her husband's hand fell short. Her blood had started to boil, and she was quickly getting to a point from which even deep breathing wouldn't bring her back.

Dr. Barnes seemed relatively unfazed by her escalating outbursts. In fact, he seemed sympathetic.

"Mrs. Reigns…" His eyes were soft, caring.

For some reason, the doctor's complacency seemed to only infuriate Arielle further. She could even feel beads of sweat forming on her forehead.

It was suddenly hot, *too* hot, in the doctor's small office. It was hot and stifling, and she could feel the walls closing in on her.

Arielle was starting to get tunnel vision.

"I understand what you are going through. I think —"

The doctor's words all melded together, fueling her rage.

Just as she was about to explode, Martin stood and wrapped his arms around her. This time she let him hold her.

You understand nothing, Dr. Barnes! I want a baby and you are a useless fucking tit. Fucking drippy-nosed, goofy-eared, bald fucking quack!

Arielle closed her eyes tightly, trying desperately to control her emotions.

Seven years; for seven years I have been trying to conceive. Seven fucking years.

For the next several moments, all Arielle heard was the sound of blood rushing in her ears and her own heavy breathing.

Calm.

After what felt like minutes, but couldn't possibly have been more than twenty seconds, her anger subsided to a dull throb — it receded just enough to allow embarrassment to creep in.

The doctor is just trying to help, she scolded herself. *Just trying to do his job.*

A moment later, she felt Martin's grip on her shoulders relax.

Calm, Arielle; Dr. Barnes is just trying to help.

The doctor reached up and scratched at the stubble at the back of his head again.

"Just one more question, Mrs. Reigns: have you ever been pregnant before?"

Arielle's eyes snapped open and she lunged at Dr. Barnes, her hands balling into tight fists.

Chapter 2

Neither Martin nor Arielle spoke for the first fifteen minutes of the car ride home. Several times, Martin had cleared his throat as if he intended to say something, but he had refrained. For the most part, this was just fine for Arielle. Staring out the window at the trees as they made their way home was just perfectly fine with her. What wasn't fine, however, was what had happened in the doctor's office.

The next time Martin cleared his throat, whatever had previously held his tongue had disappeared. And what came out of his mouth, somewhat predictably, was a joke. Leave it to Martin to joke at a time like this... at any time, regardless of the situation.

It was one of the many reasons she loved him.

"You know, that's a mean right hook you've got there."

Arielle had been staring at the raw knuckles on her right hand when Martin had started to speak, but now she turned to look at him. When their eyes met, he pulled a hand off of the wheel and pretended to cower against the door.

She couldn't help but smirk.

"Please, Masa, no mo'! I can't take it no mo'!"

Arielle tried her best not to laugh, but she lost the battle. A fountain of giggles came out of her in a spurt.

It wasn't that funny, not really, and it might have even been offensive, but she just couldn't help it. The torrid mix of emotions had bubbled over, and now it was impossible to keep them inside.

After nearly a full minute of laughing, she was left gasping for air with tears streaming down her cheeks.

The next time Martin spoke, his voice was more serious, even if the twinkle in his eye remained.

"Seriously Arielle, that was messed up."

Arielle nodded slowly. Of course it was messed up.

"We are lucky that Dr. Barnes is such a—"

Arielle turned to him and opened her mouth to say something, to defend herself, but Martin cut her off.

"Let me finish," he urged.

She closed her mouth.

"We are lucky that Dr. Barnes is such a nice guy. Woodward wouldn't have recommended him if he weren't. *And* he helped them conceive Thomas."

Arielle's thoughts turned to their mutual friends, Officer Tony Woodward and his wife, Charlene. And of course she couldn't help think of their beautiful young boy, Thomas. Thomas, with the golden blond hair and cherub-like cheeks adorned with not two but three dimples.

"I know," Arielle said softly.

She didn't doubt what her husband was saying. And Dr. Barnes seemed like he was actually a nice guy... it was just... just...

"And I'm pretty sure that if it weren't for the fact that both we and Dr. Barnes are friends with the Woodwards, he would be pressing charges by now."

Arielle stared at her husband as he spoke, and despite the condemning nature of his words—this was as aggressive or scolding as the man ever got—she found herself admiring the way he managed to keep his cool even under the most extreme circumstances.

Martin Reigns was undeniably handsome, with a strong jaw adorned with light brown stubble, which was only a shade or two darker than the neatly cropped hair atop his head. There were flecks of gray in the beginnings of his beard and more at his temples. And even though Martin often complained about the gray—*my hair is as white as Charlize Theron's ass*—his hair had just the right amount of it; it had just enough to make him look wiser and not older. Which, in her estimation, not only made him more attractive, but likely helped solidify his spot one of the best real estate brokers in all of South Carolina. A little gray, just enough to show that he had experience, but not enough to suggest that he was too old to compete with the young guns.

"I know it's hard for you, babe."

Martin ran a hand through his hair. It fell back in place, landing exactly the way it had been before. For the hundredth time, Arielle found herself wondering how it did that. With her golden locks, a simple fart in the wind could give her a cowlick for a month.

"I know it's really hard for you, but clearly—*clearly*—blowing up at the doctor is *not* the solution."

Martin made a popping sound with his tongue, reminiscent of the sound her fist had made when it had connected with Dr. Barnes's jaw.

Having completed his speech, Martin finally turned to look at her again. His lips were pressed together with only the corners slightly upturned.

This was as close as Martin got to frowning.

"What do you think?"

Arielle tried not to smile.

I think you are one handsome bastard.

"It *is* hard," she admitted at last. "But I don't want any tests—you know that. I don't... I don't like being prodded, poked, and scraped like some sort of animal before slaughter."

Now it was Martin's turn to laugh, but unlike her giggles, his exclamation was a throaty, bellowing sound that reverberated throughout the cabin.

Arielle frowned.

"No, seriously, Martin. You know how I feel about that."

Martin stopped laughing.

"I've told you before, you're more than enough woman for me."

Arielle felt herself nodding despite herself. For some reason, his words still seemed to soothe her, even though she had heard them many, many times before.

The first time he had said them to her, only about six months after they had started trying, and failing, to conceive, she had been enraged.

'You don't want kids? You don't want to have a child with me?'

But Martin had remained calm during her outburst, and she had soon realized that this was not at all what he'd meant. Martin *did* want a child, she was sure of it. And he wanted one with her. This was just his way of saying, 'If we can't, then *c'est la vie;* I love you, and you are enough to complete me.'

Arielle just wished she could feel the same.

Her eyes drifted back to her throbbing knuckles.

What was *I thinking? Punching a doctor? For what? For suggesting that I take a test? For asking if I had been pregnant before?*

But the answer to that was simple: nothing—she hadn't been thinking at all.

He thinks he knows everything. But he doesn't.

"Imagine we had a girl?"

Arielle's eyes shot up.

"How could one man deal with two women with Floyd Mayweather right hooks?"

Arielle didn't smile, not because she wasn't completely sure who Floyd Mayweather was—she knew enough to get the joke—but because she was immediately preoccupied by the idea of having a girl.

If they had a girl, she would probably have a square jaw like her father, but she would have Arielle's blond hair and green eyes. And hopefully Martin's sense of humor.

"But, seriously, Arielle, why don't we get some tests done? I will stay with you the whole time, and if you feel at all uncomfortable, we can stop immediately."

I feel uncomfortable right now talking about this.

"And I'll get tested too, of course."

Arielle scoffed at this.

"Oh, yeah, easy for you to say. All you have to do is watch some porn and jizz in a cup."

Martin laughed again, this time even louder than before.

"Yeah, they call it Sunday," he added, but Arielle ignored the comment.

"You just jizz in a cup, but I have to be fingered by a stranger. Think about it: a stranger is going to jam his fingers inside me and then use a spoon to scrape my *insides.*"

Martin cringed.

"Jesus, Arielle, that's sick."

"Well?"

"Well, let's say you do get pregnant—you are going to have to be inspected then. You know that, right?"

Arielle nodded.

"Sure. But that's different."

"How is that different?" Martin challenged.

Arielle turned her gaze back to the window before answering. As the question hung in the air, Martin pulled up to the long, winding driveway that led to their large stone house. The sun was still high in the sky, and its rays reflected off the many glass windows, creating a sparkling effect. At nearly three thousand square feet and constructed of bleached gray and white stone, their house was beautiful. But with the sun glinting the way that it was? It was surreal—a sparkling beacon signifying home.

She loved their house and she loved Martin.

But it wasn't enough.

Not for her.

"Because then we would be having a child, Martin," she replied as Martin shifted the car into park. "And I've *always* wanted a child."

Chapter 3

With the shades drawn, it was hot in the bedroom; hot *and* humid. It was so hot and humid, in fact, that Arielle felt her forehead break out into a sheen of sweat.

The fact that her heart was racing wasn't helping anything, but that wasn't related to the heat. At least not directly.

"When's the last time we were home at this hour together, babe?"

Arielle ignored her husband and stepped out of the bathroom. Eyes closed, she reached down and grabbed ahold of either side of her t-shirt and forced it downward. It was Martin's t-shirt, an old cotton V-neck that had worn thin, and even when she pushed it down it barely covered her bare ass. A quick shake of her head and her hair fell in front of her face, and she opened her eyes again. Staring through the strands of blond hair, she saw that Martin was still sitting on the side of the bed, magazine in his lap.

He hadn't noticed her yet.

Arielle gently swayed back and forth as she made her way toward the bed, imaginary music playing in her head, the iconic words of 'Lost Together' by Blue Rodeo driving her deeper into the trance.

"Ari—"

Martin swallowed the rest of the word.

Even through the blond hair that still hung in front of her face, Arielle knew that he had finally noticed her. His hands, which had been fiddling with the knot of his tie, froze in midair.

She took another step toward him and pulled the bottom of the t-shirt up slightly, rubbing it back and forth, giving Martin a brief glance of the inside of her thighs.

This was not her, this was someone else; someone had somehow transported themselves into Arielle and turned her into a sexy nymph.

She wasn't entirely sure what had gotten into her. Maybe she felt guilty about the way she had behaved in the doctor's office — *I've been a bad girl* — or maybe she was rewarding Martin for keeping his cool, for putting up with her outbursts.

Maybe she liked it.

Martin *definitely* liked it.

The man swallowed hard and his hands dropped to his sides as Arielle approached, the dangling knot of his tie long forgotten.

"Where's Arielle and what have you done with my wife?" His words came out hoarse, and Arielle had to resist the urge to giggle.

She was within three feet of him now, and she paused to lift her shirt a little higher, revealing more than just her thighs this time.

Martin's breath was coming out in short bursts, and his obvious arousal added to her own. She felt her nipples harden, and when she twisted the shirt again, the fabric rubbed against them and she gasped.

Martin reached for her — nearly lunged at her — but Arielle hopped backward just in time and his arms fell short.

"Lie down," she instructed, her own throat suddenly parched.

A look of confusion crossed Martin's face, so Arielle repeated the order more forcefully.

Martin nodded and obliged.

Arielle's eyes drifted to his khaki slacks.

Now, lying on his back, his arms spread above his head, his arousal was more than palpable—it was plainly obvious.

The tingling that started as sweat on her forehead spread first to her full breasts, then to between her legs. Soon, her entire body was thrumming, their combined sexual energy charging not just the space between them, but their bodies as well.

Arielle pushed her hands downward, driving the t-shirt nearly to her knees. Then, in one smooth motion, she hoisted it completely off her body, revealing herself in all her naked glory. She gave Martin but a second to take it all in before she leapt onto him.

His hands were on her instantly, first clutching at her sides, then grabbing her ass, her breasts, and finally her face as she lowered her head and kissed him.

Arielle felt the hardness of his cock through his pants, and she rubbed her sex up and down it, gliding her body over the whole length of his shaft. Martin nibbled gently at her lower lip, and then his hands were on her hips, driving her onto him.

After only a few seconds of foreplay, neither of them could take it any longer. Arielle reached back, unzipped his pants, and in an instant Martin slid effortlessly inside her.

Their lovemaking was hungered, fueled by lust and desire, and also by a need.

A need of Arielle to conceive.

When she felt the height of Martin's arousal, she quickly flipped over, pulling him on top of her, driving him deeper inside of her.

"In me," she whispered. "Put a baby in me, Martin."

The man's eyebrows knitted, and he looked shocked by the sudden change of pace, the sudden *businesslike* nature of the act.

He looked shocked and a little hurt.

At first, Arielle feared that she had ruined the moment, but Martin had passed the point of no return. As he grunted into the final climactic moments of ecstasy, Arielle's words echoed in her own head.

Put a baby in me, Martin. Please, please put a baby in me.

*   *   *

"Where in God's name did that come from?"

Arielle was lying nude on the bed, her knees pulled up to her chin. She had been positioned this way ever since they had finished making love.

She was not so consumed with her need that she was oblivious to the fact that the view she was presently giving Martin was far from flattering.

But it wasn't about him anymore. His role was over.

Now it was up to her, and goddamn it if she wasn't going to use every wives' tale in the book to ensure conception. Even if this meant looking like a pale, shell-less turtle waiting on its back to be picked off by an ostentatious buzzard.

"Martin? Where did you get that?"

Martin rolled a cigar between the thumb and forefinger of his right hand, turning it over to get a better view of the cigar band.

"H. Upmann," he said with an air of pretentiousness. "Magnum Fifty. From Cuba."

Arielle rolled her eyes.

"I meant who gave it to you?"

Martin snipped the end off the cigar and brought it to his lips.

"A client."

When she just stared, he continued.

"Sold the business complex on Park Ave. Got a fat commission check." He pulled the cigar from his lips and stared at it. "And a fat cigar."

Arielle gave him a moment to enjoy his cigar, but when he brought the lighter to within a few inches of it, she spoke up.

"You aren't going to light that in here."

Martin raised an eyebrow, his eyes twinkling mischievously.

"No?"

He brought the lighter closer, teasing her. The end of the cigar started to darken.

"And what are you going to do about it, Mrs. Kegel?"

She attempted to swat the lighter away, but she missed and nearly rolled over. Her hands shot out and she quickly grabbed her knees again.

Martin chuckled and leaned away from her. He brought the lighter to the end of the cigar.

"Martin!" she shouted.

"Just this once," he said. "Because when we have the baby, I will have to stop smoking altogether."

Arielle shook her head and tried to scold him, but a smile found its way on her full lips instead. He knew just what to say to get his way.

Martin didn't wait for a response before proceeding to light the end of the cigar.

It was clear by the expression on his face that he knew he had won. Her smile told him so.

And she was helpless to conceal it.

"Just this once," she affirmed, squeezing her knees close to her chest and holding her breath.

Just this once… because after this I will be pregnant.

Chapter 4

"Saint Raymond Nonnatus," Arielle whispered.

She clicked the mouse, and her face was immediately bathed in the frosty blue glow from her computer screen.

The painting on-screen depicted a man with short brown hair and an impossibly thick beard that hung nearly to the hollow of his throat. He was wearing a strange red shawl that covered his shoulders, and a white flowing gown that flooded to his ankles where it gave way to clichéd brown strap sandals. Grasped in his right hand and held out in front of him was what looked like a golden cup. The man held something else in his other hand—a scepter? A fancy mirror?—which was aimed high in the sky like some sort of beacon.

For all Arielle knew, it *was* a beacon, a signal to the heavens. *Giveth this woman a babe.*

"Nonnatus," she repeated, enjoying the way the name rolled off her tongue. "Nonnnn—"

A hand rested on her shoulder, and she nearly jumped out of her skin.

"Jesus!" she swore, turning to face Martin.

There was a goofy look on his face, one that made him look far younger than his forty-odd years. He looked like a little boy, and the fact that he was holding a bowl of cereal in one hand only perpetuated this image. His brown eyes squinted as he hovered over her, staring intently at her computer screen.

"Yeah, it could be him," he affirmed, nodding. He leaned away and brought another spoonful of cereal to his mouth. "Sure looks like Jesus."

Arielle shook her head.

"No, it's not Jesus. It's Saint—" She glanced back at the screen. "—Saint Raymond Nonnatus. The patron saint of conception."

She felt Martin lean over her again, but this time he stretched so far that she was essentially giving him a piggyback. The sweet smell of Fruitee-O's or whatever cereal he was eating mixed with the equally saccharine scent of milk filled her nostrils.

How can he eat that stuff?

"Hmm... looks like the patron Saint of crossdressing to me."

He pulled back and Arielle suppressed a smile.

Martin had a point.

"But look." She switched to another browser window. A bulletin board popped onto the screen. "There are hundreds, if not thousands, of people that swear by this guy. These woman, they—"

"—are desperate and lonely?" Martin offered.

Arielle ignored him.

"They went once, just once, and prayed to this—"

"—crossdressing makeup artist—"

"—Saint, and they conceived shortly thereafter."

Martin's expression changed from mocking to one of incredulity. He stared at her for a moment, as if sizing her up. Arielle refused to back down and stared back.

He brought another spoonful of cereal to his mouth.

"You're serious?"

Arielle nodded.

Chew, chew, chew.

"Serious, serious? Like you're going to do this, serious?"

Her gaze faltered, but only for a moment.

She clasped her hands together and lay them on her lap.

"I'm willing to try anything at this point."

Martin continued to stare, unabashedly sizing her up now.

"Nana-tits?"

"Nonnatus."

Martin made a 'What the fuck?' face and turned and went to the sink. She heard him sigh before dropping his empty bowl into the metal basin. There was an awkward moment where she just stared at his back, his hands clutching the sides of the sink, his head hung low. But when he turned back to face her, his expression was unexpectedly neutral.

"Look, Air, I'm all for having sex on a schedule like a union worker, and I even don't mind your 'orchid trying to hold onto dew' pose after sex. But, but this—" He gestured toward her computer screen. "—this *Nana-tits* is too much."

Arielle could feel her face begin to tingle. She was pretty sure that the color of her cheeks matched the crimson color of Saint Nonnatus's robes.

Anger crept in behind the embarrassment.

"Arielle, did you ever think that it's just not meant to be? That maybe we can be happy without children? Or—God forbid—adopt a child?"

Arielle's face transitioned from crimson to purple. She jumped to her feet so quickly that the computer chair rolled all the way to the far wall.

In all seven years of trying to conceive, this was the first time he had ever said anything like this. And he chose now, wearing a crappy cotton t-shirt and plaid pajama bottoms with milk clinging to just beneath his bottom lip, to say it.

Arielle lost it.

"Without children? *Without children?* Martin, what the fuck are you saying? Don't you want to have kids with me?"

Martin recoiled as if he had been struck, and his face got all screwed up. It looked like he was having a stroke.

"I—I—"

"You really don't want to have kids?"

The last thing Arielle wanted to do was cry, but she was helpless to control the tears that welled from somewhere inside her lids. This tsunami of emotions was extreme even for her. But this was what her life had become lately; just a light breeze pushing her hair out of perfect and Arielle wouldn't know if she would cry, scream, or pass out.

This time, however, it seemed like it was time to cry.

Martin recovered from the initial shock of her tantrum and quickly made his way over to her, wrapping his burly arms protectively around her.

"Of course I want to have kids, Air, you know that."

Arielle sniffed and nodded. She buried her head in his shirt, enjoying the way it smelled faintly of vanilla.

They stayed in that pose for a moment or two without speaking. She knew she should say something, that she should apologize, but she couldn't; she was too busy holding back more tears like the Hoover Dam.

"Hey, Arielle?" Martin said at last. He gestured to the computer screen with his chin. "Do you think Nana-tits is gonna breastfeed when we finally have our baby?"

Arielle laughed. She couldn't help it. Martin had a way of doing that; getting her to laugh even during the most stressful and anxiety-ridden situations.

Even when laughing was the last thing in the world she wanted to do.

Chapter 5

Of course Martin went with her.

Despite everything that he said—which ranged from mocking, to incredulous, to dumbfounded—he eventually agreed to get in the car and drive her to the church.

Just as Arielle had known he would.

Now, standing at the base of a large, bleached staircase, staring up at the ornate church, Arielle felt silly. And with the sun beating down on her, causing sweat to drip down her back before being soaked up by her pale blue sundress, she felt incredibly uncomfortable as well.

For what it was worth, Martin looked worse. She couldn't tell if it was the heat, the church, or the fact that he seemed to have put on a few extra pounds ever since he had left his real estate firm to go out on his own. But whatever it was that was irking him this day, it was clearly etched on his handsome face: his eyebrows were knitted, giving him unsightly creases at the top of his nose, and the corners of his mouth, so very often leaning upward in a grin or the beginnings of a smile, were downturned. And he, like Arielle, was covered in a thin layer of sweat.

What the hell are we doing here?

The front of the church was adorned by several massive stained glass windows. Two huge Corinthian pillars held up a peaked awning that overhung a ridiculously large wooden door.

It was a Catholic church, which made sense to Arielle. After all, not only was this the home of Saint Raymond Nonnatus, but she *was* Catholic. Not Catholic in a churchgoing, God-fearing way, but in the way a person is Jewish despite chowing down on bacon cheeseburgers on the weekend. She was a Catholic *now*, because she needed to be Catholic—it suited her purpose.

And right now she needed Saint Nonnatus.

Arielle turned to face her husband, who was staring up at the church like a layman charged with writing a dissertation on a Jackson Pollock painting.

"You ready?"

Martin's answer was immediate and unambiguous.

"No."

He opened his mouth to add something else, but decided better of it. It didn't matter; Arielle knew what he wanted to say. She knew because the same words were bouncing around in her blond skull.

What are we doing here?

"It will be quick... let's get it over with. Besides," she said, gesturing toward the awning and the large wooden door, "I need to get into the shade."

Martin nodded and hooked arms with her.

"Let's do this," he grumbled, and together they made their way up the church steps.

Arielle didn't think it was possible, but she felt more uncomfortable *inside* the church than she had been staring at the facade.

The cool church interior was predictably gloomy, with light only coming from two sources: weak streaks of colored rays of sun that squeezed through thick panes of stained glass, and a series of candles that seemed to be scattered about the church.

Like forgotten relics, the candles dripped waxed everywhere: on makeshift altars, on the handles of massive brass candle holders, and even on what looked like a tapestry-covered coffin.

And then there was the smell: the inside of the church smelled like a noxious concoction of bitter incense and must.

Arielle crinkled her nose.

As she waited for her eyes to adjust to the dramatic change in light, she began inspecting the church's other patrons. There were only a handful of people in the church, mostly women, which was odd for a Sunday afternoon—or so she thought.

Isn't Sunday their busy day?

As it was, most of the other churchgoers seemed caught up in their business, and as strange and out of place as Arielle felt entering the church, they took no notice of either her or Martin.

There was an elderly woman with long, frizzy hair kneeling on a pew, her hands clasped together so tightly that Arielle thought she might crush the plastic rosary that was intertwined between her fingers.

Another woman was weeping silently over a table of candles, a thin wooden stick with the end alight in her trembling hand, casting flickering shadows across her hawkish features.

A third woman stood in the center of the room, her head high, her eyes tightly closed. Her hands hung at her sides, palms out, as if she expected the rays of colored light in which she stood would suddenly beam her up and out of the church... and maybe off this earth.

What are we doing here? Arielle wondered for what felt like the hundredth time. *What are we doing in this place of death and mourning? Of sadness? We are not like this.*

She turned to stare at Martin.

He looked constipated. Or maybe like he was having a stroke.

We are usually *not like this.*

"What do we do now?" Martin asked out of the corner of his mouth.

When he turned to face her, he clearly didn't expect her to be staring at him. His eyes bulged.

"What?"

Arielle shook her head.

"Nothing."

Martin tapped the toe of his light gray loafer.

"Well, what do we do now, Mother Teresa?"

Arielle went back to scanning the inside of the church. She didn't bother answering her husband, deciding instead that her efforts were best spent searching for divine inspiration.

The truth was, she had no idea what to do next. She couldn't remember the last time she had been in church, but assumed it had been when she still crapped in her pants.

"Air? What—?"

Arielle shushed him.

Her eyes gradually made their way back to the woman hovering over the table with all the candles. She was pretty sure that this was where you lit candles for the dead—the exact opposite reason why they were here—but for some reason she was drawn to that spot.

"Come on," she grumbled, giving Martin's arm a tug.

The table of candles was pressed against the side wall, and Arielle dragged Martin over to it. The woman with the shaking hands had since lit her candle and now hovered over it, humming, her back to them.

When Arielle was just a few feet from the table, she noticed it: a figure wearing red-and-white robes, just like she had seen on the Internet. It was a painting of Saint Raymond Nonnatus in a tacky gold frame leaning up against the wall. Just in front of the picture was a dark ceramic bowl, inside of which were a handful of small turquoise stones.

"There," she whispered, extending a finger toward the painting, trying her best not to disturb the mourning woman.

Martin nodded, but the confused look on his face remained.

"I think we take a—"

The woman hovering over the candles turned to face Arielle.

She was younger than Arielle might have expected based on her pointy features. Her smooth face was covered in strands of jet-black hair that were nearly indistinguishable from the streaks of teary mascara that marked her cheeks.

"Please, my—"

The woman had begun saying something as she turned, but when her eyes met Arielle's, her expression immediately changed. The woman's dark eyebrows furrowed, her eyes somehow became beady, and something akin to recognition crossed her face.

"*Filius obcisor,*" the woman hissed.

Arielle cringed and shrunk away from her.

What the fuck?

Martin, who didn't appear to have even noticed the weeping woman, reached into the bowl of turquoise stones.

"Air, I think you put one of these in if…" He pulled out one of the stones and rubbed it between his fingers. It was smooth, like marble.

The woman with the black hair turned to Martin, and Arielle took another step backward. Her heart raced. She could feel all of the muscles in her face go slack, as if the anger and hatred in the strange woman's eyes had somehow taxed her ability to form an expression.

Inside, her mind was twisting into a carnival pretzel.

"You already took one out," she spat.

Martin finally acknowledged the woman. Whatever hold the woman had on Arielle apparently did not extend to him.

"Huh?" Martin held the stone up so that it caught a ray of stained glass sunlight. "This? It's just a—"

"You already took one out!" the woman hissed. "You are supposed to put one in."

Martin made a face as he tossed the stone back into the bowl, where it landed with a loud clack.

"It's just a rock," he finished with a shrug.

The woman turned back to Arielle.

"*Filius obcisor!* You took one out, you don't get to put one back in! *Filius obcisor!*"

"I put it back," Martin informed her, but his comment went ignored. "Didn't you see?"

Arielle felt like crying.

"*Filius obcisor!* You took one out!"

Who is this fucking psycho and what is she saying?

Martin stepped between them.

"Woah, now. I don't know—"

"A LIFE FOR A LIFE!" the woman suddenly screamed.

The tears that had been welling behind Arielle's eyes suddenly evaporated and were immediately replaced by fury.

She stepped past Martin and grabbed the woman by the arm.

"What the *fuck* did you say?"

Spit dribbled from Arielle's lip, but she refused to wipe it away. She squeezed the woman's triceps so hard that her fingers started to ache.

"What did you say?"

The woman failed to acknowledge either Arielle's words or her grasp. Instead, her expression twisted into a sneer. Her face, which before might have before been described as cute if pointy, was suddenly all angles and shadows; hideous.

"*Filius obcisor.*" The woman's voice was barely a whisper now.

"No, not that. What *else* did you say?"

The shock that had gripped Martin suddenly thawed. Apparently realizing that the bizarre situation was about to reach a head, he leaned over and tried to separate the two women. It took him three tries to pry Arielle's fingers from the woman's arm.

"Let go, Arielle," he grumbled.

Arielle ignored him.

"What did you say?" she repeated between gritted teeth.

None of the malice she laced her words with seemed to matter; the stupid fucking words—*Filius obcisor*—that the woman uttered were some sort of anti-venom.

"Arielle, let's get out of here."

Martin tried to turn her, but Arielle held her ground.

Did she really say what I think she did?

She couldn't let it go… the only person who had ever said that to her had been—

"*Filius obcisor!*"

"What did you say to me, you fucking bitch?"

"Woah! Arielle, calm down. Let's just get out of here."

She felt Martin's hands grab her by the shoulders and attempt to guide her toward the door. This time she let him; if she didn't, she knew that Martin would eventually just pick her up and haul her out of there, whether she wanted to leave or not.

"*Filius obcisor!*"

The strange words sounded as if they were coming at her in stereo now, and Arielle managed with great effort to tear her eyes from the psycho with the black hair. The other two women that had been in the church when they had arrived were now staring at her, their own lips twisted in matching sneers.

"*Filius obcisor!*" all three women shouted in unison.

What the fuck?

Arielle didn't know if she said the words, if Martin had, or if she just thought them.

But they had never been more appropriate.

What the FUCK?!

The woman in the pews stepped into the aisle and her rosary, clutched so desperately only moments earlier, fell to the ground in a clatter, unwanted, useless.

"*Filius obcisor!*" she hissed.

The third woman was still standing in the glow of the stained glass, but now her head was facing forward and her eyes were not trained on Martin, who had succeeded in getting them both within a few feet of the large wooden door, but on her.

In her.

"*Filius obcisor! Filius obcisor! Filius obcisor!!!*"

Chapter 6

Filius obcisor.

Filia obcisor.

Filius et filia eversor.

"Goddamn it, Arielle! Wake up!"

Arielle's eyes shot open. Everything was blurry, and at first she thought she was drowning. Her blond hair was plastered to her cheeks, stuck to them as if she were underwater.

"Help!" she croaked, but despite the wetness that engulfed her, the words came out dry and hoarse. She tried to raise her head, but couldn't.

"Arielle!"

Someone was shaking her, and when she finally managed to blink her eyes clear, she realized that she wasn't underwater after all.

She was lying in her bed, her hair and face so drenched with sweat that when she moved, it oozed out of her pillow like pus.

The hand eventually stopped shaking her, but Arielle's body kept on trembling. She felt like sitting up, but her body felt too heavy, too tired to move.

If she had been underwater, she would have been wearing concrete shoes.

"Arielle? What the fuck, Arielle?"

Martin's handsome face came into view, but this time he wasn't smiling.

Come to think of it, he had been *not* smiling nearly as often as he had been smiling over the past few days; an oddity for him.

"You were shouting something, something crazy... you sounded like the psychos in the church."

Arielle closed her eyes tightly and held them like that for a moment.

Was I dreaming?

If she had been, she couldn't remember. The only thing she remembered was a turquoise stone, falling and falling and falling...

When she finally opened her eyes again, they immediately fell on the solitary picture frame on her wooden bedside table.

It was the only photograph she had of herself as a child — her only link to her past, before she'd been found and her memories kick-started. She must have been four or five in the photo — it was difficult to tell based on the poor quality image — with a shock of long blond hair that was tied in a braid and lay over her chest. There was a woman standing beside her who she had, over time, convinced herself must have been her mother. The woman was wearing a dark outfit that looked almost robe-like in the grainy black-and-white photo. It was strange, wearing what looked like a bathrobe even though they were clearly standing outside. Aside from obviously being outside, there really was nothing descript about the landscape; the picture quality was just too poor to make out any details. Which in itself was also odd, given the fact that if she had been four or five at the time — even if she had been six, which was unlikely — then the photo must have been taken at best in the late seventies. Regardless, there was a man behind both Arielle and her mother; her father, most likely, but he, like the dark shadows that surrounded the subjects, was nearly unrecognizable. It wasn't a good picture, or even a nice picture, but it was the only evidence of a childhood she didn't remember.

Arielle blinked hard again and the image of her younger self, complete with a missing front tooth, faded into memories that didn't exist. She squeezed her eyes tight, forcing tears out of the corners. When she started seeing spots, she eased the pressure and opened them again.

This time, her focus went immediately to an object lying directly in front of her framed picture.

It was small, like a marble, but it wasn't a perfect sphere. Instead, it was oblong, with one side extending further than the other.

"Martin?" she whispered, slowly raising her head again and beginning to sit up. "What is that, Martin?"

As her vision continued to clear, the object came into more acute focus.

"Martin! What the fuck is that, Martin?"

"What?" Her husband was immediately beside her, helping her up. "What is it?"

Arielle shrugged him off and pointed at her bedside table.

"That! What the fuck, Martin?"

"What, the picture…?"

"Not the fucking picture, *Martin*! The fucking stone! The goddamn rock! Where did you get it from?"

She didn't dare take her eyes off the stone, but she knew by the way Martin's hands reached for her again that he knew exactly what she was referring to.

She said it anyway.

"*That* stone."

It wasn't a question, although it probably should have been. Instead, it was a statement.

"It's just a stupid rock, Air."

Arielle scooted backwards, further burying herself in her husband's arms. It wasn't that she needed comfort, although this wasn't an unwelcome side effect, but more because she wanted to get as far away from the turquoise stone as possible.

Filius obcisor.

She shuddered.

"It's not *just* a rock, Martin. Where did you get it from?"

Martin gently turned her to face him.

"From the church... I grabbed it as a, ugh, a souvenir."

Souvenir?

The image of the woman with the dark hair and gaunt features, the one with the trembling hands lighting a candle—a physical representation of someone she had lost. A child, maybe? She had been at the table with the painting of Saint Nonnatus, after all.

Filius et filia eversor.

"Souvenir? *Souvenir?* Women put those stones in the bowl as a prayer to conceive. What the fuck were you thinking, Martin?"

'*You took one out already.*'

If Martin's hurt expression was any indication, she was being too harsh. But still... a fucking souvenir?

"I thought... I dunno, a good luck charm?"

Arielle remember what else the woman in the church had said and her heart skipped a beat.

Martin had meant well—the man's upturned eyebrows and boyish expression said as much.

"You shouldn't have taken that."

Martin averted his eyes like a child caught stealing the last cookie from the jar.

"I know. I'll throw it out."

Arielle shook her head.

"You need to take it back."

He leaned away from her.

"Take it back? With those psychos? I'll throw it out, but—"

Arielle turned and stared her husband directly in his hazel eyes.

"You can't throw it out, Martin. It's someone's wish, someone's hope. You need to take it back."

Martin rolled his eyes.

"Fuck, alright, I'll take it back, then."

Arielle nodded and then threw her head back onto the pillow. It landed with a wet *plunk*.

"What time is it?" she asked, staring at the ceiling.

There was a pause as Martin scrambled for his watch on the bedside table.

"Almost six."

Arielle closed her eyes again and lay in darkness for almost a minute.

It was Martin who broke the silence.

"Air?"

"Yeah?"

"What were you saying in your sleep?"

Arielle's breath caught in her throat.

"Nothing—gibberish. I was asleep."

Another pause, but this one was different. It was almost as if she could hear Martin's brain working, trying to figure out if she was telling the truth.

"And those women in the church? What were they saying?"

Filius obcisor.

"I have no idea," she lied.

She knew, because she had looked it up on the Internet the second they had gotten home.

Filia obcisor.

"I don't know," she repeated.

"Okay."

All of a sudden, Arielle felt her stomach flip.

Oh God.

It felt as if she had a whole nest of worms writhing through her intestines.

Her cheeks puffed with gas and she belched.

"You sure?"

Arielle couldn't answer; her mouth suddenly filled with vomit, and she threw the duvet back and hopped to her feet. She bolted to the en suite bathroom, tasting the worst combination of bile and last night's dinner.

As sick as she was, she wasn't ill enough not to answer Martin's query in her mind.

Filius obcisor.

Son killer.

Filia obcisor.

Daughter killer.

Chapter 7

The best thing about running is the shoes.

Arielle stared at the words on her computer screen, hoping that they magically improve on their own.

They didn't.

That's stupid.

She erased the line, and rewrote it.

The best thing about shoes is feeling the run.

Her head slumped in her hand.

Also stupid. This is all bullshit. The best thing about running is the Big Mac you can enjoy guiltlessly afterward.

One of her largest clients had commissioned her to write the copy for their new shoe launch. An impossibly lightweight running shoe with essentially zero sole. Normally this job would be a breeze for her, a simple task of putting together a few catchy lines that her client would be happy with.

But today was different. Today, she was distracted.

Arielle stretched her arms high over her head, groaning as she did. Then she took a sip of coffee—it had gone cold—but as gross as it was, it served to momentarily relieve her dry mouth, which was enough.

"What about… you have enough soul to run," she said out loud.

Soul/sole. That was good, that was nice. A play on words—everyone always likes those.

"You have enough soul in you to run, you don't need any more on your shoe."

Not great, but good. Something to work with.

Arielle heard the door open, and she immediately cracked a smile.

A few moments of jingle-jangling keys later, Martin hollered at her.

"Honey, I'm home!"

Arielle smiled so hard that her cheeks started to hurt.

"In here," she replied, turning back to her computer and resuming typing.

Soul/sole. I can work with that.

A few seconds later, Martin came into her "office," which was just a simple desk pressed up against the wall adjacent the kitchen. Their house had an actual office—two, if you counted the room that had officially become Martin's dirty laundry haven—but she liked this spot better. She liked it because it was right beneath a large window that overlooked the backyard. On sunny days like today, she could bask in the warm glow without having to worry about mosquitoes or melanoma.

Martin crept up behind her and wrapped his arms around her neck. She turned into him and kissed his forearm.

"What you working on, Air?"

Arielle stared at the words on the screen.

"Copy for a new running shoe ad."

"*Sole-less, not soulless. Just run.*" He read from her screen. "Not bad, not bad at all. Let's just hope no redheads buy the shoe. Could be sued for false advertising."

Arielle laughed.

"Fine," she said, and erased the sentence.

Martin pulled back from her.

"Just kidding, babe. It sounded good."

Arielle shook her head.

"Naw, just wasn't right... wasn't perfect."

Martin let go of her neck and retreated to the kitchen.

"Keep at it, then."

Arielle followed her husband's reflection in the computer screen as he made his way to a cabinet above the stove and pulled out a rock glass.

She loved looking at Martin when he wasn't paying attention. There was something about the way that he always seemed to be smiling even when no one was around that was just so *him*. It was as if he were always remembering the punchline to a joke that was running on loop in his brain.

It was one of the reasons why she had fallen in love with him.

It was Friday, and there was no rush to Martin's movements. He first cleaned the glass with a paper towel, then made his way over to the liquor cabinet. After a fleeting inventory of his scotch collection, he pulled out his favorite: Talisker 18 year.

This, unlike his perpetual boyish grin, was *not* something that Arielle loved about Martin: his penchant for scotch. And Talisker in particular, or any of the other peaty scotches, was one of her least favorite. It smelled of acrid barbecue, and it made *him* smell like an old man.

And he wasn't old.

Neither was she.

They were young and in love and...

The wooden cork made a small popping sound when Martin removed it from the bottle, distracting Arielle from her thoughts.

He still didn't know that she was watching him, and for some reason this excited her.

Martin brought the bottle to his nose and inhaled deeply. He pulled back a bit when the full brunt of the smell hit him, and Arielle chuckled.

Apparently, even he wasn't immune to the smell of the stuff.

"What?" he asked, turning to face her for the first time since she had started observing him. "You watching me again, perv?"

Arielle didn't bother turning. Instead, she met his eyes in the computer screen reflection.

"Get over here," she ordered.

Martin took a sip.

"Yes, ma'am."

As he sauntered over to him, still in no hurry, she typed a few more words on the screen.

"I want your opinion on this... need your *expertise*," she whispered.

"It better be good," he said with a smile. "It's blasphemy to interrupt a man before his first sip of scotch."

Arielle said nothing as Martin leaned over her to get a better view of the screen.

A second later, his revered glass of scotch fell to the floor.

* * *

"I could stay here all night *and* all of tomorrow," Arielle whispered, running her fingers through Martin's short brown hair. She leaned in and kissed him on the lips. "All night, all day."

They had made love again, only this time it had been different. This time it had been slow and sensual and her climax had been near earth-shattering.

"Wow," Martin said.

Evidently, the experience had been the same for him.

She smiled, enjoying this thought. For so long, their love-making had become, as he appropriately referred to it, a unionized event; a ritual, a work-like process with an ultimate goal.

This time, however, there had been no clear objective... aside from pleasure, of course.

And that objective had been met in spades.

"Wow," Martin said again.

Even during the entire forty minutes that their bodies writhed together in sweaty bliss, his face had been the same: incredulous.

And it had been that way ever since he had read the words that she had typed on the screen: *I'm pregnant.*

Just the thought made her heart skip a beat.

I'm pregnant.

She took a deep breath.

Finally.

"Wow," Martin said again.

Arielle giggled.

"Is that all you can say? 'Wow'?"

"Pretty much, yeah."

She stopped fussing with his hair.

For seven years they had tried, and for seven years they had failed.

But all that had changed.

"Hey, don't stop playing with my hair," Martin said, turning to face her. "That felt good."

"Nope, not until you say something other than 'wow'."

Now it was Martin's turn to laugh.

"Wow is a good word." He made a dramatic *wow* gesture with his lips. "Wow, wow, wow."

Arielle slipped the pillow out from under her elbow and smacked him with it.

Martin instantly flipped her over and proceeded to pin her arms above her head. She threw her head back and laughed.

"I—"

He kissed her neck lightly.

"—can—"

He kissed her collarbone.

"—say—"

He kissed her bare breast, just beside her nipple.

"—wow—"

He kissed her ribcage.

"—as many times as I want!"

With each of the final six words he kissed her belly, his mouth making a puckering sound on the extra skin that seemed to have appeared overnight.

"Isn't that right, my boy?"

Arielle stopped laughing.

Filius.

She reached down and grabbed his head and eased him back up to eye level.

"How do you know it's a boy?"

Martin's eyes were twinkling and he was grinning.

"Oh, it's a boy, I can tell."

Arielle frowned.

"You can't know that."

Martin flipped onto his back and lay beside her. With both of them staring at the ceiling, his right hand slowly snaked out from his side and gently brushed the hollow of her throat.

His touch was gentle, tickling. Just the way she liked it.

"I know everything," he whispered, his hand creeping lower.

Martin's touch didn't linger when his finger brushed against her hardened nipple, but Arielle gasped nonetheless. And when his hand slid beneath the sheet and made it to the inside of her thigh, she moaned.

Any thoughts of the strange women in the church shouting at her were quickly vanquished by her building orgasm.

Chapter 8

"Right, left, right," a muffled voice instructed.

Arielle followed the orders, driving her taped knuckles into the worn punching bag in rapid succession.

Perspiration dripped from her forehead, turning the few tendrils of hair that had fallen from her ponytail into dark, wet strips that clung to her red cheeks.

"Good," the voice said. "Now finish with a hard left hook."

Arielle lowered her hands to her sides and shook her arms out to loosen them as she jogged on the spot.

"You ready?"

The man's voice was clearer now as he leaned around the side of the punching bag to stare at her.

He was just as handsome as ever, in a completely different way than her husband... which was probably the reason why she had fallen for him.

Fallen for him? Fallen?

Arielle balled her fists.

One time. A mistake, a stupid fucking mistake. I didn't fall for him. I love my husband.

Kevin Dreiger was tall, black, and absolutely shredded. As was expected, given the fact that he had been a champion boxer in his not-so-distant youth, but had since resigned himself to run his own boxing school. Arielle knew little of sports, and less of boxing, but she had been intrigued by Kevin's story when he had first let small details about it leak to her.

It had started innocuously enough: after one of their sessions—much like the current one—she had passed by his office and had asked about the belt that was encased in a worn wooden and glass box in his small office.

"What's that?"

Nothing could have been more innocuous than those two words.

And, to Kevin's credit, he had been reluctant to talk about it. Not in an artificially bashful sort of way, but because it appeared as if he truly missed the sport. It pained him to talk about it.

But there were no secrets in the Internet era, and it had revealed all to Arielle.

At the height of his career, just as he was coming into the big money fights, Kevin endured a twelve-round brawl with Kenny 'Big Toe' Bard. Kevin had won by unanimous decision, but he had spent nearly a month in the hospital trying to remember how to do the most rudimentary of things: brush his teeth, feed himself…he even had to remember how to sleep.

Not surprisingly, Kevin didn't want to talk about this, save for mentioning that he could have kept competing. And, based on his physique, she didn't doubt that part. But the risks had been too great for him, so he had resolved himself to be here— to run a boxing gym that he opened. It mustn't have been an easy decision, as she had read some ridiculous rumors about how much the promoters had thrown at him to fight again.

Or so the story went.

"Arielle? You ready? You look lost."

Arielle shook her head and let the motion travel all the way down to her taped hands.

She cleared her throat, and took her eyes off of Kevin's handsome face.

One time. A mistake. Only one time.

Kevin smiled as if he knew what she was thinking.

"Left, right, left."

Arielle drove her fists into the punching bag. She finished with the left hook even before the instruction came out of Kevin's mouth. Her final punch had so much power behind it that it surprised Kevin, and he had to take a large step backward to avoid staggering. His smile grew.

She looked down at her right hand, her fist still tightly clenched. Even though it had been expertly taped, she could see a dot of blood soaking into the tape on the middle knuckle, exactly where she had struck Dr. Barnes' face.

Kevin took a step back and started to step out from behind the heavy bag, but Arielle shook her head. He wasn't wearing a shirt, and his ebony skin glistened in the poor lighting like polished glass.

"More," she said, again averting her eyes.

One time only.

"It's been over an hour, Arielle. I think—"

Again she shook her head.

"More."

Kevin shrugged and retreated behind the heavy bag again, bracing himself against it. He knew when she got this way that the punches were going to come hard and fast.

"You're the boss," he said, his voice muffled again. "Left, right…"

Arielle drove her fists into the bag, grunting heavily with each punch.

One time only.

Chapter 9

"You nervous?"

"No—why would you ask that? Do I look nervous?"

Martin shrugged.

"Not really." He paused. "Maybe. I'm nervous."

He looked over at her and smiled. Arielle smiled back.

"Hey, what do you think about this whole sympathy weight thing? Think I'll look good with an extra twenty or thirty pounds around my gut?"

He pushed his stomach out, straining it against the seatbelt. Then he puffed his cheeks.

"Shut up," she replied, punching him playfully on the shoulder.

The truth was, Arielle *wasn't* nervous, even though she knew she probably should have been, given what they had been through.

And then there was Dr. Barnes.

Martin had insisted that they see another OB/GYN, but Arielle had put her foot down. It was important to her that it was Dr. Barnes that saw her, not only because an apology was definitely in order, but a little part of her—a small, teeny-tiny piece of her brain—was proud of the fact that she had conceived *without* the tests he had been so insistent on.

I didn't need your tests.

Gloating about this was petty and childish, which she was acutely aware of, but she was pregnant, and weren't pregnant women allowed to be a little irrational sometimes?

Just the thought of being pregnant made her hands subconsciously fall to her belly in a protective fashion. For the past few weeks, she had caught herself rubbing at the small pouch of excess skin without even knowing it. She had tried to convince herself that it was to soothe her sore abdominal muscles—a consequence of puking nearly every morning for the past three weeks—but this was a lie.

After seven years of trying to get pregnant, she felt the need to protect the tiny cluster of cells growing in her womb.

Protect them, then it, and then him or her. That was her goal now.

Nothing else mattered, least of all a little abdominal soreness.

"Air?"

She turned back to Martin.

"Hmm?"

"I said, 'Are you gonna play nice'?"

Arielle made a face.

"With Dr. Barnes," Martin clarified. "No more right hooks?"

Arielle smiled and resisted the urge to look down at the knuckles of her right hand. The bruising had long since healed, but just the sight of the ridges of her pale hand reminded her of what she had done.

"No, no right hooks. Promise."

Martin raised an eyebrow, clearly doubting her. Arielle chuckled.

"No, for real, no punching this time. I swear."

"And you're really sure you want to see *him*? You don't want to see a different doctor?"

Arielle turned her gaze back to the window. It was another incredibly sunny day out as summer slowly came into full bloom.

July… that means I'll be giving birth in spring.

To Arielle, it seemed like the perfect timing: giving birth in the spring meant summer walks with the stroller.

"Dr. Barnes is fine," she replied. "Besides, I owe him an apology."

Martin laughed as they pulled into the doctor office parking lot.

"Yep, you sure do."

Arielle considered punching him on the shoulder again, but decided against it.

Her punching days were over.

*   *   *

The good news was that there was nothing on Dr. Barnes's face suggesting that about a month ago he had suffered from a vicious right hook.

The bad news was that the doctor wasn't smiling, which, in Arielle's estimation, was never a good thing.

"So," the doctor began. The man was looking down at a chart in his hands, presenting the top of his shiny bald head to her and Martin.

"Wait, Doc, before you begin, I need to say something."

The doctor raised his eyes but kept his head cocked downward. Martin leaned forward in his chair, propping himself up as if he might need to spring up at any moment to prevent her from pummeling the doctor. The scene was so bizarre that Arielle almost laughed, but she managed to stifle the sound at the last moment. Hormonal or not, laughing at a time like this probably wouldn't go over well. She had, after all, popped Dr. Barnes a good one the last time she was there.

"I feel very badly about what happened last time I was here... and I'm incredibly embarrassed. It obviously wasn't your fault that I couldn't get pregnant, but I think—"

Her desire to laugh suddenly transitioned into a deep sadness and a need to cry. But, like the chuckle, she forced this away too.

"—it's just... it took so damn long to get pregnant, you know? And I always wanted children, and I mean *always.*"

She realized that she was rambling and decided to end the awkwardness before she talked herself into a corner.

"But that doesn't matter now, does it?" she finished with a broad smile.

Dr. Barnes didn't return the expression. Instead, the man methodically flipped through the file in his hands as if she hadn't said anything at all.

Arielle made a face.

Did he not hear me?

But then the doctor laid the file on his desk and turned to her, staring directly into her eyes.

"Thank you," he said. "And I'm very happy to hear that you and Martin managed to conceive."

His response was curt, direct, to the point. Evidently, it would take some time for the doctor to become friendly with her again.

That's okay, Doc, I have nine months to make it up to you.

Out of the corner of her eye, she saw Martin settle back into his chair.

Good, at least he *is loosening up.*

"But I feel compelled to let you know that my wife was none too happy about my bruised jaw." He brought a slender hand to his face and rubbed the left side of his chin. "And if it happens again, well..."

Arielle shook her head.

"No way… Like I said, I am so sorry. Won't happen again. Ever."

Dr. Barnes nodded.

"Alrighty," Martin piped in. "Now that we've gotten that awkwardness out of the way, what's next, Doc?"

Arielle answered before the doctor had a chance.

"Blood test," she said simply.

Both men in the room turned to look at her. She shrugged.

"What? I've been trying to get pregnant for seven years, you didn't think I would do some research?"

Martin's gaze moved from her to the doctor and he shrugged.

It was his *'What do you want me to do?'* expression.

"You're right, Mrs. Reigns—"

"Please, Arielle."

"Blood test first, Arielle. We need to confirm that you're pregnant. But I also want to talk to you about your habits, and how things might change, including your emotional state, your body, and…"

Confirm that I'm pregnant?

None of the other words registered with her.

"Oh, I'm pregnant, Dr. Barnes. There's no question about that."

Her hands subconsciously fell to her stomach and started kneading the area gently.

Dr. Barnes raised one of his gray eyebrows.

"Morning sickness?"

Arielle inhaled sharply.

"Oh yeah."

The man looked to Martin for confirmation, who made a face and nodded vigorously.

"How often?"

"Once a day, maybe twice."

"Is it food or just bile coming up?"

Martin scrunched his nose.

Well, if you think this is gross, you have another thing coming...

"Mostly bile."

The doctor reached back onto his desk and quickly filled out a prescription.

"Promathezine," he informed her, holding out the sheet of paper. "Take every four hours as necessary."

Arielle hesitated before taking the paper.

"It's been seven years, Doc; I've actually been looking forward to this part."

She offered what she thought was a convincing smile. The doctor didn't retract his hand.

"That's a first. But it's good to have on hand, just in case. As I said, 'as needed'."

Arielle shrugged and politely acquiesced, taking the paper and jamming it into her purse.

"Come sit in this chair and we'll get blood drawn, and then follow up with a pap smear. Usually we don't do the pap this early, but because you are here, and given your—" He paused again, eying her as he selected his words carefully. " —aversion to tests, I figured we'd get it over with?"

Arielle wasn't sure if it was a question or an instruction, but she nodded anyway.

Now, it didn't matter. Now, she would allow aliens to finger every orifice to make sure everything was fine with the baby.

Arielle rolled up her sleeves and pulled down her pants as instructed, and after filling three vials of blood and having her insides scraped, she returned to her seat beside Martin.

"As you've obviously done your research, I don't think I need to tell you that you shouldn't drink or smoke or do any drugs at this point."

Arielle rolled her eyes.

Martin reached over and shook her arm.

"You hear that, honey? No more doobie aperitifs."

Arielle shrugged him off, her eyes intent on Dr. Barnes. The bald man, clearly not amused, shook his head.

"I'm not just talking about street drugs, but cold and headache medicines, too. You need to be careful, Arielle, especially given your advanced—"

The man hesitated as if he had just realized that he was about to swear.

Advanced age. Say it, Doc. I won't hurt you.

Again.

Dr. Barnes cleared his throat.

"—given your advanced condition."

Arielle almost laughed again.

Hormones; it's my hormones.

"No Advil, only Tylenol. Do you guys want to wait around for the blood test results, or would you prefer to wait for my call? It should only be an hour or two."

Martin turned to Arielle.

"Up to you."

"No, that's fine, Doc." She patted her stomach and laughed. "Anyways, it's a friend's Fourth of July party, and we're gonna be late as it is."

Martin nodded.

"Gonna miss the tequila shots."

Dr. Barnes's thin lips pressed together tightly.

"Well, listen, someone will give you a call if anything strange pops up on the blood test or pap. Other than that, I'll see you back here in two weeks to do a preliminary ultra-sound—just book an appointment with the secretary on the way out."

Arielle thanked the man and apologized again for what had happened last time.

"You just take care of yourself, now, okay? Being pregnant can have a dramatic effect on your mood and emotions."

Martin piped in before she had a chance to say anything.

"What, Arielle? Emotional? No way, not my wife..."

Arielle leaned over and punched him playfully on the shoulder. Out of the corner of her eye, she caught Dr. Barnes leaning away from her, a frown plastered on his clean-shaven face.

Chapter 10

"Do we tell them?"

They were almost at the Woodward's place, running only about an hour late for their friends' annual, if a few days premature, Fourth of July party.

The mood inside the car was one of elation, what with both of them glad that the encounter with Dr. Barnes had gone so, well, *uneventfully*. Still, the heightened mood was not going to stop Martin from making jokes about the middle-aged man.

"They say we should wait until the three-month ultrasound before we tell people," Arielle answered. "What do you think? Tony and Charlene know we have been trying for so long. And besides, Charlene is a hawk. She will know right away if I'm not drinking."

Martin bit his lip as he mulled this over. A moment later, they pulled into the driveway of the Woodward's modest ranch-style home.

"I could make you virgin drinks, pretend like I'm putting alcohol in there."

"Too sneaky. Too *tricky*."

"Well, I'll leave it up to you, then, Mrs. Mayweather. I don't want to make the wrong decision and get punched out."

Arielle laughed.

"Are you going to hold this over on me forever?"

Martin jammed the car into park and opened his door.

"Nope, not forever. Just until you are too old and decrepit to punch me." He shadowboxed in the summer air. "Or until you lose your title."

Arielle said nothing; she knew Martin well enough to know that if she commented, it would only egg him on. Instead, she slowly pulled herself out of the car and into the bright sun.

The iconic vocals of Brad Nowell belting out 'What I Got' led them directly to the backyard. As they got closer, Arielle thought she heard the equally recognizable sound of sausages sizzling on a barbecue over the music. And even if she couldn't hear them—if she was just imagining the sound—she definitely *smelled* them. And she was ravenous.

Eating for two.

She felt a little bit like Daredevil, what with her pregnancy enhancing her senses. Which probably wasn't *always* a good thing. Case in point, Martin's Talisker 18.

"We'll play it by ear," she whispered to Martin as he swung the gate open.

The Woodward's backyard was small, roughly ten by twenty feet, but like most proud homeowners in Batesburg, South Carolina, even the small patch of grass between the flag-stones and the back fence was fastidiously manicured and a vibrant, almost inorganic shade of green.

Arielle barely had time to take it all in before someone spotted them.

"Hey! Martin! Arielle!"

Tony Woodward waved a beefy arm high in the air, as if he were signaling to them over the immense crowd... of six or seven other partygoers. Eight if you counted little Thomas, who was not yet two.

Tony was a large man, even by Carolina standards. With crossly cropped hair, the style of which bordered on military,

and small, beady eyes and matching mouth, he always reminded Arielle of a small man trapped in a fat suit. He was
wearing a grease-smeared apron with the words '*Kiss the 'Cue*',
which were only just legible amidst a spattering of mustard and
ketchup stains. He was standing in front of an open barbecue
with tendrils of grease-saturated smoke drifting up in front of
his face.

Martin made it to Tony first. Without hesitation, he grabbed
the big man in a bear hug. Martin was not a small man by any
means, but even he had a hard time getting his arms even halfway around Tony's broad back.

"Smells good, my man," Martin said as they disengaged.

"Glad you could make it."

Tony leaned over and kissed Arielle on the cheek.

"And welcome to the party to you, too, beautiful," he said
with a sly grin.

If the man's slurred words weren't a tipoff that he was well
into the sauce, the four or five empty Budweiser bottles littered
around the barbecue were another clue.

And why shouldn't he be? It was the *almost* the Fourth of
July, after all.

"You smell good," she blurted, then immediately turned
red.

"I do, do I?" Tony winked at Martin. "You hear that? Your—
"

"I mean the meat, jackass," Arielle said quickly.

Tony's small mouth puckered into an 'o' shape.

"I'm sorry," he mocked. "Please don't hit me!"

Arielle's jaw dropped.

"Oh my God," she turned to Martin. "You told him?"

Martin offered a surprised expression.

"No way!"

"Martin!"

She felt a hand on her shoulder and turned back to Tony. The man was chuckling, the thick skin beneath his chin quivering like warm Jell-O. Even though Tony had been a big man ever since Arielle had met him, it still amazed her that a man of his *stature* was an officer of the law. If nothing else, it served as great fodder for her and Martin's friendly banter when they imagined him running after someone who had just knocked off the corner store.

'He's deceptively fast,' Martin would always say.

Cue Arielle's predictable eye roll.

'Yeah, right.'

'For real.'

'Downhill, maybe.'

"Relax, hon, it wasn't Martin." He hooked a meaty thumb over his shoulder. "Charlene over there went to see Dr. Barnes about some *woman* problems, and she asked about the shiner."

"It was his jaw, sweetie, not his eye," a tall, lanky woman said as she made her way out from the house via a set of sliding doors. She was wearing a yellow sundress and held matching glasses of pale green liquid in each hand.

"Charlene!"

The woman smiled a droopy smile and made her way over to them. Charlene was all elbows and knees, which made it difficult for Arielle to tell from her awkward gate if she too, like her husband, was already half in the bag.

When Charlene kissed her on the cheek, the sickly sweet smell of margaritas confirmed her suspicions.

"Take one, sweetie," Charlene said, offering her one of the drinks.

"Just gimme a sec," Arielle replied awkwardly. "Actually, do you think I could have some water first? I'm super thirsty."

Charlene raised a thinly painted eyebrow. Even her expressions were angular.

"Water? You don't need water, my love, what you need is alcohol. After all, it's the *Fourth of July!*"

Martin laughed and the other partygoers, two other couples—the Allens and the Dupries—raised their beers from their respective lawn chairs.

"Doug, Marnie," Martin said, acknowledging the Allens first. He said hello to the Dupries next, although Arielle could tell from the way that he called them exactly that—*Dupries*—that Martin had forgotten their names.

"Hi Cindy and Ron," Arielle chimed in quickly, rescuing her husband's poor memory. "Happy early Fourth of July!"

Tony's voice drew her back to the delicious BBQ.

"Perfect timing, Marty. Dogs are almost ready, and I gotta tell you, I am starving." Tony rubbed his considerable belly through the apron. "And you know the rules at the Woodward's place: first come, first serve. If you come too late, you don't get fed."

Arielle's gaze drifted to the grill. There were at least two dozen sausages sizzling away, and another half dozen chicken breasts coated in some sort of thick white sauce that was being licked by flame.

Charlene rolled her eyes.

"Oh God, Tony. You remember what the doctor said? You need to cut out the meat."

Tony's quip was immediate, a clear indication that this wasn't the first time that Charlene had reminded him of his health—or *unhealth*, as it were.

"Can't do it, sweetie. I was born a red-blooded American Meatatarian, and no quack doctor with a degree from community college is gonna tell me what to eat."

"He went to Harvard, dumbass. They don't have medical school at community college."

Tony winked at Arielle, and it was her turn to roll her eyes.

"Meh, potayta, potata. Besides, if I don't like what the doctor's got to say, I can just throw him a right hook, i'nt that right, Arielle?"

Arielle gave him the finger.

"You mention that again, and I'll be sure to land one on your chin… if I can find it."

Tony laughed a hearty laugh, and Martin mimed stepping between them to break up a potential fight.

The Woodwards were a bizarre couple, what with Tony being a mountain of a man and Charlene a thin, angular woman. But it worked—*they* worked. Arielle and Martin had met the Woodwards more than a decade ago, when they had first moved to Batesburg. Martin had sold his first house to Woodward, a smaller yet similar ranch-style home to the one that they were currently visiting—which, incidentally, Martin had also sold to them—and they had kept in touch ever since. They weren't what Arielle would consider *best* friends, partly because they led different lifestyles—case in point the Woodwards's affinity for drinking and partying, while the Reigns preferred a much more low-key lifestyle.

And although Arielle wouldn't dare say this to anyone, they were of different classes as well.

Just look at the contrast in their homes.

Arielle shook the negative thoughts away; today was a day for celebrating.

"And where's little Tommy?" Arielle asked, changing the subject. Her eyes scanned the yard for the little guy.

"Thomas," Charlene corrected. "And the little beast is right over there, happy as a clown!"

Arielle spotted Thomas just to the left of the sliding doors that Charlene had exited moments ago.

The boy was impossibly cute, the perfect combination of his parents' features. He had a round head with big blue eyes and thick red lips. His blond, nearly white hair was running a little long, and the ends had curled upward from the heat and humidity.

Arielle's heart nearly broke.

I'm going to have one of those.

Ignoring Tony's continuing prattle, Arielle made her way over to the toddler, who was so content in bouncing up and down inside some sort of saucer contraption that he didn't notice her approach.

When she got nearer, she squatted on her haunches and just watched, waiting patiently for Thomas to spin around and look at her.

The boy didn't smile when he finally noticed her, but her presence was enough to cause him to cease jumping. He stared at her with his giant marble eyes like a man inspecting a newly discovered species.

Who is this mammalian creature that doth squat before me? his marbles asked. *What does said creature want? Does it also provide sustenance and nurture from its udders?*

"Hi," Arielle said simply. She reached out and rubbed a dot of ketchup from the corner of his mouth.

The boy didn't respond to either her words or the gesture.

"Hi Tommy," she repeated. This time, the boy answered in the cutest little lisp-voice.

"Thomas," he corrected, jutting his lower lip defiantly.

"Oh, I see. Well, little Thomas—"

The boy shook his head, his curly blond hair whipping about his face.

"Not little."

Arielle laughed. The boy was so cute that her cheeks hurt from smiling.

"Well now that you're all grown up, I guess I can tell you a secret. I—"

Something bumped into her back and she was momentarily distracted. It was Charlene with her two martini glasses in hand. Some of the tequila-laden liquid splashed to the flagstones below, but Charlene failed to notice. Or maybe she did and just didn't care.

"And what's this secret, hmmm?" her friend asked, playing along with Arielle and her son. "Take the drink, Air, you're too sober for this party."

"I can't," Arielle said without thinking.

One of Charlene's thin eyebrows migrated up her flat forehead like a malnourished caterpillar.

"You can't? Why—?"

When Charlene saw the tears in Arielle's eyes, she stopped talking. Arielle waited for a moment as the woman's gears ground, trying not to laugh or cry or *something.*

Charlene's gaze bounced from Arielle to Thomas and back again. When her eyes landed on Arielle a second time, they went wide.

"Shut up," Charlene said, to which Arielle nodded. "Shut up!" she repeated more forcefully this time.

Now both of them were crying.

"Shut up!" she said a third time, and this time she shoved Arielle backwards so hard that she had to dig her heels in to stop herself from stumbling over Thomas.

Charlene raised both of her glasses high in the sky. Before Arielle could stop her, she let out a cry reminiscent of frat parties and sorority celebrations.

"Wahoo! Tony, we have some celebrating to do tonight!"

*   *   *

Tony's face was a deep shade of red when he finally made his way back downstairs.

"The little monster is finally napping," he informed them in a huff.

Arielle had come inside to get out of the heat, and she was sitting at the table with Charlene having a glass of ice water. Martin had remained outside manning the grill, as a few late-comers had arrived to the party. Despite what Tony had said earlier, he wasn't going to let any of his guests '*leave with an empty gut.*' So Martin had volunteered to put some burgers on the grill while Tony put Thomas down for a nap.

Arielle and Charlene had spent the last ten or so minutes catching up, which, of course, had mainly focused on Arielle's pregnancy.

Tony collapsed in the chair beside his wife like a sack of rotten onions.

"Monster," he gasped between breaths. "Evil, evil boy."

Deceptively quick, my ass.

He turned to Arielle.

"Did you know that he once shat all the way up his back to his hairline? No joke. Up to his hairline."

They all laughed.

"Anyways, Arielle, I—" Tony glanced at Charlene. "—*we* are so happy for you guys. I know how much you wanted this."

Arielle had cried so much recently that she feared dehydration, and took another sip of water to compose herself.

"Thanks," she said, and was about to add more before the sliding door suddenly opened.

Martin poked his head in, which Arielle noted was nearly as pink as Tony's had been.

He's into the sauce too... but it's a party, so who cares?

"Hon, your phone is blowing up over here. Rang like five times in the last two minutes. You wanna grab it? I have to feed the hungry dogs."

He had a beer in one hand, and was holding her phone out to her with his other.

"Quick, before the burgers burn," he added.

Arielle pulled herself out of her seat, picking up her water as she moved toward the door.

"Thanks," she said, taking the phone.

Her battery was running low, and the screen had dimmed, making it difficult to see.

"I'll be right back," she said to the Woodwards as she followed her husband into the sun.

She took a sip of her water as she scrolled to the missed calls.

Had Martin broke the news, maybe? Was it people calling to congratulate her? She remembered what he had said when they had first arrived a couple of hours ago.

'You decide if you want to tell.'

No, Martin wouldn't do that.

What, then? It couldn't have been Charlene who spilled the beans—I was with her the whole time, and she hasn't touched her phone. Tony, then?

All of her missed calls—of which there were four, and not five as Martin had said—were from the same number, one that wasn't in her contact list and she didn't recognize it.

She called the number back and when the voice answered, her heart fell into her stomach.

"Dr. Robert Barnes's office, how may I help you?"

Chapter 11

"No, I can't come in today. I'm at a party. Can't it wait for my next visit? I booked a follow-up in a couple of weeks."

There was a pause on the other end of the line.

"I think it would be best if you came back in today, Mrs. Reigns."

Arielle shook her head. She pictured the woman, a squat, troll-like creature with skin tags hanging from her doughy face.

"What's the rush? Why can't you just tell me what's up?"

Another pause. This conversation was starting to annoy her and she still didn't even know what it was about.

"Mrs. Reigns, Dr. Barnes specifically asked that you come back in today."

"Is it my pap? Abnormal cells?"

She had read about this; it's not uncommon for pregnant woman to have abnormal pap smears.

It was usually nothing to worry about.

The secretary sighed.

"Mrs. Reigns, please just come in."

Martin called her name, but she shooed him away. Her patience was wafer thin, and it was threatening to crack.

"Fine, I'll come in, but not until you tell me what the issue is."

"Our policy is not to reveal personal information over the phone."

That was it. The final straw.

Arielle lost it.

"Just tell me what the *fuck* is going on!"

There was a longer pause and Arielle started to pace. She knew that everyone at the party was now looking at her, but she didn't care. If this was about the baby…

"Mrs. Reigns, I'm sorry, but your blood tests came back and you're—you're—"

"Oh, for fuck's sake woman, spit it out!"

"Mrs. Reigns, I'm sorry but you *aren't* pregnant."

The words slipped out of the secretary's mouth with as much empathy as an accountant.

"What? Did you say *aren't*? That's impossible."

Her words came out in a strained whisper.

"We tested all three vials of blood, Mrs. Reigns, and the…"

The woman's words all melded together.

Not pregnant.

The glass of water slipped from her hand and shattered on the flagstones.

Not pregnant.

"That's impossible," she repeated. "I took the pregnancy test and I have fucking morning sickness, for Christ's sake."

There were concerned looks on the faces of the other partygoers now, but she paid them no mind. Somewhere far away, she heard Martin calling her name, but she ignored him, too.

Dr. Barnes's secretary's words detonated in her head like a bomb.

Not pregnant.

"Mrs. Reigns, sometimes when you really want something, the mind has a way of—"

"What the *fuck* are you saying? I fucking puke every morning! What. Are. You. Saying?"

She was gripping the phone so tightly that her fingers were starting to ache.

Then the woman on the line had the gall to sigh.

"This is why we don't usually reveal personal information over the phone."

She sensed that Martin had come near, but she turned her back to him. When she felt his arm slip around her waist, she pushed it away.

"You're gonna fucking lecture me, you stupid fucking twat?"

Martin reached for her again, but she shoved him so hard that he stumbled backward.

"Mrs. Reigns—"

"Don't 'Mrs. Reigns' me, you stupid goblin. I fucking pay—"

At some point during her tirade, Arielle realized that the line had gone dead, either because her phone had run out of power or because the secretary had hung up on her. It didn't matter which; she continued her tirade anyway.

"—your goddamn salary, you stupid bitch. So don't you *dare* sigh at me. And it isn't my fault that you haven't been laid in years, you crusty asshole. Why don't you hit the gym once in a while? Then maybe you'll get laid."

Seething, Arielle threw the phone to the ground, where it shattered into at least a dozen pieces of plastic. Her vision red, she stared at the broken glass and plastic that littered the flagstones.

Not pregnant? Not pregnant?

Only after the ramifications of those words began to settle did she look up and observe her surroundings. Martin was staring at her, his mouth wide, his hands at his sides. He was wearing the stupid '*Kiss the 'Cue*' apron, and this only enraged her further. At some point during her shouting, Charlene and Tony had also made their way outside and were standing just behind

Martin. The other couples had likewise stopped what they were doing—drinking, mostly—and had turned to face her. It was as if the entire world had stopped, as if everything was frozen in time like in a bad sci-fi movie. Except for her, of course; Arielle could see, hear, and smell—*God, the smell of rendered fat is disgusting*—everything. Even the music seemed to have stopped.

Silence; there was silence and dread and disgust. And then a wail suddenly filled the air.

It was Thomas; beautiful baby Thomas.

Evil, evil monster.

When Tony's eyes flicked back toward the open sliding doors in response to his son's cries, something inside Arielle snapped.

"What the *fuck* are you all looking at?"

"Air—"

Arielle glared at Charlene.

"Don't fucking 'Air' me, you drunk," she said, pointing a finger at her. "You don't deserve children."

Something happened to Charlene's face; her lips suddenly flipped downward, and all of her angular features suddenly became like softened rubber.

"Arielle!" Martin shouted as he moved toward her.

"Don't," she warned, immediately halting his progress. She turned to Tony. "And you, with your little fucking asshole of a mouth... you don't deserve Thomas or Tommy or whatever the fuck you call him either. *Evil monster? Evil monster?!* I would kill for a *monster.*"

"Air," Martin said again, almost whispering this time. His face had transformed into a mask of horror. "What's wrong? What happened to the baby?"

"There is no baby!" She threw her arms into the air and spun around, presenting herself to all the party guests. "You hear that, everyone? There is no fucking baby. Hope you're all happy."

She stopped just short of a bow.

What happened next only infuriated her further: nothing. Apparently, everyone was so shocked or confused that they failed to react to her outburst.

Her vision blurred as tears started to flow, and she wiped at her face with the subtlety of a blacksmith. When she turned back to Martin, she was surprised to see that there were tears in his eyes too.

No, you don't get to be sad, Martin. I'm the one who is sad. Not you. I wanted a baby, not you with your 'I'm enough woman for you' bullshit. I wanted the baby… needed a baby.

You didn't even fucking want it.

She remembered the words she had whispered almost every night for the past seven years, and they made her cringe.

Put a baby in me, Martin.

"You had one job to do, and you couldn't even do that," she spat at her husband.

Something in Martin's face broke, and tears spilled unabated over his handsome cheeks. He opened his mouth to say something, but before he could offer a reply, Arielle turned and ran from the backyard, leaving everyone with three parting words: "Fuck you all."

Chapter 12

Arielle walked for a good hour, not really knowing or even caring where she was going.

It wasn't fair. None of it was fair—definitely not the part about her *not* being pregnant. Or that the Woodwards had a kid while her fucked up body wasn't able to carry one.

A life for a life.

And she didn't care what the troll at Dr. Barnes's office said, *she* had been pregnant. The woman could talk all the psychosomatic bullshit that she wanted, but she *had* been pregnant.

Had.

But wasn't anymore.

Arielle eventually found herself at a small convenience store about fifteen minutes from her house buying, of all things, a package of cigarettes.

She hadn't smoked in more than five years. In fact, she had quit around the exact same time that she had started her boxing classes. At the time, she had told Martin that she was just making some changes to become healthier, but the truth was that she knew that quitting smoking and getting into shape would improve her chances of conceiving.

Everything she had done, from quitting her stressful ad agency job to work more reasonable hours from home, to quitting smoking, to working out, to limiting her alcohol intake to just a few glasses of wine on the weekend, to trying every goddamn trick in the book, including being assaulted by some psycho churchgoers, was in order to try and get pregnant. And, in the end, it had all been worth it because it had worked; she had conceived.

But now *this*.

"Give me a bottle of wine, too," she told the man behind the counter.

"What kind would you like? I have a brand new —"

Arielle pulled her sunglasses down her nose, revealing her raw lids and cheeks that were still wet with tears.

"Does it look like I care? Just give me a bottle—any bottle. Something cheap."

The man behind the counter with thick, bushy eyebrows and deeply tanned skinned frowned, but obliged.

"Seventeen fifty-six."

Arielle paid and headed to the park near her house. Even on regular days—not just on days as *fucked* up as this one—she often found herself at this park at some point during the afternoon. It was a great place for her to take a break from trying to come up with creative copy for a new client or just generally to clear her head.

It was just a small, simple park, with one swing set and plastic slide, but there was almost always a child or two playing with their nanny during the warmer afternoons. Arielle typically sat on the bench, drinking a coffee and watching the laughing children with a smile on her face.

Today, however, it was probably a blessing that there were no kids in the park. Because today she wasn't sipping coffee, but drinking sour red wine from a bottle wrapped in a brown paper bag. And she wasn't smiling, either; she was grimacing with every drag from a cigarette.

Less than three sips of the wine and an equal number of drags later, her head started to spin... most likely from the nicotine more than the wine.

"What the fuck am I doing?" she whispered.

She looked down at the cigarette, a brand she didn't even know, and then the crumpled brown bag concealing a wine bottle, the name of which she also didn't know.

"Seriously, what the *fuck* are you doing, Arielle?"

Go home, apologize to Martin. Then think of a way of how you can somehow make it up to the Woodwards.

She shook her head.

Did I really say that horrible stuff?

She hadn't been thinking, clearly, but *it just wasn't fair.*

Her throat and lungs burned from the smoke, but she took another drag anyway as a sort of penance.

Why can't I have a baby? Why can't I just let Dr. Barnes do his stupid tests and figure out if there is something he can prescribe to help me conceive?

These weren't just rhetorical questions, but ones that she had posed to herself for years, ever since...

Stop it. It wasn't your fault; she made you do it. You can't keep punishing yourself for something that you had no choice in.

With trembling hands, she brought the brown paper bag to her face and took a swig of the wine.

Although she had told Martin many, many times that she remembered nothing of her childhood, that wasn't *exactly* true; there was *one* thing that she remembered.

Maybe I could have stopped her — run away, maybe. Or hidden it better.

Another gulp of wine, another hard pull from the cigarette.

I was just so scared. I was young and terrified and...

Arielle tossed the cigarette to the ground in disgust.

"Stop it," she scolded herself.

You don't get to feel sorry for yourself. You're being a baby — an immature child. A child drinking wine at a park and smoking.

She was more than disgusted with herself; she was ashamed and appalled.

Arielle took a deep, shuddering breath, and ground the still lit cigarette with her heel.

Grow up. You desperately want a child, and yet you consistently act like one. Maybe you should accept the fact that maybe you aren't fit to be a mother. What did someone famous once say? Some things just ain't meant to be.

Arielle took one more sip of wine and then screwed the cap back on. Part of her wanted to smash the bottle right there on the ground, like she had destroyed her phone at the Woodwards's. A *big* part of her wanted to do just that. But, like an addict trying to get sober, she knew that the pain and regret that would chase the few minutes of satisfaction would just sink her lower. Still...

No. This self-pitying has to end.

She had to grow up and face the facts, no matter how much they threw a wrench in her master plan.

It wasn't the first time that she had considered just giving up all hope of having a child, but this was the first time that she felt like she meant it. All it had taken was to blow up at her husband, the Woodwards, and a bunch of people she barely knew, and find herself crying in the park, drinking wine out of a bag and smoking cigarettes. What she was going through definitely didn't qualify for *rock bottom* on any global scale—she was not naive enough to think that it was—but she didn't know how it could get any worse for *her*.

"Get over it. Move on."

Saying the words out loud seemed to empower her decision and, surprisingly, it actually felt good to say them. It was like a weight was lifted off her shoulders.

Can I do it? Can I really move on?

Martin had repeatedly told her that she was enough woman for him... but the real question was, was he enough for her? After going so many years wanting, *expecting*, to have a child, could she be content with just having Martin to love and to hold?

Arielle rose from the park bench and stretched her legs, which had already started to stiffen up from all the walking.

She didn't know the answers to these questions, but she did know that they wouldn't be answered here, in this park, or anytime soon, for that matter.

As she dropped the nearly full bottle of wine into the wire trash bin, a flash of orange suddenly crossed her peripheral vision. A Frisbee flew within inches of her still outstretched arm and skittered across the sandy park.

What the...?

Arielle turned in the direction that the Frisbee had come and caught sight of a young girl—four, maybe five years old—with long blond hair high-tailing it toward the park, waving a hand high above her head.

"Throw it back!" the girl hollered.

Arielle stared at the girl for a moment without moving. Then she surprised herself by smiling. It was hard not to; the girl was incredibly cute, with a small, upturned nose and rosy red cheeks. She was wearing a navy t-shirt with the words '*I luv Mom*' written across the chest in pink glitter-type.

"I'll get it!" Arielle shouted back, surprised at how quickly her mood turned.

Hustling back into the park, she reached down and grabbed the orange disk, squeezing it tightly in her fingers. It was an uncomplicated piece of plastic, just a flat, circular disk with a half-inch curled lip, but when she picked it up, it induced a strong emotional reaction in her.

Did I play with one as a child? Is that it?

Frustration at not being able to remember threatened to overthrow her pleasure, but she wouldn't let it.

So what if I can't remember? I can pretend, can't I?

"Throw it back!" the girl repeated. Her wide grin revealed two missing front teeth.

She was so cute it made Arielle's heart ache.

I luv Mom.

Arielle's throw was true, and the Frisbee whirled through the air, aimed directly at the young girl's navy t-shirt. At first, she thought she might have thrown it too hard, and cringed a second before the girl reached out and snatched it without hesitation.

Arielle clapped her hands together in both relief and surprise.

"Thanks!" the girl shouted, turning away from the park.

Arielle glanced around quickly for the girl's parents, but saw no one. The park was strangely empty for a sunny Sunday afternoon.

"Wait!" Arielle yelled, her maternal instincts taking over. The girl didn't acknowledge her cry.

Arielle's eyes kept darting back and forth, trying to figure out where the girl had come from.

She can't be out alone, can she?

The girl was almost out of view now, and without thinking Arielle broke into a jog, following after her long blond braid.

She was nearly in a full sprint by the time she hit the street corner, and as she turned, she stopped so abruptly that she almost tripped and fell on her face.

The girl with the blond hair was standing just around the corner, the Frisbee dangling in one hand. Arielle had nearly run right into her.

"Jesus," she said between deep breaths, "you scared me."

She brought a hand to her chest as she heaved. The girl's light-colored eyebrows lowered suspiciously.

"Why are you following me?"

Arielle took another deep breath and finally managed to straighten her body.

"I just... I just wanted to know where your mother was."

"Do you know my mother?"

Now it was Arielle's turn to make a face.

"Well, no, but—"

"Do you have any kids?"

Arielle looked away. Somehow, with those five words, this girl had made her feel both confused and ashamed at the same time.

"No," she admitted quietly.

The girl shrugged.

"I need some more friends to play with," she said simply.

Now it was Arielle's turn to offer a suspicious glance. This girl was confusing the hell out of her.

"What's your name?" Arielle asked.

The girl's face suddenly changed from wary to cheerful.

"I have to go," she said. "It was nice playing with you."

And with that, the girl whirled on the heels of her sparkling high-tops and sped off. This time, Arielle let her go, parent or not. Clearly this girl was able to figure things out by herself. Still, the entire encounter left a strange taste in her mouth.

What the hell was that all about?

She watched the girl's wagging braid fade into the sun.

With another deep breath, Arielle straightened and glanced around. She realized that despite having visited the park at least a dozen times this summer alone, she had never been on this street.

She found the green street sign above her head: Grove St.

Grove Street? Never even heard of it.

Her eyes drifted downward, and attached to the same pole that held the sign she saw a white sheet of paper. It looked like it had been hastily taped on, with clear tendrils of plastic tape hanging from each of the corners. The paper must have recently been posted too, as it was too white, too *crisp*, to have been up there for any significant amount of time. Normally, Arielle wouldn't have paid an ad like this a second thought. But this was no normal ad; there was one handwritten word in thick black ink that held her attention fast.

A word that had a specific meaning for her.

One that seemed to call to her, begging her to read more.

Just six block letters, but they were enough to draw her in. Six simple letters that spelled *MOTHER.*

Chapter 13

Only crackheads, prostitutes, and bookies use payphones in the cell phone era.

Or so Arielle had thought.

Well, you can add desperate women who want to conceive to that list.

The phone rang so many times that she almost hung up.

One more, one more—just one more ring.

As she listened to the phone ring, she realized that her thoughts were an odd microcosm that mimicked her decision to make the call: just one more chance—one more chance to try and make things right.

MOTHER.

The handwritten block letters had drawn her in, and the irony of her being drawn in by expert copy was not beyond her. The copywriter being coerced by copy.

MOTHER.

You will get pregnant and you will deliver a healthy child. 100% success.

It was the simplicity of the ad that pulled her attention, and it was the assumption that kept it. The ad never asked if the reader wanted a child, it simply assumed that they did.

MOTHER.

Those six letters were the key.

And here she was, cowering in a phone booth that smelled like weed and shit and—

"Hello?"

Arielle shook her head.

"Hello?" she replied, trying to force the desperation she felt from her voice.

There was a pause, leaving Arielle unsure of whose turn it was to speak next. She heard a soft crinkling sound, like an old leather wallet being twisted, and somehow she just knew that the woman on the other end of the line was smiling.

MOTHER.

"Coverfeld Ave."

The woman's voice was scratchy, as if she had spent the night shouting, but, almost paradoxically, it had a soothing quality to it.

Just thinking about this made Arielle clear her own throat.

"Sorry? I just—"

There was an audible *click*, and for the second time in one day, the person on the other end had hung up on her.

Fuck.

Coverfeld Ave? What the fuck am I doing?

*   *   *

For some reason, the fifteen-minute walk home only took eight, and getting changed, packing a small overnight bag, and getting into her car only took half as long as that.

It took a total of twelve minutes from the time she hung up the payphone to make it home and get ready to leave.

Arielle refused to believe that her speed was due to excitement over the newest prospect—over *Coverfeld Ave*—because this was a stretch, even for her; replying to an ad pasted to a light pole and a mysterious voice on the phone—a strange voice, an *old* voice, *MOTHER*'s voice—and expecting that somehow hidden in there was the secret to getting pregnant was borderline insane.

At best, it was a scam. At worst... well, at worst she would have to put her years of boxing training to the test. Perhaps Dr. Barnes's face had just been the opening act—the undercard, if you will.

Still, even knowing these facts, Arielle employed cognitive dissonance to keep her rational brain out of the equation. She was like a physician who was also a religious zealot; the two completely incompatible ideologies were nestled quietly and comfortably in different corners of the room. Like a complacent couple, without speaking or interacting, they couldn't rightly argue.

Nevertheless, she took almost everything out of her wallet save a few twenties and one piece of ID. Without a phone, she had to resort to the somewhat archaic act of searching the Internet for directions. Although there were about a dozen Coverfeld Avenues in the southeastern United States, there was one of them in particular that she kept turning back to. This Coverfeld Ave was located less than two hours away near Elloree, which was probably the reason why it seemed so *right* to her. Arielle had never been to Elloree, but she knew that it housed a large swamp whose beauty was best encapsulated by its name: Stumphole Swamp. While it was impossible to tell from Google Maps the details of any houses or compounds—*women's shelters?*—on Coverfeld Ave, it ran right along the swamp, which also felt right for some reason.

The woman's strange, harsh yet soothing voice on the other end of the payphone—*"Coverfeld Ave"*—suddenly repeated in her head.

In the swamp, she thought. *Coverfeld Ave definitely runs smack in the middle of the swamp. And this woman's house is probably right in the center.*

Her mind locked up as she debated whether to leave a note for Martin; some half-assed explanation of where she was headed (which he likely wouldn't believe) and how sorry she was (which would come off as insincere). In the end, she decided against it for two reasons: one, she had been such a crusty bitch that she doubted a hand-scrawled apology on the back of the grocery list would cut it, and two, she was a bit perturbed that Martin hadn't actually been there when she'd jogged home from the payphone. The latter was a ridiculously selfish notion, no doubt, but she was in a ridiculous mood. And the last time she had done something *this* horrible—an image of Kevin's face filled her mind, and she shook it away—and had left a note, it had not been well received.

Maybe Martin is out looking for me.

The alternative was that he had given up on her, that this afternoon's outburst had been the final straw... that after seven years of pressure to have a child, this most recent eruption might have broken even his rock-solid resolve.

Arielle did her best to force thoughts of either Martin or Kevin from her mind as she tossed her bag into the backseat of her Audi. Ignoring these thoughts wasn't easy; every time she pictured her husband, he was making the face he had made the night they had made love after she'd told him she was pregnant—it was his 'wow' face. But as Arielle put the car into reverse and backed down the driveway, her husband's phantom face changed. It changed in a way that reminded her of how she had screamed at him, of all the terrible things she had said. Martin's face, like his heart, had broken.

This better work, because I don't know if he'll forgive me this time.

Chapter 14

For once, Arielle wished that she had been wrong.

Not only was Coverfeld Ave *near* Stumphole Swamp, but it ran right through the damn middle of it.

She had no idea what she was looking for, and her driving slowed to a mere crawl once she turned onto the almost hidden road. There were no houses—none that she could see, any-way—and the way her tires continually spun in the soft mud made her wonder if anyone had even driven their car down the street within the past century. In fact, she was perplexed that Google had actually given this shithole the dignity of including it in their Maps. But, hey, it was probably part of their plan for global domination.

And why global domination would include this shithole, would include Coverfeld Ave, only Google knew.

Arielle's mindset had gone from excited at the unlikely pro-spect of finding Mother to just wanting to get the hell out of this creepy place—to drive anyway but on this damn mud-packed road. But then she saw something, and her mindset shifted once more.

Lying in the mud by the side of the road was a familiar shape covered in rotting moss.

It was a mailbox.

Muttering 'shit' over and over again like some demented mantra, Arielle slammed her car into park and sat there for a moment, staring at the unmistakable shape of the mailbox in the mud. The stake that had once rooted it into the ground was completely gone, leaving just the box portion. Squinting hard, she thought she could make out numbers emblazoned on the side of it with a Sharpie. A fucking *Sharpie*—like whoever lived there couldn't be bothered with actual fifty-cent numbers from the hardware store.

1818, the numbers read.

1818 Coverfeld Ave.

A shudder ran through her. For some reason, she knew that this was *the* place, that she had somehow found the place—the exact place—that Mother had directed her to. This, despite only being given a street name. A common sounding street name, nonetheless.

Shit, shit, shit, shit.

Her eyes flicked to where the driveway should have been, but of course there wasn't one; there was only a trail of mud that led from the road—and even the word 'road' was more a reflection of the use of the dirt-packed terrain that her Audi struggled through than any resemblance to an *actual* road—and through the long, thin, and generally leafless trees that were indigenous to the swamp.

Arielle sat in the car for a moment with the engine off. Her eyes drifted from her left—the swamp, a stagnant, boggy inlet of Stumphole covered in a blanket of moss—to her right—the mud-packed trail that led though the spindle-like trees to where she assumed must be a house in the distance.

Back and forth her eyes whipped until she feared getting dizzy and closed them tightly. Her hand subconsciously went to her forehead, massaging her temples with the pads of her fingers.

What in God's name am I doing here? And how the fuck did I even find this place?

She didn't want to—*couldn't*—answer the question with any rational response, so instead she threw the car door open and stepped into the stagnant air.

She expected it to smell bad outside, given the thick patch of green-brown vegetation in various states of decay that suffocated the swamp bank to her left.

Arielle scrunched her nose.

But this time, she *had* been wrong; it didn't just smell *bad,* it smelled God-awful. There was the unmistakable scent of rotting leaves and something else... an underlying funk that was difficult for her to place. Sulfur, maybe? Eggs left out in the sun too long?

Regardless, the smell was horrible, and she immediately switched to gulping air through her mouth instead of breathing through her nose.

She checked her watch next, then turned her gaze upward to the pathetic tendrils of sunlight that leaked through the tall tree trunks. The trees themselves weren't completely devoid of leaves—*wrong answer number two, Steve*—she realized; rather, all the foliage had congregated at the top, forming a canopy so dense that it was more like a professorially made brick-and-mortar awning than something organic... which she cared very little about, save for the fact that it trapped the nasty smell like a greenhouse.

Arielle adjusted her shoes next—grateful that she had chosen to wear flats on this day, what with the Woodwards's barbecue—and then shifted her blue sundress. The underlying reason for these innate rituals was not beyond her—basically doing anything and everything to postpone turning up the mud drive of 1818 Coverfeld Ave—but this realization did nothing to hasten her step.

What the fuck am I doing here?

Adjusting her dress, fixing her hair, and tree-gazing were all better than trying to wrap her mind around that incessant question.

With a deep, open-mouthed breath, Arielle eventually turned to the mud-packed drive and took her first step. And another. And another. With the fifth or six step, she finally saw the house.

The urge to turn and run, to get back in her Audi and haul ass back to her urban life with her husband, was so strong that she nearly succumbed. It was only the thought of returning home to face Martin, with no hope of ever getting pregnant, that kept her moving forward.

Arielle realized that she had probably been staring right at the place when she had first looked up the drive, but it blended in so well with the trees that she hadn't seen it.

It was a large, Victorian-style home with heavily washed-out red bricks that bordered on gray, which was one of the reasons that it was nearly indistinguishable from the thin trees that both flanked and surrounded it. If someone wanted to build a two-story house with the intention of camouflaging it in a swamp, then 1818 Coverfeld Ave would most definitely serve as a formidable template.

The right half of the building was set in front of the rest, and was covered with a large, peaked roof and a bay window that was boarded up with plywood. A roofed porch was off to the right, above which were several rounded-top windows. These windows weren't boarded up, but might as well have been: the thick black curtains that hung in them completely blocked out the interior. The brick, in addition to being a washed-out gray, also had to contend with tendrils of dark green moss that reached nearly to the roof.

It was getting late in the day, and deep shadows shrouded the porch, making it difficult to make out much of anything beyond the front rail.

Arielle glanced down at herself and then back at the house about forty paces up the muddy walk.

The scene was so absurd that she nearly laughed out loud. It was as if Alice from Alice in Wonderland had found herself lost in front of an abandoned crack house.

Screw Alice in Wonderland, this is Alice in the Crack Den.

Arielle took a deep breath in through her nose and immediately gagged. The smell was worse near the house, and she had forgotten to breathe through her mouth.

Spitting a hunk of phlegm on the ground beside her loafer, thoughts of regret, confusion, and disapproval again flooded her mind.

What am I doing here?

If she hadn't driven for the better part of two hours, and if she hadn't exploded at the party, she would have left the creepy place right there and then.

Probably.

But then there was, '*A life for a life.*'

There was always that.

Her hand made its way to her stomach, and she massaged the still swollen abdominal flesh through the thin material of her dress.

Where did you go? You were in there once, but now where did you go?

Knowing that if she continued down this path she would break down into tears and collapse in the mud, Arielle forced her hand away from her stomach.

No. No self-pity. You are here to get things done. One hundred percent guarantee, remember?

Part of her knew, and *had* known ever since picking up the payphone, that this was borderline insane, but it was all she could think of that would help move her forward.

Arielle gritted her teeth and took another few steps toward the house.

I'll knock, then leave, she compromised. *After all, there is no way someone lives here—not in* this *place.*

The air suddenly stirred, and a shiver traveled up her spine. After the sensation passed, the cool air was actually a welcome relief to the stifling stillness of a few moments ago. The moving air also served to clear out some of the foul smell from the roof of her mouth and nose, for which she was also grateful. She was almost able to breathe through her nose again.

Amidst the sound of rustling leaves high above her and the *drip, drip, drip* of water somewhere behind her slowly filling the swamp, she started to pick up another sound: a rhythmic creaking noise, like a rusty chain being gently caressed by the wind.

Has it been there all along and I just didn't hear it because of the crazy shit running through my head and my loafers being deep-throated by the mud?

The sound unexpectedly increased in both tempo and volume, and a vision of the hawkish woman in the church, the one with the tears still wet on her cheeks and trembling hands, suddenly filled her mind.

Filius obcisor!

It wasn't really the words that had frightened her, although they'd carried an undeniable condemnation, but it was the *way* the words had been spoken.

Filius obcisor!

They had been uttered like the words of a grieving father at the sentencing of his child's murderer. They had been filled with sadness, malice, and vengeance.

I shouldn't be here. I need to leave.

This sentiment was so jarring that it actually stopped her forward progress.

I need to leave this place. I need to leave now.

And this time she would have—Arielle would have spun her heels in the mud beneath her feet and high-tailed it back to her Audi and gotten the *fuck* out of there—except the creaking suddenly stopped.

The sound had been coming from the porch, of that she was now certain. Squinting hard, Arielle leaned toward the house.

There was someone on the porch.

A woman.

An old woman.

"Arielle, is that you?"

Chapter 15

The porch swing creaked once more as an old woman craned into view.

Arielle could only stare; any words that she had prepared to say, which, granted, were bizarre in and of themselves—*Hi, I'm here for a baby? Oh, hi there, we spoke on the phone? I'm looking to get pregnant*—stuck in her throat like an over-sized olive.

The woman staring at her from the porch swing had a face like worn leather. A ribbed sun hat had been pushed back from her face, revealing high cheekbones with enough creases to make a relief map of Utah blush. The woman's thick blue eye-shadow and pale pink lipstick stood out on her heavily tanned skin. Gray hair seemed not to fall out from beneath her hat as it appeared to *crawl* out, only to give up just above her shoulders.

As Arielle watched in what could only be described as sheer wonderment, the woman brought a thin, wrinkled hand adorned with several large turquoise rings into view. She placed a cigarette between her lipstick-marred lips and slowly inhaled. A moment later, she exhaled, and when the smoke cleared, the woman leaned forward even farther, revealing ear-rings that matched her turquoise rings.

Filius obcisor.

They looked eerily like the stones from the church, the ones that desperate woman threw into the bowl beneath the painting of Raymond Nonnatus—like the one that Martin had stolen.

"Arielle?" the woman asked again. Her voice was the same as Arielle had heard on the other end of the payphone, which seemed to not only be separated by an inordinate amount of time, but the vast reaches of space as well.

What the fuck am I doing here?

She gaped, unsure of how to respond.

The woman looked away as she took another drag of her cigarette. When she turned back to Arielle, she was grinning.

"Of course it's you, Arielle." The woman patted the spot on the porch swing next to her. "Come, sit beside me."

A slurping sound came from her left, and Arielle immediately swung her head in that direction.

For the second time in less than a minute, her heart skipped a beat.

At first, she thought that two of the long, thin trees had been chopped down and were going to crush her. But when they articulated in an awkward, uncoordinated fashion, she realized that they weren't trees but *legs*.

She tried to step backward, but her feet stuck in the mud, and it was all she could do to keep from falling on her ass.

And she gaped. She couldn't help it.

The man that shambled toward her was so tall that his face was obscured by shadows, his head blocking out the sun. He must have been close to seven feet tall, dwarfing her five-and-a-half-foot frame. Dressed in a red-and-black checkered shirt and a pair of soiled overalls that stopped just short of his ankles, he looked like a caricature of an emaciated lumberjack. His feet were plunged so deeply into the mud that he had to pull his leg at least a foot out of the ground before putting it down again. And when he did, he revealed a knotted mess of mud that lacked any semblance of a foot. If she were a betting woman, she would have put her money on him not wearing any shoes.

In the end, all of Arielle's preparation for what to say should anyone be home at 1818 Coverfeld Ave—and now *two* people!

Who woulda thunk it?—were for naught, as two words spilled out of her.

"Jesus, fuck!"

She tried to move her feet again, but the mud held fast. Her hands instinctively balled into fists, and she stopped just short of raising them in front of her face as Kevin had first taught her so many years ago.

Punching would do no good here; she could not possibly fight this giant of a man, no matter how uncoordinated he appeared.

The porch swing creaked loudly from somewhere off to her right, but Arielle kept her eyes trained on the man who simply stood there, teetering on one foot about ten paces from where she was rooted.

"Jessie!" the woman from the porch hollered. "Back off!" She let out some bizarre a hiss/whistle combination, and the man responded immediately with a head nod and a sound that might have been construed for agreement. Then he planted his leg in the mud, the movement accompanied by a horrible suckling sound, and turned without another word.

Arielle watched him awkwardly shamble back into the trees, her mouth still wide.

What the hell was that? Jessie?

When he finally retreated out of sight, Arielle took a deep breath, her heart rate returning to somewhere near normal.

The wind had died, and the foul air had returned.

"Don't be bothered by him, sweetie. He's harmless. Just an overgrown oaf that takes care of the yardwork for an old woman."

Arielle glanced around briefly at the muddy lane, the overgrown moss creeping up the side of the house, and the tall, branchless trees that raced up to a canopy that nearly blocked out the sun entirely.

Yardwork?

"Completely harmless, my dear. Now, why don't you come here and sit beside me?"

The woman's grin returned, and against her better judgment, Arielle took two deliberate steps forward.

Two steps. That was all it took before her rational mind kicked into gear again, telling her that this was ridiculous, probably even dangerous. But the other half of her mind was curious. Interested. *Determined.*

And, as usual, the latter won out.

There was something about the woman's voice, something that drew Arielle in. The soothing quality that had been apparent on the phone seemed amplified in the calm, swampy air.

"Who are you?" Arielle asked breathlessly. Despite her years of training, moving through the muddy driveway was proving exhausting.

The woman brought the cigarette to her lips and took another drag. Then she smiled, revealing a perfectly white and perfectly straight set of teeth that couldn't possibly have been her own.

"You know who I am," she replied simply.

Arielle continued toward the porch, finding herself nodding as she put her muddy shoe on the first wooden step. Like the rest of the house, the porch was a bland gray, the color of microwaved meat.

The woman's smile grew.

"You know who I am, sweets," she repeated.

Her smile was so wide now that it seemed to literally stretch from ear to ear, nearly splitting her leathery face in two.

Arielle sat down beside the woman, breathing in her lavender scent. It was too cloying for her taste, but it was still a welcome relief to the general sulfurous funk of the swamp.

"Mother," Arielle heard herself whisper.

The woman nodded.

"That's right, sweets, you can call me Mother."

*   *   *

When the sun weakened to the point that it could no longer penetrate the dense canopy above, Arielle and Mother decided to head inside.

For some strange reason, Arielle had spent what felt like hours talking to the woman, opening up about nearly everything. She'd told Mother, this *stranger*, about her desperate desire to bring a child in this world and her inability to do so. She went as far as to talk about what the events of earlier this afternoon, about how she had snapped at her friends and her husband. And the whole time, Mother just sat and listened. She didn't crack jokes like Martin would have, or go glassy-eyed like Charlene Woodward was apt to do. Instead, the woman appeared to genuinely listen—she wasn't just thinking about how to respond while Arielle spoke. She did what was so rare in a society obsessed with instant gratification and judged merit based on the number of upturned thumbs. No, the woman simply *listened*.

When Arielle's tale made it to seeing the numbers *1818* emblazoned on the mailbox and nearly driving away, she exhaled deeply.

Mother took a drag from what must have been her tenth cigarette and smiled.

"Come, let's go inside. I have something that will calm you down. And then we can really chat."

The interior of the house was not much different from the outside: everything was a dreary gray, from the couch to the ornate bookshelf, and everything was seemingly covered with a thin layer of dust.

Mother sat in a large wooden rocker by the bay window and instructed Arielle to take a seat on the couch. Arielle half expected a puff of dust when she sat, but the stale air in the house remained relatively clear as she sank into the worn cushion.

Mother snapped her fingers, and Arielle heard a stirring from somewhere behind her. Drawing her head from her hands, she swiveled and, like when the hulking Jessie had somehow sneaked up on her, Arielle was taken aback.

Two young girls who couldn't have been older than four or five bounded into the room from the doorway leading to what Arielle assumed was the kitchen. With identical blond pigtails and small, upturned noses, Arielle wouldn't have questioned her if Mother had told her that they were twins. Still, the girl on the left was a little larger, and based on the way she stood a half a foot in front of what Arielle presumed was her sister, it was clear that she was the dominant one.

"Girls," Mother said with a wan smile, "would you be so kind to get our guest a nice, warm glass of milk?"

The girl in front nodded.

"Yes, Mother."

Together, the two girls receded back through the doorway.

Mother? She couldn't possibly be—

"Now," the woman with the blue eyeshadow and pale pink lipstick continued, "a pretty woman like you *deserves* a child."

Arielle felt herself nodding despite herself.

"You are very beautiful. When I was younger, I—"

Something in the woman's face changed; a flicker, a shimmer, passed across her worn features. Then she laughed.

"Oh, listen to me. I'm just being a silly old lady." She laughed again. "Today is not about me, sweets, it's about you."

Arielle cleared her throat.

"That's—"

The woman's eyes suddenly darted to above and behind Arielle and she let out a small burst of air, making the same whistle/hiss sound that had driven Jessie to action.

Arielle whipped her head around, her brow furrowing. It wasn't just the two girls returning to the room this time, but *three*.

The blond head of a third girl peeked out from around the corner. She had a long braid and was wearing a t-shirt with the words *'I luv Mom'* on it.

It was the same girl from earlier in the day, the one with the orange Frisbee. Arielle was almost sure of it. But when she blinked, the girl was gone.

How can it be?

"Hey," she said, turning back to Mother. "Is that the—?"

Mother shook her head.

"You should drink some of the warm milk. It'll calm you down."

"But—"

Mother shushed her.

Arielle wasn't sure that she needed *calming down*, but she was feeling parched. The last thing she drank was some sour wine at the park. So when the two girls suddenly appeared in front of her, the larger one, the one that Arielle was now convinced was at least a year older than the other, holding out the pint glass of milk, she took it.

Arielle smiled at the girl, who had yet to say a word.

"What's your name, little one?" She turned to the other girl when the first offered no response. "Is this your sister? And the other girl? That your sister too?"

Mother made that strange whistle/hiss sound again and the girl averted her eyes. A blink, and they were gone.

Who are these girls, and how can the girl with the Frisbee possibly be here?

Arielle brought the pint glass to her mouth and she took a sip. The warmth and sweetness of the liquid surprised her.

"Don't worry about the girls," Mother said. "They just stop by every once in a while to help an old woman with some chores."

Arielle thought about what Mother had said about Jessie.

'He just does the yardwork.'

Well, if Mother is telling the truth, Jessie is just about the worst fucking gardener that ever lived.

Her eyes scanned the dusty coffee table between them.

And these girls are God awful at 'chores'.

Arielle took another sip of the warm milk with Mother watching on intently. She felt like a superhero and Mother was an evil villain who had poisoned her drink and was watching her to make sure she drank it all.

"A life for a life," Mother whispered, and Arielle's eyes rocketed up.

"What did you say?"

Arielle had intended to snap at the woman, but the words came out slowly with a strange drawl.

"Whaaaa d'ju saay?"

Mother just smiled.

Arielle licked some of the liquid from her upper lip and decided that she had had enough milk. Clearly, she was no superhero, but she wasn't so sure that *Mother* wasn't some sort of twisted villain.

'Villain.' What a strange word.

She rolled her tongue.

Villlll-aiinnnn.

When she went to put the glass on the table, her hand seemed to move in slow motion, as if migrating through a thick ether.

"You *deserve* a child," Mother assured her as she leaned back in her chair and began rocking slowly back and forth. This action, like her voice, seemed to soothe Arielle. "And I can guarantee that you will have one of your own."

The woman smiled again, and Arielle found herself smiling along with her.

"But there is one condition. One promise that you must make."

Arielle's head began to swim, and she blinked hard, trying to clear both her blurred vision and her foggy brain.

It seemed to work, as the next time when Mother spoke, she leaned in close and listened carefully to her instructions, making sure to pick up on every detail, every nuance in the strange woman's velvety-smooth voice.

Chapter 16

The car ride home was admittedly murky for Arielle. Any clarity that had struck her in the old woman's gray house had quickly dissolved after taking the first sip of that curious milk.

But the woman's words, those were still clear. It was just the minor details, like who had been in the house with them—there had been others there, hadn't there been?—that had fled her.

Mother's instructions were as clear as the to-do list that she typed on her cell phone every Sunday night.

Cell phone… where is my cell phone?

The door was open when she finally made it home, and the lights were still on.

She found Martin in the kitchen wearing only an undershirt and jeans, a glass of scotch clutched firmly in one hand. He didn't immediately notice her when she walked in, so she took a quiet moment to observe him.

His hair, usually perfectly flopped to one side, was a damp mess atop his head. He looked softer than usual; his muscular physique seemed somehow flaccid, an odd sallowness that extended to his cheeks. It wasn't just tonight that had taken its toll on Martin, she knew, but it was the culmination of the past seven years. Despite his continued assertion that she was *more than enough woman for him*, Arielle knew that he too wanted children. Why else would he volunteer to coach the Real Estate Brokers' children's little league team without a child of his own? Why else would—

Martin suddenly sighed and his head slumped, his eyes closing slowly. Feeling now that her observation was beginning to border on voyeurism, Arielle cleared her throat to announce her presence.

When he turned to her, it was patently obvious that he had been crying, what with his red eyes and the wet track marks on his cheeks. Arielle wasn't sure what reaction to expect out of her husband, so she just stood there, her muddy feet rooted on the hardwood, her hands hanging at her sides.

In the end, his reaction was better than she could have ever hoped. Martin rushed to her, scooping her up in his arms. Arielle was so taken aback by this that she didn't raise her own arms in time and they were pinned to her sides. He buried his head in her neck.

"You're back," he whispered. The smell of scotch on his breath mingled with the sweat from his pores. It wasn't the most flattering combination, but she was so oversaturated with foul smells that she barely noticed. "Thank God you're back. Where the hell did you go?"

Despite asking the question, he didn't wait for her to answer. Instead, he pulled his head away and shouted over his shoulder.

"Woods! Woods! Arielle's back!"

Arielle immediately regained control of her body and she gently pushed her husband away.

"Woodward is here?" Her eyes went wide. "Tony's here?"

Martin didn't need to answer. Instead, Arielle heard someone enter the room, sucking out the oxygen, and even without turning she knew that it was Tony Woodward.

Facing Martin after what she had said and done was one thing, but facing Woodward was something that she didn't think she could handle right now. Instead of turning, she grabbed for her husband, and this time it was she who hugged him. As she did, she leaned up and whispered in his ear.

"Please make him go. I need to talk to you."

Martin pulled back to look at her more clearly. Seeing the seriousness in her expression, he nodded subtly.

Old; he looks so old. Old and tired.

Keeping his eyes trained on Arielle, he spoke.

"Woods, Arielle's fine... we, uh, we need some time alone."

Martin's eyes darted upward, and there was a silent exchange between the two men that Arielle didn't catch. A moment later, the oxygen returned to the room as Woodward vacated it. A few seconds after that, she heard the sound of his car start through the door that she had forgotten to close, and then it faded into the night.

Arielle was surprised that she hadn't noticed his cruiser parked out front when she had pulled up, but she shook this away too. She hadn't been thinking clearly.

But now she was.

Now everything was clear again.

'You deserve a child, sweets.'

When Martin turned back to her, Arielle leaned in and kissed him full on the lips.

He pulled back.

"Air? What the—?"

Arielle leaned in again and kissed him. She felt him try to push her away again, but she pulled him in tighter with her arms, and then her tongue.

Mother's leathery face and pale pink lips flashed in her mind, her soothing voice uttering her instructions.

'Go home tonight, sweets. Leave this place and drive your beautiful body back to your beautiful house. And then make love to your beautiful husband.'

When her tongue darted into Martin's mouth, teasing, inviting, the man couldn't resist, and despite the horrible things she had said and done, he began to kiss her back.

She pulled him tighter, and felt the front of his jeans begin to stiffen.

And after you make love, come back here. Come back here with the child brewing inside of you, and stay here until he or she is born.

Arielle slipped one of her hands from the small of his back and reached down to the front of his jeans, squeezing his manhood gently.

Martin's breath against her lips hastened, and Arielle couldn't suppress a small smile.

*   *   *

Martin had been so exhausted that he hadn't asked Arielle too many questions, for which she was grateful. He hadn't made any jokes, either, which concerned her a little.

After making love—in the kitchen, no less, without even bothering to close the front door—they had made their way up to the bedroom, where Martin had promptly passed out. He hadn't even finished his scotch.

Arielle, on the other hand, had lain beside him with her eyes wide for several hours, the afternoon's events cutting through her mind like a riptide.

'Go home tonight, sweetie. Leave this place, and drive your beautiful body back to your beautiful house. And then make love to your beautiful husband. And after you make love, come back here. Come back here with a child brewing inside of you, and stay here until the child is born.'

It was ludicrous, of course, but what wasn't? Was it less or more ludicrous than holding her knees to her chest, trying to will Martin's sperm to collide with her egg? Was having sex based on a lunar cycle as crazy?

She swallowed hard.

Who knows—how can one measure degrees of desperation? Is there a scale?

What she did know, however, was that if there was a scale, she was at the high end of crazy.

This was her last chance.

A life for a life.

Arielle gently lifted Martin's arm from her stomach and laid it across his chest. Then she slid out of bed.

Ludicrous, surely, but that wasn't the most disturbing thing that Mother had said.

The most disturbing thing was the old woman's *'one condition.'*

Arielle pulled her jeans on without waking her husband.

'There is one condition, sweets,' Mother's words echoed in her head. *'One very important condition that you* must *consider before agreeing to this deal.'*

She pulled her sweatshirt over her head, keeping her eyes trained on Martin as long as possible, prepared to freeze if he stirred even a little.

But Mother's words didn't matter—her "condition" meant little to her now, and would mean less when she was pregnant. And it would mean nothing at all when her child was eventually born. She would humor the woman for now—would go through her charade, stay in her gray house—but on the off chance that she did bear a child, she was out of there, never to return again. She would leave Mother's leathery face and the swamp stench in her Audi's rear-fucking-view.

She was about to turn and leave, but hesitated for a moment. Blue moonlight spilled through the slats of the blinds, illuminating Martin in what looked like wisps of blue smoke.

He'll forgive me. He knows how much this means to me. He has to forgive me.

Martin's face was flaccid, his lower lip quivering with every breath. His right arm lay across his chest, his hand resting over his heart.

Arielle quietly made her way to the bed and hovered over her husband. Then she leaned down and kissed him gently on the cheek. When she pulled back, she was surprised by the tears that had formed in her eyes.

"I love you, Martin," she whispered.

And when this baby that you put into me tonight is born, we will be a family again. I promise.

Arielle backed out of the room, Mother's pale pink lips moving in her mind.

'There is one condition, sweetie. One critical condition that you must *consider before agreeing to this deal.'*

For once, Mother had waited for an actual response out of her. So she had done what anyone in her position would have done to keep the conversation moving: she had nodded.

'You can have a child, sweets, but when this child turns four, you must bring her back to me.'

Arielle opened the front door and stepped into the night.

Bring her back?

She made a face and resisted turning back and offering the same parting salute that she had offered the guests at the Woodwards's party.

Bring her back? Like hell I will.

Part II – Nurture the Seed

Chapter 17

"Look, I just want to know if you've seen her." Martin turned his palms upward to indicate that he didn't want any trouble. "That's it."

The shirtless man leaned out from behind the heavy bag and turned to the twenty-something woman in the pink sports bra and matching shorts who was hopping on the spot.

"Take a break, Janelle. Grab a drink and meet me back here in ten."

"Sure," the woman replied. She stopped jumping, brushed a piece of sweaty blond hair from her face, and began to walk away.

They waited for the woman to recede out of earshot. When she had made her way to the front of the gym to grab her water bottle from a bag whose color—*surprise!*—matched her sports bra, the smile on Kevin's face faded.

Martin cleared his throat and stared at the much younger man. Even though he himself was a bit of a lunch-hour gym rat, he looked like a couch potato compared to Kevin. Shit, the man's muscles had muscles. Even beyond his physique, however, the man was intimidating. It wasn't *just* his reputation, his history as a boxer, the scars that were nearly completely buried in his eyebrows, or the cuts on his lips that the man's beard only did a half-decent job of covering up; it was all of these things, all of them together.

But Martin wasn't here to fight.

"I just want to know if you've seen her, is all."

Kevin fully stepped out from behind the heavy bag, and for the first time Martin noticed that the man's hands were knotted into fists. Big fists.

Martin responded by raising his palms higher.

"Look, I don't care about anything but finding her. That's it, I promise."

Kevin's eyebrows lowered on his shiny forehead.

"That's it," Martin reiterated.

His fists relaxed just a little.

"Haven't seen her."

Martin tilted his head to one side, trying to determine if Kevin was telling the truth.

"Really. I don't care about *anything*" —he stressed the word— "except for finding her."

"Really?"

"Really."

"That why you brought the nine-nine?" Kevin hooked a chin toward the door.

Martin turned.

"Damn it," he muttered under his breath.

He had told Woodward to stay out of sight, not to come in unless it was absolutely necessary. And while it looked as if the man had heeded Martin's advice when he had taken up post just outside the door, part of his gut, complete with the iconic navy uniform, was clearly visible through the glass.

Martin turned back to Kevin.

"I'm desperate, man, I just want to know if you've seen her... I don't care what happ—"

"I haven't seen her. For real. She missed her last two sessions. Haven't heard from her or seen her since... last Friday?"

Martin felt his heart sink. Last Friday was just before the Fourth of July party at the Woodwards's. The night Arielle had gone missing.

For a brief moment, Martin just stared at the man before him, knowing that he had bedded his wife. On some level, Martin knew he should be angry, that he was *expected* to be furious, incensed even, but he wasn't. Instead, he felt an odd sadness for the punch-drunk boxer. After all, Kevin needed to try and steal what Martin had in order to give himself happiness. If anything, Martin thought he caught an air of anger towards *him* from Kevin. And *that* was sad. Truth be told, he wasn't really angry at Arielle for her indiscretion, either. After all, Arielle was like an empty vessel, or a plastic cup peppered with holes. No matter how hard you tried to fill it with soda, beer, wine, spirits... it didn't matter. No matter what you poured into it, it just slowly trickled out the other end. Which was probably why she wanted a child so badly, and why she had slept with her boxing coach. And it all stemmed from her childhood, or lack thereof.

Martin had known Arielle for more than a decade, and during all those years she had told him very little of where she was born and how she was brought up. It wasn't a case of her being secretive; it was, more simply, that she just *didn't know*. In fact, she couldn't remember anything before the age of twelve, when she was adopted by the two elderly people she referred to as Aunt and Uncle. And when they died a few years back, Arielle was alone—except for him, of course. She had him.

But apparently that wasn't enough.

And tiny glimpses of memories weren't enough for Martin, either; he had been compelled to find out more. A number of years back, he had approached Woodward with a favor: could a police officer find out information about where Arielle had come from? Could he find out anything at all about her past? Martin's intention had always been to surprise Arielle with anything he found, but when Woodward had come back with a hospital record nearly a year later—well, he wasn't cruel enough to share it with her.

"What happened?"

Martin snapped out of his head.

"What?"

He loved Arielle more than anything in the world. And now she had disappeared, and he felt as if *his* past had been stolen. That *his* memories were also muddled. Despair must have shown on his face, because when Kevin addressed him again, his tone was softer this time, as was his body; all the tension had left the man.

Martin didn't want to fight. Martin just wanted to find his wife. His lonely, desperate, and confused wife.

"Did something happen? Where'd she go?"

Martin shook his head.

"I dunno."

"Well, I haven't seen her, man."

Shit.

Martin reached into his pocket and pulled out a business card. Holding it out to the man who had fucked his wife was absurd on many levels, he knew that, but what else was he to do? He *had* to find her. And if this man could help him, well... he would suck it up. But despite Martin's frankness, Kevin seemed less than inclined to help. As it was, the man just stared at the card as if Martin were handing him a rotting fish.

It took a few moments, but Martin thought he finally interpreted the man's expression.

Kevin was questioning how Martin could lose Arielle—he blamed Martin for her disappearance, which was unsettling.

Could it be that there was more to their relationship than a fling?

It was something he had considered, but thought it unlikely. The real question was, did it matter?

Martin shook his head; it *didn't* matter, not really. What mattered was finding Arielle.

"Please," Martin pleaded.

Kevin finally took his business card.

"Please call if you hear from her. I just need to know she's okay."

Martin didn't wait for a response. Instead, he turned quickly and made his way to the door.

When he passed the woman with the vibrant sports bra, he could feel her eyes on him; she was staring at him with all the subtlety of an elephant inspecting a mouse. Martin focused his attention on Woodward's muffin tops that spilled into the doorway.

Kevin can have this woman, as long as I get Arielle back.

"Let's go, Woods," Martin said as he pushed the door open.

Woodward turned to him, a concerned expression on his round face. Seeing Martin, his face took on an 'is everything all right' appearance.

"Yeah, everything's fine," Martin replied to the unasked question. "Except your damn hips. Goddamn muffin tops always getting in the way."

Woodward smirked. Martin didn't.

"Let's go find my wife."

Chapter 18

Martin Reigns

298 O'Brien Lane
Batesburg, SC
29006

July 17, 2016

Martin,

There's not much that I can say to you now—I know that. There is probably nothing that I can say that will make what happened okay. But I'll say it anyway, if nothing else but to try and ease my mind: I'm sorry.

I'm sorry that I acted the way I did, and I'm not just talking about at the Woodwards's party (although I'm very sorry about that, don't get me wrong). I'm talking about the past seven years. I know it hasn't been easy for you, and the whole time you've been nothing but support-ive—you've never made me feel bad for it. I know things—I know *I*—have changed a lot since we married… and it's unfair that I have become a very different person from back then. I know this has to be frustrating, especially because you are pretty much the exact same as way back then (and that's a good thing!). Okay, maybe a little different—more gray hairs, ha!

I don't mean to beat a dead horse, but I have changed so much because I want to have a child—

have wanted one for as long as I can remember.
And I *deserve* a child to share my love with. *We*
deserve a child. So I'll say it again: I'm sorry for two weeks
ago and I'm sorry for the past seven years.
You've been kind, sweet, and supporting, and I
hope to pay you back for this one day.
And that leads me to where I am now—to where
I went. And you're not going to like my answer.
The truth is, I can't tell you exactly where I
am right now. But I don't want you to worry. I
am safe here. Mother, the woman who runs the
place, says I can tell you a bit about *what* the
place is, just not about *where*. The truth is,
I'm not totally sure where I am. I guess, at
its core, it's a place where women who are
struggling to conceive can come and be safe, to
talk, and (most importantly) to get pregnant
(no, not that way, perv—remember my visit that
night? *That* was the night). I know that sounds
weird, but all the heavy lifting has been done
already (wink, wink), and now it's all about
nurturing the baby that you put inside me.
Silly, I know. But it's my—our—last chance.
Worst case scenario, I learn a lot about myself
over these next nine months and come back as a
better wife for you. And as a mother. Please,
God, I hope to come back a mother.

It's the weirdest thing, too (okay, the whole
thing is weird, I can see you chuckling now);
Mother has these earrings and rings that look
exactly like the stones from the church. Like
exactly… same color, same shape (bigger, but
still). Weird, huh? Maybe there was something
tp Saint Raymond Nonnatus. Who knows.

Anyways, I feel… different. I don't know If
I'm pregnant yet (Mother says that will take
some time to know for sure—they don't take blood

here), but we are all hopeful. Right now it's me, two other women (for now; Mother says people come and go), and the girls. The girls are super helpful; there are three of them, all between five and seven. Celeste is the oldest, Madison is in the middle, and Hanna is the youngest. They call each other by their names, but I'm pretty sure they're sisters. They have the sweetest blond, almost white hair. They call Mother 'Mother', but everyone calls her that. She is way too old to be their actual mother. Best I can figure it is that they are Mother's grand or great-grandchildren helping her out. They don't talk about it much—the kids don't talk about *anything*, really—but I'm guessing they are just doing her a kindness.

Sleeping quarters are nice, if a little plain. I share a room with one of the women here. Melissa. She's kind, a bit older than me (I know!), but she is eight months pregnant. She's a bit of a bigger woman (I'm being nice here), so she doesn't have the typical huge belly hanging off of her—more like she has excess skin everywhere (yeah, that kind of bigger). Still, she says she can feel the baby kicking, although when I place my hand on her belly, I can never feel it. In a couple of months, maybe I'll feel my own kicks… one can hope, right?

The food is probably the worst thing about this place. Well, I guess it's not the food, exactly, but the *milk*. I don't know which is stranger: that they basically force-feed this stuff to us, or that it tastes a little off, a little too sweet to be *just* milk. And it makes me feel, I dunno, a bit *weird*. I often get sleepy after finishing my glass (one pint, no more, no less). Mother says that that's a good thing, that the milk is infused with iron and other nutrients to help make sure that the baby grows. I dunno about that, but if there's a chance it's anything other than just gross, I'll suck it up. Literally.

We get out and walk twice a day—once in the morning and once at night. The smell is bad here, almost as if the swamp is rotting or something. Let me tell you, the walks aren't my favorite part of my day. But Mother says that they too are important, so I'll suck them up as well.

I know what you are thinking, and I can assure you I haven't completely lost my mind... at least, not since coming here. And no, we are not burning bras on the lawn every night and cursing the evil penis.

This is my last chance, Martin. I know that now. If this doesn't work, then that's it. It's over. I don't get how Mother can guarantee success, but whenever I ask about it, she just says it's about a state of mind. Which is why I *have* to stay here. She says that if I leave, the chances of me having a live birth are about the same as if I never came here—and we both know how well that worked out. I don't know if I feel pregnant, *per se*, but I definitely feel different. And the good news is that I haven't been sick yet, like before.

I think it's the milk.

I know this is an impossible request, but please don't worry about me, Martin. Again, I don't know how to explain this without you thinking I am even crazier than you already do.

I'm sorry. I really am. I never wanted any of this. All I ever wanted was a child.

And you. I want you, too. I know you always said that I am enough woman for you, but I'm not. No one is; you are too good for me or any one woman. But maybe if there are two of us... maybe if we have a baby girl... then maybe that will be enough.

I love you, Martin, and I hope you still love me.

Please write.

XOXO
Arielle

Chapter 19

"The phone is completely trashed. I tried giving it to my IT guys to see if they could get anything from it, any incoming or outgoing call information." Woodward hesitated. "Nothing. They couldn't pull up anything."

Martin put his scotch glass back on the counter and shut his eyes.

The two of them were leaning on his kitchen island, standing across from each other. Woodward had arrived about ten minutes ago at about eight, after having gone home to change out of his work uniform first.

Woodward was a good friend, there was no denying that. He had come by nearly every night since Arielle had gone missing. For the first few nights — weeks, even — they had discussed strategies on how to find her; where they should look, who they could call, just what the *fuck* they were supposed to do. The problem was that their options were limited because *officially* Arielle wasn't a missing person. *Officially*, a grown woman who goes ape-shit at a party, comes home and fucks her husband, then packs a bag full of clothes and takes her ID with her isn't *missing*.

No, that scenario didn't typically qualify as a description of a missing person. That described a woman who had met someone — who had left her husband for another life.

But that wasn't Arielle. Despite her previous indiscretion, that wasn't her.

No way.

Martin opened his eyes and took a sip of his scotch. Woodward did the same as he patiently waited for a response. When Martin offered none, the man continued.

"But the lab report came back on that mud that Arielle tracked through the hallway."

Martin's eyes snapped up.

The mud; he had forgotten that Woodward had taken that to friends in the lab to see if they could figure out where Arielle had gone between storming out of the party and arriving home late that night.

"And? What'd they say?"

"Worth checking out. The mud was from a swamp here in South Carolina. The lab said that they have narrowed it down to one or two specific regions based on microbial content."

Martin made a face and Woodward laughed.

"I know, fucked up what they can do now, isn't it? This broad in the lab did it as a favor for me, so..." He shrugged.

Martin took another sip of his scotch and then raised an eyebrow.

"She owed you a favor, did she?"

Woodward laughed again. Despite his immense size, the man's laugh was on the high-pitched side. And when he laughed, the thick skin beneath his chin—Martin assumed there was a chin in there somewhere—quivered.

"Long story. Anyways, Stumphole Swamp is probably our best bet—where we should start first. What do you think about this weekend?"

Martin mulled over his friend's proposition for a moment. He had a big deal closing at the new supermall—he was hoping to get Best Buy and Walmart to anchor either end—and it was something he couldn't really miss.

Or could he?

His numbers had taken a nose-dive ever since Arielle had split about a month ago. And if they kept going south for much longer, the other partners were going to speak up, regardless of what he was going through.

Jesus, was it really that long ago? A full month without her?

There would come a time, he knew, where he would have to concede that Arielle had just left him. She'd wanted so badly to have a child that it had consumed her. And when she'd failed at that, it was as if she had failed at *life.*

The thought made Martin shudder. Until now, he had refused to exercise *that* possibility. Arielle wouldn't take it that far, would she? Was she so torn up about not being able to carry a child that she would harm herself?

No.

Martin refused to believe it.

He finished the rest of his scotch in one gulp, aware that Woodward was eying him suspiciously.

There may come a time when I give up, but not now. Not yet.

"This weekend," he confirmed, "let's find Arielle this weekend."

Let me get my life back.

Chapter 20

Martin Reigns

298 O'Brien Lane
Batesburg, SC
29006

August 14, 2016

Martin,

I can't believe it. Ha, I can barely write, my hands are shaking so much. I missed my period (TMI, I know)! I feel… different, too. I know this is it. I spoke to Mother this morning, and even she couldn't help but smile.

I'm pregnant. For the second time in just over three months, I'm pregnant!

I'M PREGNANT.

I feel like shouting, like crying, like punching the wall. I guess this is what it means to be pregnant—all my emotions bubbling up and overflowing. I mean, I feel the same things as before, only now everything is more *heightened*. And where before I could shut some of these off, now that I'm pregnant there is no way to stop them.

But I don't care because I'M PREGNANT.

I'm putting on some weight, too, much faster than last time. I guess without my boxing classes, these twice-a-day walks—I'm beginning to feel a little like a puppy now—aren't really cutting it.

BUT I DON'T CARE.

Sorry about this letter… I mean the writing and the wet paper (those are my tears of joy, BTW).

They're still pumping me full of this milk… yech… I don't know if it's just that I hate it more and more each day or if it's getting thicker (I know, nasty), but I can barely stand it. And after every glass (twice a day, just like the stupid walks), I get so damn sleepy.

Anyways, I haven't heard from you—you never replied to my last letter—so I hope you are not still pissed. Maybe you are. But hopefully my news helps you forgive me!!!

XOXO
Arielle

P.S. Melissa—the one I was rooming with—had her baby. A beautiful if tiny baby girl named Olivia. So cute. It's weird, though, Melissa looks exactly the same now as she did before giving birth (remember what I said about her being a bigger woman?). I mean, exactly—soft all over. Oh well. After I give birth, I'm gonna hit the gym hardcore. But only after I heal up and look after the baby. The baby comes first.

P.P.S. I'M PREGNANT.

Chapter 21

Neither Woodward nor Martin knew exactly what they were looking for. But all they were *seeing* was swamp.

And swamp.

And more swamp.

"Fucking hell, who knew there was this much swamp only two hours from Batesburg?" Martin grumbled.

Against his better judgment, they had taken Woodward's cruiser for the drive north. Martin thought that it might send warning bells to someone if they were, for reasons he didn't want to consider, hiding information about Arielle. But Woodward had insisted for pretty much the exact same reason.

'If they aren't scared yet, they will be when they see the cruiser. Especially if they are the Deliverance types.'

Yeah, that was probably the last thing Martin wanted to see today—some cross-eyed hillbilly strumming a banjo.

"Are we sure that the mud came from here?" Martin asked, if for nothing else but to change the subject of the thoughts in his head.

The road—if you could call it that—was so narrow and poorly defined that Woodward had to keep his eyes trained on it at all times to avoid getting the cruiser's wide tires stuck.

"Nope," he replied out of the corner of his mouth. "They could only tell me that the mud that Arielle tracked through the house was from up north. Just figured that Stumphole would be the best place to start, given that it's the largest swamp in the hood. Besides, I used to camp here as a kid, so I know the area a little."

Martin made a face.

"You camped here?"

Woodward chuckled.

"Yup. Dad was a sadist, what can I say?"

"*People* camp here?"

"Nope. Not people; just me and my dad—that's it. Was really the only time we did anything together. I think it was more about him getting away from my Ma than any sort of bonding experience with me. But every year for four days in the summer, we would drive up to Stumphole and set up camp in the mud."

Martin stared out the window.

Who in their right mind would camp here?

"Yup," Woodward said as if he were reading Martin's mind. "Just me and Pa."

Then he went on to hum a few bars of the Deliverance song.

Martin smirked and turned back to the window.

Mud—why didn't I notice that Arielle was covered in mud when she stormed in that night? Am I such a simple man that the only thing I cared about was getting my rocks off?

But that wasn't fair, and he knew it. After all, she had basically thrown herself at him.

You could have said no. You could have asked her where she'd been, and that it didn't matter that she had run her mouth at you and the Woodwards. You could have told her that she was forgiven.

That thought struck a chord with him, and it resonated in his mind.

Did I make her do this? Did she feel so badly about what happened that she needed me to console her? Was her throwing herself at me just a test? A test that I failed miserably?

"Marty? You all right?"

Could she have—could she have felt so badly that she… that she hurt *herself*?

Martin shook his head.

"Marty?"

"Huh?"

"I asked if you were all right. You looked… spooked."

"Fine—as fine as I can be." He cleared his throat, and was about to leave it at that when a thought popped into his head. "Hey, question for you: can you track Arielle's credit cards? Bank cards? Find out where she's been spending money?"

Woodward's face twisted and he shifted his considerable girth in his seat. It looked like he was either constipated or try- ing to hold in a fart. Martin didn't let him off the hook; he con- tinued to stare at his friend, whose own gaze was locked on the road.

"Ah, Marty, I dunno, man. I don't think I can do that."

"Can't or won't?" Martin pressed.

Woodward squirmed again. Now he looked as comfortable as a first-time drug mule crossing the border… in one of those countries that had a severe penalty for drug trafficking. Like beheading severe.

"You want me to be honest?"

Martin nodded cautiously. It was clear that Woodward had had something like this—an answer like this—prepared and had just been waiting for an opportunity to use it. And appar- ently the opportunity had arisen. No one said, *'want me to be honest'* without needing to get something off their chest.

"Shoot."

"Truth is, I *can* probably get someone to check Arielle's credit cards. But I'd be breaking federal law, man. That wouldn't be like calling in a favor to the lab to check out some mud… that would be breaking *federal law*. And"—he tapped the gold star on his chest—"even this wouldn't protect me from going to prison. Remember what happened with, ugh, with the other thing, too. Maybe it's a can of worms we don't want to open, my friend."

The 'other thing' that Woodward was referring to was what he had found on Arielle. About how his digging at Martin's behest had revealed a police record and a hospital report from about a month before Arielle started living with her 'Aunt' and 'Uncle.' A report about a twelve-year-old girl wandering nude through the streets of nearby Creston.

A girl with blood running down the insides of her legs.

A girl with no home, no memory, and no parents.

Martin shuddered.

Woodward was right; that had been a mistake. One that he had refused to share with Arielle.

Some things were just better left unknown.

Martin made a sound that was halfway between a grunt and an affirmation.

"You're right. I'm sorry," he grumbled.

I shouldn't have put him in that spot. He—he shouldn't even be here with me. This is my thing. It's my Arielle.

But his tongue had uncharacteristically loosened of late, with him saying things that normally would have remained locked up tight. And when he did say things, what were once playful jokes had turned mean-spirited.

It had started with encouraging several of his smaller clients—new couples, mostly—to take shitty deals for their homes when he knew they could haggle for at least an extra ten or fifteen grand. Not big money in the grand scheme of things, but big for Batesburg. And fifteen grand was fifteen grand—who couldn't use extra cash? Then there was him smoking cigar after cigar inside his house... cigars that he couldn't even taste anymore, and whose enjoyment had long since dissolved.

And then there was the mall deal. He could have been diplomatic about it and asked a favor of one of his partners to take the deal, even though it was his—they probably would've understood, considering the shit he was going through. Or he could have lied and told them he wasn't feeling well.

They would've understood.

Shit, *he* would have understood.

But he hadn't done any of that.

Instead, he had made up some lame excuse that he couldn't even remember in order to yell at his partners and then leave in a huff, muttering something about taking a few days off and hoping that they would pick up the slack.

It wasn't fair.

It wasn't fair to ask Woodward to break the law.

It wasn't fair that he and Arielle couldn't have a kid.

It wasn't fair that she had run away.

Martin closed his eyes and forced his thumb and forefinger into them.

He was getting desperate, which meant that this was likely one of the final steps before he gave up and moved on.

But he didn't want to move on, not just yet.

Fuck, why did you have to take off, Air? Why couldn't you just be content with all of the things we have? With each other?

"Weird..." Woodward muttered.

Martin pulled his fingers out of his eyes.

"What?"

Woodward extended a pudgy finger over the wheel.

"There. You see that?"

Martin saw nothing—just more of the mud road and miles of moss-covered swamp. Exactly the same thing they had been staring at for the better part of five hours.

"No," he answered.

"There. The tire marks. At the side of the road." Woodward brought the cruiser to a stop. "See how they are deeper and then shallow, then deeper again? Look, see there?"

There were indeed fresh-*er* tire marks in softer, wetter areas of the mud that hadn't been packed by whatever few cars had passed over the past week—or month, or year.

"That pattern—the deep indentations, then shallower ones, then deeper ones—that only happens when someone pushes or pulls a car and then takes a break every few meters. The car settles with the rest, making it even more difficult to get it going again."

Martin shrugged; he now saw what Woodward was referring to, but he didn't know what it meant. Could someone have taken Arielle's car? But if they had her car, wouldn't they have her keys, too? Why didn't they just drive the car? Someone had run out of gas? But then why push the car?

Woodward took his foot off the brake and the car crept forward at a snail's pace. His eyes were fixed on the side of the road, but Martin, for the life of him, couldn't tell what the hell he was looking at now.

"There!" Woodward suddenly shouted excitedly.

"What?"

"There!" he repeated, bringing the cruiser to a stop.

Martin squinted hard. He raised his eyes from the tire marks and stared at the trunks at a half dozen emaciated trees.

Birch trees? Do birch trees grow in swamps?

"You see it?"

Martin shook his head.

"See what?"

Woodward grunted as he shifted his body and leaned over into the passenger seat. This time when he flicked his chubby index finger, it passed within a few inches of Martin's nose.

"There."

And this time Martin did see it.

There was a mailbox lying by the side of the road, one that someone had obviously tried to cover with heaps of rotting moss. They had done a shitty job, and Martin could see the familiar shape clearly now that it had been pointed out to him.

"Yeah," Martin said, nodding vigorously, "I see it."

He pressed the trigger on the door and the window rolled down, affording him a better look.

"I think..." He squinted hard in the fading light. "I think it says eighteen on the side of it—can't really tell because of the moss."

Woodward shook his head.

"No, not eighteen. Eighteen eighteen."

Martin shrugged.

Could be, but what does it matter?

"Why would someone cover it up?" he said, thinking out loud.

Woodward jammed the car into park, causing the vehicle to lurch in the mud.

"Don't know, but I'd say that it's just cause to check it out. What do you think?"

There was a twinkle in his eye when he said this, and Martin wasn't sure if he liked what that meant.

Chapter 22

Martin Reigns

298 O'Brien Lane
Batesburg, South Carolina
29006

September ?, 2016

Martin,

I still haven't heard from you… you can't still be mad at me, can you? I mean, I—we—finally did it! I'm pregnant… for sure I'm pregnant now. I'm putting on more weight. Mother says I'm 8 weeks now. 8 weeks! Can you believe it? We don't have calendars here, and since I broke my phone (no phones allowed anyway, bad for the baby, Mother says), I really don't know what day it is. What I do know is that the sun is setting earlier and it's getting cooler every day. So much so that I had to borrow a light jacket for the evening walks. I think it was Melissa's… it's still quite large (she was a big woman), but I think I can grow into it. I *know* I will grow into it.

Mother says I can get letters, but I can't have visitors. Not yet. She says I am sensitive—sorry, *the baby* is sensitive—to outside interference now. I know, I know. I don't believe half of this shit… ha, not even close to half. But fuck, who knows. It's working. Mother says in a few weeks I might be able to feel the baby move. Says it'll feel like tiny little bubbles in my stomach. I'm so excited!

Also, about Mother. She looks like she's actually packing on weight too. Weird. There are two new women here, both pregnant, Joan and Jamie. JJ, I call them, although not to their faces. They're always together. JJ are older than even Melissa, and I don't talk to them much. They are strange… I think Joan (or is it Jamie?) talks to herself at night. Oh, and they talk to each other a lot, but usually only after milk time (yeah, it's a thing—like, 'you know what time it is kiddies? It's milk time!'). Anyway, JJ whisper back and forth, and occasionally I pick up some words here and there. Most of it is about not having a husband, and their fears about whether or not they can raise a child alone. I think they might dyke it out and raise the babies together (between you and me). Their collective age must be pushing a century, but, like me, they're pregnant. I had my doubts (their fleshy stomachs aside), but hey, Mother says this is a non-judgmental space. You can bet that I'm fitting in just peachy.

Aside from our walks, there really isn't much to do. Most days I just sit in my room, or in what I now call the 'lunch room,' and read books. Been digging into some of the classics (not my first choice, but that's all Mother has) like Twain and Dostoyevsky (sp?). I tried Tolstoy, but War and Peace is impossible. Seriously. There are about a billion characters, and every one of them has a name that is some derivation of Peter… Piotr, Petra, Peetie, etc…

I miss you, Martin. I miss your stupid jokes and everything about you. I miss spending time with you, just hanging out. Please, I need a letter or something to let me know you care. The last thing I want is to be stuck in a three-some with J and J. Our celebrity name would be JAJ… sounds like some sort of Japanese manga character. See? I suck at jokes. I need you to keep telling them.

Write me.
Please.
I love you.

XOXO
Arielle

Chapter 23

"Well? You ready?"

"For what?"

"To go up to the house."

Martin furrowed his brow. They were standing on the side of the mud-packed road staring into a line of thin tree trunks.

"House? What are you talking about, house?"

Woodward sighed and extended his finger.

"Jesus, Marty, what's wrong with you? You blind? There's a house right there."

Martin tried to follow the man's finger like he had with the mailbox, but this time he saw nothing.

Except for the trees. There were those. And they were everywhere, dotting the muddy landscape like ill-placed spears.

"What the fuck are you talking about?"

"Fuck, Marty, there's a fucking house right there! Forty feet up the walk."

Martin blinked rapidly three times, trying not only to clear his vision but also his mind. It had fogged over even before they had exited the car, and now that they were exposed to the sheer funk of the swamp, his confusion had only gotten worse. And so had his headache.

"Woods, I don't—"

Tony Woodward made his way over to him with surprising speed despite his size and the suctioning mud and grabbed him around the shoulders. He stunk like sweat, but even this was a relief compared to the sulfurous swamp. Martin went slack and allowed Woodward to turn his body. Then, staring down the man's finger like the sight of a gun, he saw it.

"There, you—"

Martin pushed the other man's hand down.

"I see it," he replied softly.

In the distance—more like sixty feet than the forty Woodward claimed—there was a washed-out gray Victorian house. Martin guessed it had been built in the late 1800s, or maybe even before that. It was tough to tell because, like the mailbox, it blended into the trees with amazing precision. And, like the mailbox, it too was covered in moss.

"Yeah," Martin said, his heart fluttering for some reason. "Let's go check out the house."

Chapter 24

Martin Reigns

298 O'Brien Lane
Batesburg, SC
29006

October

Martin,

Marty. I never call you that anymore; I wonder why that is. I'm feeling strange a bit these days. I'm growing fast; you should see my belly. Everything is big—ha, so much for training. It's gonna take forever to get this off. It's all worth it, though.

It's getting cold here. And my room is not so nice anymore. There is some cold air coming through the walls at night, and last night I think I heard a mouse. A mouse! Mother says I'm paranoid, but I dunno. Why would there be a mouse in here? Mother says that you can't visit because that's bad for the baby—the stress is bad—but I can be up all night freaking out because I'm cold and I think a mouse is gonna shit on my face? Like, c'mon.

At this point, I don't even know if you would come if she would let you. Are you still mad? Why are you still mad?

JJ are mocking me, I think. Talking behind my back. I think they are going to ask me into

their lesbian triangle. They think I can't
raise a kid alone, but I know I can.

I just don't want to.
Please Marty, write me back.
Please.
I'm begging you.

XOXO
Arielle

Chapter 25

"All right, so you know those Deliverance jokes?"

Woodward nodded.

"Well, don't make any more of them. Too real. Too close for comfort, know what I mean?"

Woodward pulled his foot out of a wad of mud that suctioned to his police shoe. He swore.

"Fucking A," he said. "I mean, look at this shit. Looks like no one has been here in a hundred years."

Martin lifted the corner of a porch swing that hung from the rotting roof by two chains. There was a burnt smudge on the left side of the swing that looked like someone's ass had caught fire and they had thought it a good idea to put it out on the seat. The chains were so rusty that thick flakes of coppery metal fell away when Martin let the swing go again.

"Creepy," Woodward muttered as the thing creaked and cawed like an old woman crooning.

Martin turned to his friend and watched him try to navigate through the mud and up to the porch. Woodward was so heavy that his feet sank in to nearly his ankle bones, and when he lifted that leg, it only drove the other one deeper. Martin knew that the clichéd quicksand that you saw in movies didn't exist, but this was pretty damn close.

"Wait! I don't know if this porch can support your fat ass."

"Very funny," Woodward replied. But when he finally managed to step on the first worn deck board, it groaned in protest.

Marty laughed.

Despite all of this—Arielle leaving, them at this creepy fuck-ing place doing God knows what—he laughed.

Laughter. Giggling.

What the fuck is wrong with me?

The porch held, and eventually Martin and Woodward found themselves side by side roughly six inches from the front door.

"Well?"

"Well."

"Do we knock?"

Woodward shook his head.

"No, *I* knock. Officer of the law and all that."

And then he knocked, rapping his chubby knuckles off the door with such ferocity that Martin thought he saw the rotting wood flex beneath them.

The sound echoed through the house as if it were completely empty.

Martin's mind started whirring.

So much for this idea.

The problem was, if this failed, Martin had no idea what to do next, what else he could do to try to find Arielle. He was at his wits' end.

Woodward's knocking snapped him back into reality.

When there was no reply this time, Martin spoke up.

"Let's just go, man, this is fucked."

He could feel his hopes fading fast.

Martin tugged at his friend's shirtsleeve and was about to turn when Woodward resisted.

"No way. I didn't fucking drive two hours to turn around. And I definitely"—he alternated raising each of his mud-cov-ered shoes and pant legs—"didn't ruin my fucking shoes to just turn around."

"What do you want to do?"

"I'm the law, remember? I'll just kick it down. Rambo style."

Marty couldn't suppress his smile.

"Okay, first of all, Rambo was not a fucking cop. And secondly, what happened to federal crime? Going to prison and all that?"

"Meh, fuck it," Woodward said with a shrug. Then he raised his mud-covered shoe and drove it into the base of the door.

Chapter 26

Martin Reigns

298 O'Brien Lane
Batesburg, SC
29006

December

I'm scared, Martin. One of the J's had their baby… I'm having difficulty telling them apart for some reason… and it was fucked up. She looked fine, just kind of big all over and soft (not as big as Melissa, but close), then she said she felt sick and Mother came and took her away.

But she came back, Martin, she came back and she was *fucked*.

J was in a wheelchair and she looked dead. I'm not joking, she looked horrible. Jessie was parading her around while me and the other J were shouting at him to get the fuck out of here and get a doctor, but the man was just going about his business as if nothing were wrong. She was in a gown of some sort, and it was almost entirely soaked with blood. I don't know if it was the wheelchair or the fact that she was just wearing a nightgown instead of the thicker clothes that we all wear—yeah some real convent shit—but she was HUGE! Her belly was massive. I mean, what the fuck, Martin. She went from just looking fat like me to having a massive belly and bleeding everywhere. Shit, she was so pale with the blood dripping onto the floor and the wheelchair leaving blood tracks… I'm going to have nightmares. I think she's dead. But that wasn't the worst part. Fuck, Martin, I think I could hear the baby crying, like it was faint and wet and muffled, but Jesus Christ, can you hear a baby crying when it's about to be born? Like, inside the body? I don't know—that sounds crazy—but I swear I heard something like it.

A fucking baby crying after birth should be a happy thing. This was absolutely horrible.

Please, Martin. Write me. I can't do this on my own.

Fuck, I hope J isn't dead.

Arielle

Chapter 27

The house stunk nearly as bad as the air outside—a thick, pungent mix of mold and staleness. And with every step they took inside, they stirred more dirt and dust.

And more smell.

"Fuck," Woodward swore between sneezing bouts into his sleeve.

"I think you're right. I'm not sure anyone has been here in years."

Martin looked around the room as he spoke. They were in what was clearly some sort of family room, complete with a wooden rocking chair and a couch across from it. There was a network of spider webs clinging to the chair's rockers, a clear indication that it hadn't been moved in some time. The couch was much the same, but instead of spider webs, it was covered in a thick layer of dust.

The inside of the house pretty much matched what Martin had expected based on the dilapidated exterior.

And it was very depressing.

Arielle wasn't here; never had been.

Woodward likely saw the despair painted on his features as he pushed by him.

"Not everything is as it seems," he said, clearly trying to comfort his friend.

No kidding, Columbo.

Martin almost said the words, but bit his tongue. He didn't feel like joking anymore.

"There's nothing here, Woods. Let's just go."

Woodward ignored him and continued farther into the house.

"I'm going into the kitchen," he said as he swiped his finger along the back of the couch, creating a clear line in the dust.

"Waste of time," Martin muttered.

He stood three feet inside the doorway, staring into the room, his mind wandering, trying to come up with something new. Some new way to track his wife. Some new way of convincing himself not to give up. To not get desperate.

It took what felt like an hour of just staring before he realized that there was something amiss with the scene before him. Everything seemed in (or out) of place, depending on how he looked (or stared) at it. The dust, the old-fashioned rocking chair with spider webs, the fabric couch, the wooden table between them. Everything was exactly the way it should have been. Except for one thing... one little thing.

"Martin! Hey, come take a look at this."

Martin's eyes were fixed on the small table situated between the rocking chair and the couch.

"Just a sec," he hollered back.

There was a small, clear patch on the dust-covered tabletop.

"Marty? There's a lock here, on the floor in the kitchen. It was under a rug."

Shut up, Woods.

The clear area was the size of a —

"Martin! Get your ass over here! I think it's a door!"

The size of the bottom of a pint glass.

"What the —?"

There was a serious of rapid, consecutive thuds from somewhere down the hall that were so quick that Martin didn't have a chance to turn before he felt strong hands on him. Big hands.

Hands so big that it only took one of them to wrap completely around his throat.

Chapter 28

Martin

298 Brien Lane
Batesburg
2906

January

Okay, I think I overreacted in my last letter—in case you even bothered to read the thing. J is fine; she came back a couple of days ago and showed us her brand-new baby girl. Like Melissa's baby, she was tiny but super cute. And J looks okay too; still fat, but at least she has regained *some* color in her face. Shit, Martin, I really thought that she was dead. She told us that she had some emergency C-section that left a nasty scar, but that she is healing up nicely and will be going home soon.

That was scary, really scary.

Back to my baby—*our* baby. Fuck, Martin, why don't you write me?—Mother says it might come early. I don't really see her much anymore... sometimes she looks almost as bad as J did... but when she comes in, she just puts her hands on my stomach and feels around a bit. Nothing invasive, which is perfect for me. I have no idea how—or if—she can tell anything by doing that, but she says it's her "experience." And I guess she must be doing something right. I mean, J was nearly fifty years old and she had a baby...

almost fucking died (yikes), but had a healthy baby girl. Mother must know something.

Still, I'm scared, Martin. And I'm tired, so fucking tired. I haven't felt the baby move in a while. It's the milk, I'm sure of it. The stuff is nasty. I think I puked because of it. I'm not too sure, but my pillow stunk like some overly sweet cocktail in the morning. But then they brought another glass. As if they were watching me. And they made me drink it, the fucking girls—these Children of the Corn girls who always seem to be around, like they don't have any parents of their own—just waited until I drank it. Told me they couldn't leave until I finished it. I gagged. And then I got sleepy again. Slept. Heard the mouse. Mice. There are more of them now. And the walls here are wet.

I tried to refuse the milk at lunch a couple of weeks back. And when I did, the girls came and sat with me. They were nice at first, but then when I said that I didn't want it, they just waited. And waited. And waited. We sat there for about 3 or 4 hours (I don't know for sure because there aren't any fucking clocks in the place) and they just fucking smiled at me with their perfect little smiles. Even the one with no teeth—Madison? The one with the Frisbee from the park?—has a perfect smile. And then eventually I started shaking. Almost like I was having a seizure. And they just watched. I knew Mother was watching too, although I couldn't see her. I just knew it.

I drank the milk. I didn't want to, but I did.

I did it because I didn't want to hurt the baby. Please, Martin, I can't do this on my own. I know that now. I am so tired, so damn fucking tired and foggy. Can't think straight, it's pregnancy brain for sure.

I thought about running away. Sneaking the fuck out of here and running to you, but I'm beginning to think that you don't want that. After all, you haven't replied to me yet. And Mother promised me the letters were going out.

Have you found someone, Martin? Is that it?

I want out, Marty. I want to take the baby and go. I *need* to get out.

I need you to come get us.

If it's a girl, I think I'll name her Hope, Marty. I dunno why, I guess I just like it. Hope for a new life, a new family, new beginnings.

Please write me. Please don't forget about me.

Arielle

Chapter 29

"Marty? Marty! You okay in there?"

Martin couldn't move; he could barely breathe. The hand that clutched his throat was so strong that he feared that if he just turned his head even a little, let alone tried to escape, his throat would be crushed.

Attempting to speak was out of the question.

"Marty?"

Martin heard his friend pull himself to his feet even amidst the heavy breathing coming from somewhere high above him.

His own breaths were coming out in short bursts. His heart was doing the same with his blood.

A few seconds later, Woodward stumbled into the room. When he raised his head and stared at Marty, his eyes went wide. Then his eyes kept traveling upward, and upward, and upward, until it seemed as if he was staring at a spot near the ceiling.

And then something snapped in him and Woodward stumbled backward while at the same time grabbing at his gun on his hip. It took several attempts before he managed to free it from his holster.

Martin's eyes bulged so much that he feared they might pop from their sockets. If what Woodward saw, a cop for more than eighteen years, caused him pause, then he could only imagine what kind of man gripped him.

Woodward put two hands on the gun and pointed it at a spot above Martin.

The hand around Martin's throat tightened.

"Put him down! Put him down, now!" Woodward shouted.

Someone, or something, grunted above Martin.

"Why are you in my house?" The voice was deep and scratchy, the consonants melding together in a mumble.

Woodward seemed to have collected himself, and the next time he spoke, his voice was strong, assertive.

"Put him down, now!"

Martin had never seen his friend like this—the entire time he had known Woodward he had *never* seen him like this. His soft, doughy friend had suddenly gotten hard.

"Why are you in my house?" The man's voice was like sandpaper stroking a bassoon.

Woodward seemed unfazed.

"Put. Him. Down."

And then, miraculously, Martin felt the hand on his neck release. Air suddenly rushed into his mouth and throat, burning as it traveled all the way down to his lungs. He fell to the floor in a heap.

"Now step back."

Martin, still gasping on the floor, heard a shuffling noise as the *thing* behind him receded, making the stale air easier to breathe.

"You broke into the house."

The words were stated matter-of-factly, and Martin cringed. He tried to turn and look up at whatever had gripped his throat, but his body failed to respond.

"Look, I'm putting the gun down, okay? But if you move, I'm going to raise it again, and this time I'll use it."

There was no response.

"You have to nod or say something, or else I'm going to keep it aimed at your head. Do you understand me?"

There must have been some sort of nonverbal exchange, because Woodward eventually lowered his gun.

"What's your name?" Woodward asked, shuffling toward Martin.

"You broke into the house. Mother will not be happy."

Mother? What the fuck?

"We were called here, some disturbance," Woodward answered quickly. "We thought someone was in trouble. I can see that it was just a prank. We're going to leave now."

There was a long pause, and then there was a series of footsteps behind Martin. He instinctively buried his head in his hands, fearing that he would be picked up again. But when someone touched him, it was from in front, and not from behind.

It was Woodward.

"Get up," his friend muttered.

With Woodward's help, Martin obliged, pulling himself off the dusty wooden floor.

"My name is Jessie. I'm the gardener."

Woodward hooked his arm around Martin's waist and together they stood.

"Okay, Jessie, we're sorry for the inconvenience. Like I said, it must have just been a prank. Happens often."

"Mother said I'm not allowed visitors."

It was clear that there was something wrong with this man, but Woodward did an expert job of masking his feelings. He nodded.

A few more steps and they reached the door.

Martin coughed and cleared his throat, and then he turned and caught his first glimpse of what had grabbed him by the throat.

"What the—?"

But Woodward yanked him and they stumbled onto the porch before he could get the words out. Before he could fully comprehend the tall, spindly creature that was standing in the doorway.

With linked arms, they hurried backward past the rusty porch swing, and then back into the mud. When Martin felt the familiar sucking sensation of his shoes in the soft ground, he regained use of his limbs and separated from Woodward. Still, he stayed close to his friend; he felt safer walking backward with Woodward, knowing that if something went wrong, the man would be able to quickly whip out his gun again. He just didn't know how many bullets were in there, or if they were enough to take down *that* man.

By the time they were within spitting distance of the cruiser, the shape of the man that had eclipsed the top of the doorway had been completely enshrouded in shadows and was no longer distinguishable.

Maybe Martin had imagined him. *It.*

A hard swallow, and the pain that accompanied the normal physiological action, was proof enough that he hadn't.

His heel struck something hard, and he immediately jumped to one side, a curse clawing its way out of his raw throat.

Martin looked down in time to see the rusted, dented mailbox spinning in the mud, the number 1818 twirling like a pinwheel flower.

"Fuck, man," Woodward whispered in his ear. "What are you looking at? Let's get in the car and get the fuck out of here!"

Chapter 30

Martin

298 Brin Ln
Batesbrg, SC

Feb

   Baby is coming soon Mother told me . I m gonna
be a mo ther soon.

    You do nt care u hhhate me .

   Whe nthe baby s born I am going to leave this
place and never come back . I m sorr y abo t
vererythig

   Good by Marti n I lov u

   Arielle

Chapter 31

It was nearly a month after what happened at Coverfeld before Martin reached out to Woodward again. It was strange, really, how those events had somehow set Martin free. It was coming on three months that Arielle had been missing now, and as with most things—like pain, especially pain—the acuteness of reality faded with time.

He still missed her, and he was still searching for her. But a small part—a tiny, nearly infinitesimal part—had moved on.

Selling houses and making it up to his partners for being such a dick helped occupy his mind most of the time. But that didn't mean that he didn't love her. It didn't mean that he didn't miss her.

Then Woodward called and it changed everything again.

Martin hated the part of him that wished Woodward had never called.

"You all right?"

Woodward sounded tired.

"Yeah," Martin said, unsure of how to address his friend. Time apart, even as little as a few months, changed things between people—made things as awkward as a first date.

There was a long, uncomfortable pause that Martin eventually broke.

"Woods, I just wanted to thank you for, you know..."

"For what?"

"Well, for coming with me. For being a good friend during this hard time. For—" At this point, Martin could feel his face getting red, and he hoped that taking a breather would let Woodward know that it was okay to jump in at any time.

He didn't.

"For, you know, helping me when the hick strangled me."

"And?"

And what? What the hell?

Martin swallowed hard.

"And for, and for—"

Woodward's laugh halted Martin's awkward speech.

"Just fucking with you, man. No problem. Listen, what happened on Coverfeld was fucked up. I wanted to lie low for a bit, make sure the ogre didn't place any calls about us breaking in there. It was fucked-up shit, man. We could—" His voice lowered. "We could have gotten into real shit. I mean, what if I'd had to shoot the guy? If he'd kept choking you? Then what?"

Martin didn't want to think about it. Besides, it hadn't happened—the man had let him go—so why torture themselves with 'what-ifs'?

"No kidding," he said instead. He could feel cold, thin fingers wrapping around his throat, squeezing and squeezing...

"Fuck."

"Fuck is right. Anyways, did you look into 1818 Coverfeld Ave? You find anything?"

Of course Martin had looked; he had used any and all of his Internet research skills in addition to his access to real estate records. And both came up with the same answer: 1818 Coverfeld Ave didn't exist.

"Yeah, but came up dry. Nothing. Nada."

He thought he could hear Woodward's chins flapping as he nodded in agreement.

"Put another request in here to see if anything came up on police records. Came up blank, as well. It's like a ghost house.

1818 Coverfeld Ave doesn't exist according to any public—or police—record that I could find."

Martin exhaled.

"It's like a ghost house," Woodward repeated. "With one giant fucking Deliverance-type ghost living there. Fuck, a gardener? For real? There was no gardening going on there."

Martin almost chuckled, but then he felt his throat constricting and his smirk became a grimace.

"So weird," Martin muttered after swallowing hard.

"So weird," Woodward admitted.

*   *   *

Martin awoke gasping for air, his hand immediately reaching for his chest. He thought he was having a heart attack.

Blinking in the darkness, he tried to calm his heaving body.

Fucking hell.

He'd been having a nightmare, a good old-fashioned nightmare in which he was trapped in the fucking house—1818 Coverfeld Ave—and the tall, lanky fucker with the skinny hands was chasing him. And no matter where he went, he always ended up in the family room staring at the circle of clear space on the coffee table. The space that looked exactly like it had been made from the bottom of a glass. Like a glass had been there only minutes before Woodward had kicked the door in. There *was* someone there.

Yeah, and he was a fucking eight-foot monster.

Sweat dripped into his eye and he rubbed it away—it stung like a bitch.

There was something else about the dream, something else that had seemed out of place at the house. He tried to think back without reliving the nightmare experience of the man chasing him.

It wasn't about the house, he realized; it was when they had left the house, when he had kicked the stupid mailbox that someone had tried to hide. The rusted rectangle had been spinning in the mud, over and over again. The number 1818 rotating around and around...

Martin stopped rubbing his eye and froze.

1818.

1818.

What if it wasn't 1818? What if it was 8181?

His heart rate, which had slowed over the last minute or so, kicked back up into high gear.

What the hell? Why didn't I think of that before?

Martin could see the box spinning in his mind, and indeed the numbers could have as easily been 8181 as 1818. They had only thought it was 1818 because when they saw it from the car it was facing that way.

"Shit," he muttered in the darkness.

The glowing green digits of the digital clock beside him read 1:16.

He wished those numbers were the other way around too, that they read 9:11. There were no nightmares after nine.

It sure as hell could *be 8181 Coverfeld Ave.*

Martin wanted to go back to sleep, to forget the horrible dream. But that was the problem; the dream had been ongoing for what seemed like forever now.

He threw his bedsheet off, surprised that it was soaked with his sweat. His first instinct was to search on his phone, but sometime during the night it had run out of batteries. With a huff, he made his way down to the computer that his wife used to use for her copywriting. It had been so long since he had powered the thing up—he used his cell phone and had a computer at his office—that it took at least twenty minutes to apply all of the awaiting updates.

At least this time the wait afforded him an opportunity to get a glass of water, which he sorely needed in order to replace some of the fluids he had lost during his nightmare. He also realized that it wasn't just his sheets that were soaked, but his boxers as well. His entire body was covered in a sheen that had dried, making his arms stick to his armpits and his thighs stay glued together. He felt gross.

Is it too early to shower?

The computer pinged and he lost the thought and instead loaded up the browser.

The first thing he typed in was 8181 Coverfeld Ave. A shot in the dark, a one-hitter.

No luck. As with any search that included a name and a series of numbers, the results were just random pages in which 'Coverfeld' was mentioned and the numbers were from some strange coding string. Definitely not the 8181 Coverfeld Ave he was looking for.

He tried a few more combinations, adding 'South Carolina' to the mix.

Still nothing.

And then when he typed "8181 Coverfeld Ave, Elloree," an article appeared with that exact combination of words.

An exact match.

His finger froze above the blue-highlighted words—the link.

Part of him wanted to turn the computer off again. Part of him was screaming for him to just shut it down. To let it be.

But part of him wanted him to click it, *needed* to click it.

Just fucking click it. Don't be a pussy.

Martin shifted in his chair, peeling the inside of his thighs away from each other. His face twisted into a grimace and he pressed the link.

The first thing he saw was the bold title, "**8181 Coverdfeld Ave, Elloree,**" just like his search string.

And then he scrolled and saw the photograph.

"No." The word escaped his mouth in a partial moan. "No."

His entire body shot full of adrenaline, a tingling that ran from his scalp to his toes.

"No fucking way. It can't be."

Chapter 32

Batesburg, SC

?

Martin,

Hope has come.

Arielle

Chapter 33

"It just doesn't make sense."

Even though Martin was speaking to Woodward, he wasn't looking at him. Instead, he was staring at the tendrils of smoke that drifted up from the end of cigar like tiny, devilish fingers tickling the air.

Woodward didn't answer.

"Do you think," he began, finally looking up at his friend, "do you think she went there? Somehow her brain was wired to go there, even though she remembers none of it?"

Woodward put his own cigar back in the ashtray and picked up the framed photograph. He was staring so hard that Martin half expected him to squint one eye and tilt his head, as if he were trying to interpret an abstract painting. Thankfully, he didn't—this was not a time for comical gestures. Instead, he put the frame gently back down on the table and then picked up his cigar again.

"I don't know, Marty. I really don't know. Have you taken the picture out of the frame?"

Martin nodded and brought his glass to his lips and took a swallow. It was no Talisker 18 in his glass—those days had come and gone—but it would do.

The two of them were again in his kitchen, this time sitting beside each other on barstools. It was almost ten in the evening, the earliest that Woodward could make it to his place—still wearing his uniform this time—which had given Martin all day to try and figure out what the fuck he had seen.

The image that he had found on the Internet—the one that his search for 8181 Coverfeld Ave had uncovered—was the exact same picture that Arielle had on her bedside table. The *exact same* photograph—*the* photograph, the only thing that Arielle had had to her name when she had been found at twelve years of age, wandering the streets naked, blood dripping...

He squeezed his eyes shut tightly.

How can this be? How can it be that she found her way back there after all this time?

It was a simplest of websites, with only the photograph and the caption that consisted of the street name and number at the bottom. Nothing to click, no other information.

It was haunting in its simplicity.

"Marty? Did you take it out of the frame?"

He didn't bother looking up.

"Yeah. Someone wrote '8181' on the back in pencil."

Another pause ensued, with each of the men taking more puffs from their respective cigars.

She ran away from me and went back there? To where she was born? Why?

Woodward reached over and picked up the frame again, turning it over in his hands.

"Do you mind if I open it?"

"It says 8181 on the back, Woods."

"I know, but can I open it?"

Martin shrugged.

After thoroughly inspecting it, Woodward placed it back in the frame again. Then he leaned toward Martin and stared directly into his eyes. Martin felt tired again, just like he had during the first few weeks after Arielle had run away, and his eyes were starting to water.

Over time, even the worst wounds became numb. But the image he had seen on the Internet felt like a bandage being torn off, revealing a bloody scar beneath. One that would never completely heal.

He just wanted it over with, one way or another.

"There is another possibility here, Martin. One that you might not like to hear..."

Martin blinked.

"Shoot. Don't hold back."

"What if" — Woodward grabbed the picture again — "what if this isn't her, Marty? What if this" — he tapped the little girl in the photo — "is just some random girl?"

Martin picked up his cigar and leaned away from his friend. The thought had actually crossed his mind.

"What if this is just a random girl, and what if someone just gave this to Arielle and she thought that this was herself as a child? She remembers nothing, after all."

Martin puffed again, a great billow of smoke covering his face for a moment, obscuring his vision. When it cleared, Woodward was holding something in his hand. A folder.

"I brought this, Martin. It's the police report from when they found her. Or at least who we think is her... you know what I mean. They didn't call her Arielle back then."

Martin knew exactly what Woodward was talking about, because he had already read the file that Woodward had in his hand. He had read it six years ago when Woodward had first shown it to him. And in it there was no Arielle Reigns, not even Arielle McLeod, his wife's maiden name. There was only a description of Jane Doe, a scared, naked, and bleeding twelve-year-old girl.

"I thought you had to return that," was all he could think to say.

Woodward frowned.

"There is no mention of a photograph in this report. No mention of her having *anything.* It is possible that one of the nurses might have had it on hand or something and, to help ease the mind of a girl who couldn't remember anything, she gave it to her. Eventually, it just became part of her memories."

Woodward sighed, as if saying this was taking a lot out of him.

"It's called false memories, and it's fairly common."

"Jesus, Woods, you're a psychiatrist now?"

Woodward leaned back and picked up his cigar. His expression remained serious.

Martin shrugged.

"So? So what if it's not really her? Even if she thinks that she was born there or brought up at 8181 Coverfeld Ave, she would have—*could* have—gone there, right? And I was thinking about the whole car tracks in the mud. You know the ones that you said looked like they were from pushing?"

Woodward nodded. The man looked as if he had something else to add, but Martin had something to get off his chest too. Something that had continued to bother him even after the rest of it had become numb.

"The whole time I was thinking, if they were from Arielle's car and they had her—"

Woodward opened his mouth to say something, which Martin assumed would have been along the lines of 'there is no evidence to show that,' but he didn't let the other man speak.

"Let me finish. So if—big *if*—they had Arielle, they almost surely would have her keys, too, right? So why didn't they just drive it?"

It was his turn to lean in.

"And then I started to think about the ogre, man, and I really doubt that that guy could actually fit in Arielle's Audi. But—*but*—he could definitely push the thing. He was definitely big enough to push it."

Martin grabbed his cigar when he finished, happy to finally get his theory off his chest. He watched as Woodward chewed his lip, clearly contemplating what he had said.

Good, he thinks it might have happened that way too. Could have. Might have.

Satisfied with himself for putting doubt in Woodward and giving him pause, Martin took another puff of his cigar and then a sip of his scotch.

The silence went on for too long.

"Well? What do you think?"

"I dunno, man."

"What do you mean, 'I don't know'? You don't think that beast that literally picked me up by my throat could push a car?"

Woodward shook his head.

"It's not that… it's…"

"Spit it out."

Woodward grabbed his forehead as if he were checking for a fever.

"No, I just…"

Martin narrowed his eyes and lay his scotch glass down on the table a little more forcefully than intended.

"Just fucking say it."

Woodward sighed.

"Okay, look, you remember when we went to see that black guy in the gym? The guy you said that trained Arielle?"

Martin nodded. Of course he remembered the awkward meeting with Kevin.

"Well, I looked into his eyes, and I hate to be the one to tell you this, but I think he might have been more than just Arielle's trainer. One time, one of Charlene's friends—"

"I know."

"What?"

"I said, 'I know.'"

"You know what?"

Martin stared Woodward in the eyes.

"I know she slept with him," then he added, "once."

Woodward's face looked like a slowly deflating balloon.

"One time, but it was a mistake."

Woodward opened and closed his mouth so many times that he looked like a giant blowfish sucking air.

Martin threw up his hands.

"Just fucking say it, man. Say whatever it is that you're thinking."

Woodward exhaled.

"Fine. I just think we need to look at this objectively. Think of the facts: your wife wanted a child so desperately—there's no secret there—for how long? Five years? Six?"

"Seven."

"Fine, seven. For seven years, she's been telling you that she wants a baby, and for whatever reason—one that I think both you and I can guess after seeing her file—she can't have one. This is strike one. She's fucking devastated, man, and embarrassed as hell. Not to mention that she knows *you* want a kid, too, so she feels like she let you down."

"But—"

Woodward ignored his interruption.

"That's strike one. Then she thinks she's pregnant, and she was probably over the moon. I get that. I saw how she was when she arrived at our party. And then the bombshell. She's not pregnant. Strike two. Tack on that she blows up at you and us in front of all of our friends. Now you tell me she slept with her trainer. Look, man, I'm really not trying to be a dick, but you *need* to look at this objectively."

"What are you saying, Woods?"

"Well, at first I thought maybe something had happened to her, but—"

"I don't care about what you thought *then*. I care about now."

Woodward shook his head.

"But now I think you just need to accept that she left you. That she found someone else, or is looking for someone else. It's not about you, Marty, I just think…"

Woodward's words faded into background, elevator music. Martin could feel his face getting red, and wondered if he had smoked his cigar too quickly and the nicotine was getting to him.

Or maybe it was just because he was embarrassed. Not so much about what Woodward had said—all of that seemed reasonable, even possibly true—but because the facts had been there and he had ignored them for this long.

"Fuck," he muttered.

Nicotine or not, he picked up his cigar and took another puff.

"But what about the tire tracks? You don't think—"

"You want my advice? Just forget about the car tracks, the rusty porch swing, and all that shit. Forget about this photo" — he tapped at the picture of what they had once believed was Arielle and her mother and father—"and—ah, shit, it hurts to say this—but try to forget about Arielle."

Martin's face got all screwed up, and his friend reached out and put a comforting hand on his shoulder.

"It'll take time, but I think it's for the best."

Martin scratched the back of his head.

"You're right," he said, his words surprising even himself.

Woodward brought the cigar to his lips, drawing smoke into his mouth. Martin leaned back and did the same.

"You're right," he repeated, more to himself than to his friend.

The question was, could he really forget about her? About the woman who was more than enough for him?

Martin exhaled a large, thick cloud of smoke and watched it rise and twirl in the air.

So random, those individual streams of smoke; each seeming to follow their own secret, hidden path through the air, through life.

And then when they reached near the ceiling, the tendrils were blown away by the spinning fan overhead, their lives, once so thick and powerful, gone. Dispersed. Eliminated.

Maybe, with time, he could start again without Arielle.

Maybe.

Part III – Harvest the Seed

Chapter 34

The warm air billowed around Arielle's naked body, clouding her reflection in the mirror. She closed her eyes and breathed the steam in through her nose. It was hot, almost scalding, but she didn't mind.

The hot air helped her think.

She reached out and scrubbed the mirror with her hand, nearly pulling it away when her skin touched the startlingly cool surface. Then she leaned back and took a good look at herself.

It had taken more than a year for her to lose the weight she had put on at Coverfeld Ave. And it had taken more than a year after that, almost two, to get her body back near to where it had been before. All things considered, her hard work had paid off.

Almost.

But no matter how hard she tried, it would never be quite the same again.

Her hands moved to her now flat stomach, her fingers finding the scar that ran from just beneath the center of her chest and extended all the way to the top of a small mound of soft blond pubic hair. It was a hideous cicatrix, a half-inch-wide gash that was lighter in color than the surrounding skin. Inside the indented scar was a crisscrossing network of disorganized fibrous tissue like threads desperately trying to keep the two sides together. And then there were the dents, the dimples of skin on either side of the wound, a permanent reminder of the staples that had once punctured her flesh.

Her fingers moved up and down the scar's length like a demented, organic keyboard. It was rough, uneven, *hideous*.

The fog in the bathroom again clouded the mirror, hiding the grimace that marked her pretty face.

If Martin were here, he would tell me that I'm still beautiful. He would kiss my scar, I know he would. He would kiss it and hold me as I cried into his arms about another void in my memory, another time and place I can't remember.

But Martin was not here. Martin was gone; he had left her, abandoned her.

She didn't blame him, though, not really. But he could have at least written her back. Just once. He could have written her back and said he didn't want to see her anymore; she would have understood that. Because even that would have shown that he cared—on some level, it would have confirmed that he still cared about her.

But not responding, that was the worst.

The letters.

She remembered the letters.

She remembered the letters, and she remembered the mice. The horrible sound of their padded paws running across the cold, wet stone floor like an eternal tap dripping into a porcelain sink. But that was all she remembered.

A shudder ran through her just as the door to the bathroom was pushed open.

"Mommy? Mommy, I can't sleep."

Arielle immediately turned and snatched a towel from the rack and wrapped it around her stomach. Then she faced her daughter, pasting a fake smile on her full lips.

"What's wrong, sweetheart?"

The girl rubbed her eyes with both hands.

"I had a nightmare," she replied with a frown.

"The same one?"

The girl nodded. It looked as if she might cry.

"The other girls, they're teasing me. Pulling my hair, telling me that I'm different. That I'm weird. That you aren't my real mommy."

Arielle squatted and took her daughter in her arms. Then, in one smooth motion, she swept her off her feet.

"It's okay, sweetheart. You can sleep with me tonight. I'll keep the nightmares away, I promise."

Chapter 35

"It's complicated," Martin replied, averting his gaze.

"Yeah, how so?"

The directness of the response surprised Martin and he glanced up quickly. The woman across from him was good-looking in the traditional sense, with long dark hair that flowed down past her shoulders, and equally dark eyes that stood out on her pale skin. Her full lips were painted a deep red. She was wearing a white blouse that was cut just low enough to show off the top of her breasts, to let anyone who might be interested know that they were indeed full, but not so low as to look sleazy.

"Well?" the woman raised her Styrofoam coffee mug and gave it a swirl. "I have a lot of coffee left, you know?"

Direct. No skirting issues with this one.

And Martin liked that; it was one of the major reasons why he had agreed to be set up with her. That and her full breasts, of course.

He took a sip of his coffee, and the woman's mouth twisted into a frown.

"I'm not getting involved with someone who's complicated, Martin," she informed him.

"No, Stace, it's not like that. It's, well—" he took a deep breath, "—well, I have a wife, but…"

The woman, who gave the air of keeping her emotions close to her substantial chest, let her guard down, her eyebrows moving upward in surprise.

"You're married?"

She picked up her coffee cup and swirled it again, suggesting that while a moment ago it was full, it might now suddenly be emptied. Or maybe she was just no longer thirsty.

Martin shook his head.

"My wife left four years ago. Just packed up and left. I'm working on the divorce now, but because she just disappeared, these things take time."

The woman's expression went from surprised to intrigued.

"Really? And you say it's *not* complicated?"

Again Martin shook his head.

"It's not. She left and I've moved on. Haven't seen or heard from her in years."

He could tell that Stacey wanted to press for more, wanted to know details about how their relationship had ended, but the woman was as astute as she was direct, and the wall he began erecting was something that she picked up on quickly.

The truth was, he hadn't thought about Arielle in a while. He had done what most men would given his situation, at least men that were embarrassed and hurt: he buried his feelings in his work. And eventually one week bled into another, and his concerted efforts to find Arielle became less and less concentrated. Staying away from Woodward had helped, as was separating himself from that life—his past life. Which included selling their home and moving into a bachelor pad in the city. Going to new bars, restaurants, most of which he had successfully helped buy or sell, as was the case with most commercial buildings in Batesburg—a welcomed side-effect of burying his feelings. And then the divorce idea had been proposed by the firm that helped with his real estate transactions. That too had been a hard, but necessary decision.

And now this: four years later he was on a date. Sure, it was only a Friday afternoon coffee date, but it was a date nonetheless.

A step forward.

"Would you look at that," Stacey said suddenly. "Coffee's all done."

Martin frowned, thinking that he had scared her away. It was his first date in a long, long time, and he liked Stacey.

The woman threw her head back and laughed.

"Just kidding, Marty."

Marty; Arielle used to call me that.

He shook his head and forced himself to smile back at her.

"Actually, I *am* done my coffee. But maybe next week we can do this again?"

Martin raised an eyebrow.

"You only drink coffee once a week?"

She laughed again.

"No, silly. Next time you get to take me out to dinner. Which I eat every night, by the way."

Martin's smile transitioned from forced to legitimate.

"Great. Let me take you to your car," he offered, standing.

She shook her head.

"Nope. The next time you'll see me will be at dinner."

Martin nodded.

Her directness—he liked that. At nearly forty-five, he had no time for games.

They parted ways with a semi-awkward hug, and Martin left the coffee shop on foot. It was a beautiful afternoon and with the sun shining high in the sky, he had opted to walk from the office instead of drive. Thankfully the heatwave that had seemed permanent just a few days ago had broken, making his walk pleasant.

As he made his way back toward his office, he was surprised that the smile that Stacey had put on his face remained. It felt good to speak to someone of the opposite sex outside of the office. *Really* good.

Am I officially 'dating' now, is that it? Can I say that?

It was a strange thought, but it was also a *good* thought.

Martin made a sharp turn onto his office's street, and bumped right into a woman in a dark dress, nearly knocking her to the sidewalk.

"I'm sorry," he said, taking a step toward the woman who was huddled over, clutching her stomach as if she were winded. "You okay, ma'am? I didn't see you. I was just enjoying this beautiful weather." Martin attempted a smile, but the woman remained in a crouched position and his concern quickly grew.

He moved closer to her and rested an arm gently on her back. She was all skin and bone beneath the dark dress.

"Ma'am? You okay? I didn't—"

The woman finally raised her head and Martin froze midsentence. Strands of black hair hung in front of her face, but they were so thin that Martin could make out hawkish features that seemed to bury dark, deep-set eyes.

And he recognized that face.

"I—I—didn't—" he stammered.

He recognized the woman's face, but couldn't place it right away.

The woman appeared to recognize him too, as her sunken eyes seemed to widen. Then she straightened her body with what seemed like considerably effort and grumbled something.

In an instant, the woman was off at a considerable clip down the sidewalk, leaving Martin gaping.

What did she say?

It sounded Greek or maybe it was an Italian dialect.

It sounded like, *filing something.*

Filing Oscar? Was she from one of the clerks down at the city hall? Someone who filed my deeds of sale?

Martin shook his head.

No, that wasn't it.

He continued to stare as the woman made it to the street corner, still moving quickly as if she were late for an appointment.

As she reached the corner, she raised her hand to flag a passing cab. Martin focused on those trembling fingers, realizing that this too reminded him of something. Not an open hand, as she was gesturing now, but a closed hand delicately holding something.

Fingers that had once held a small piece of burning wood.

Filia obcisor.

"Wait!" Martin shouted, finally mobilizing. "Wait!"

He broke into a jog just as the woman closed the car door.

Martin stopped running and stared at the car is it passed, his eyes meeting the woman's through the window.

It was the woman from the church all those years ago, the one that had been standing at the painting of Raymond Nonnatus holding a candle for someone that she had lost.

It was the woman who had shouted at Arielle, one of the three that had chased them from the place of worship—the place that neither of them belonged.

Chapter 36

Arielle snuffed out her cigarette beneath her heel as soon as a woman walked into the park with her young son in tow.

"Careful on the stairs, Hope," Arielle hollered to her daughter as she watched her blond hair bounce up the plastic set of stairs for what felt like the hundredth time. In a moment, she would reappear at the bottom of the slide, a giant smile plastered on her face.

"Okay, Mommy," Hope shouted over her shoulder.

Now it was Arielle's turn to smile.

There was no question that Hope wasn't like other girls. For one, she was reserved, quiet—an introvert. Or, as Arielle preferred to consider her, a deep thinker. This didn't bother Arielle. In fact, Arielle herself had become quiet ever since she had moved away from Batesburg. If nothing else, her moving away necessitated becoming more secretive, and while at the outset this had proven difficult for her, in the end it was a good thing. In the end, she'd learned more about herself and what made her tick. And that *had* to be a good thing.

Adopting a slight variation of her maiden name—McLernon—Arielle had taken Hope and traveled south immediately after she had left 1818 Coverfeld, eventually settling in a small town in Georgia. It was far enough away from her past life so as to not be recognized or tempted, but it wasn't so far away to completely forget about where she had been.

Starting—or *re*-starting, as it were—her copywriting business hadn't been all that difficult, at least when it came time to acquire or reacquire clients. What had been difficult, however, was completely giving up on her other business; losing the name, shutting down the website, emailing her old client list. *That* had been hard. Not technically, of course, but psychologically. It had been hard because it was something that she couldn't readily undo. Theoretically, she *could* return to Batesburg, she *could* move back into her house with Martin, but what she *couldn't* do was email her list again and say, "Hey, look, ignore the last email, I'm baaaaack." If nothing else, her clients demanded consistency.

In the end, the need for fresh income had forced her hand.

Arielle was deep in thought when she first caught the woman walking toward her out of the corner of her eye.

Of course the woman chose the bench right beside hers. Mothers always did that for some reason; assumed that just because they were at the same park and that they both had a child that you wanted to talk. To make friends. That you had something in *common*. In fact, the only thing that surprised Arielle about this woman was that she didn't sit directly beside her.

Eight benches in this park, Arielle counted, *and she chose the one next to me.*

Still, despite her apathy, she couldn't help but watch as the woman bent and tended to her son.

"Petey, be careful on the swings, okay?"

Swings? The boy can't be more than two years old, and he's going to go on the swings by himself?

Petey nodded and tried to turn, but his mother grabbed him just before he took off. He was a cute kid, with shaggy blond hair cut straight across his forehead.

Thomas. He looks like Thomas Woodward.

"Not so fast, cutie-pie!" The woman rubbed some sunblock into his button nose.

Arielle was curious where she got the sunblock from, as there was no bottle in sight. Did she have a repository in her wrist? Like Spiderman's webs?

These were secrets that only moms knew, ones that Arielle was trying to discover.

The boy tore away from his mother and made a beeline directly for the swings.

Swings? Really?

Arielle turned her attention back to her own child, and when she didn't immediately see her, her heart skipped a beat.

She snapped to her feet.

"Hope? Hope!"

Her daughter poked her blond head from behind a plastic steering wheel atop the play structure, and Arielle breathed deeply.

"Yes, Mommy?"

"Nothing, sweetie, keep playing. Just make sure I can see you."

"Okay, Mommy."

And with that, she ducked back down behind the plastic that was painted to look like wood. A pirate ship, a fort, a firetruck; whatever you wanted it to be.

Arielle fell back into her thoughts, trying her best to discourage the woman on the bench beside hers—who she just absolutely knew was staring at her—from striking up a conversation. Mostly because all of these conversations were the same.

And boring as hell.

Arielle didn't think about Martin all the time, just most of the time. It got especially bad when she wasn't with Hope; in the evenings, or when Arielle needed a break and sent Hope off with their babysitter. Truth be told, the idea of raising Hope by herself wasn't something that she was terribly excited about.

She was, despite what she had been through, a new mom, after all, and reading books, watching shows, even practicing wasn't like the real thing. And it bothered her when people tried to pretend it was. Go watch all the hockey games on TV that you can feast your eyes on. Read every book on strategy, stick-handling, hitting, defense, everything you can possibly find. Now go step on the ice. Do you feel ready? You're good to play in your first game?

Hell no.

And parenting was the same thing.

But Arielle had been left with no alternative. She couldn't rightly go back to see Martin, to try to explain herself perhaps better than she had in her letters. Mostly because that would be impossible; for one, she couldn't *remember* much, if any, of her time in the house, much less *explain* it. The good news—or bad news, depending on what day it was—was that she had some experience with not being able to remember. And even if her amnesia suddenly lifted, there was no guarantee that Martin wanted her back. In fact, if his lack of response to her letters was any indication—and why wouldn't it be?—he wanted nothing to do with her.

Maybe one day. But not today, because there was another reason for her not going back. One that was less *tangible,* but at the same time much more *real.*

She had to keep Hope safe. And Martin, too.

A voice suddenly echoed in her mind, a calming voice, one imbued with a strangely pleasant hoarseness.

'There is one condition: when the child turns four, you must bring her back to me.'

Arielle swallowed hard and again located her daughter's blond head bobbing up and down on the play set in front of her.

No fucking way.

"Stay where I can see you, Hope," she repeated, her throat suddenly extremely dry.

Arielle reached down into her purse to grab a stick of gum, and when she sat up again, the woman was sitting beside her.

"Shit!" she yelped. "You scared me."

The woman before her had a round nose, round chin, and round face that matched her round body. Short and squat, she looked nothing like her string bean of a son.

How does that happen?

"I'm sorry," the woman said, making a pouty face.

Ah, so there's the resemblance.

"I'm MacKenzie," the woman continued, holding out her hand.

Arielle just stared at it.

Can I leave? Is that breaking some unwritten mother code? Will I be voted off the island?

"Hi," the woman said again, all smiles.

Arielle considered smiling back, but spared the woman—this *MacKenzie*—what might have been the worst acting job ever.

"Hi," she said simply, not bothering to shake hands. To her disappointment, the woman simply lowered her hand; her shit-smear smile remained plastered on her face.

The woman sat down right beside Arielle.

Typical. I bet she'll want to chat about some mundane crap now.

MacKenzie didn't disappoint.

"How old is your daughter? She's beautiful."

Arielle cleared her throat before answering.

"She's four."

Just saying that word—'four'—out loud made her cautious.

You're safe. No one knows you are here—nobody.

"And beautiful blond hair. So long and shiny. The only one I know with hair like that is Petey. Ha, he might have hair long enough to braid by the time he's four. Did she get it from her father?"

No, you dolt, she got it from me, Arielle almost said. Then she remembered that she had cut her hair short and dyed it a dark brown. At the time, it had felt very *femme fatale,* but it had quickly grown old. It felt fake, and she had grown to hate it.

Realizing that the woman's doughy face was still aimed at her, she racked her mind for a response. Part of her felt badly for the woman, for the way she was treating her.

Did she have to be so cruel? If this was to be her life, shouldn't she should try to form healthy relationships with others? Didn't Hope deserve a stable, healthy environment to grow up in?

Still, no amount of self-denigration would make her feel like talking to this woman or anyone else at this moment.

Arielle cleared her throat and was about to answer —'My husband is bald,' she might have said—when there was a cry from her left.

MacKenzie immediately jumped to her feet and ran to her son who had, somewhat predictably, fallen from a swing and now lay on his back, crying his face off.

A swing, by himself, at two years old.

Arielle shook her head and turned her attention back to the slide.

"C'mon, Hope, it's time to go home."

'When the child turns four, you must bring her back to me.'

Another shudder coursed through her. It was strange, the tiny tidbits that she remembered from her time at 1818 Coverfeld. They weren't even the satisfying kind, the kind where she could place exactly who she was with and what time of day it had been, what they were doing. No, these bastardized memories had all blended together. Time had had little meaning at the house, that much Arielle was oddly certain about.

"Excuse me! Excuse me, can you help me? Petey's nose is bleeding and it won't stop."

For a split second, Arielle took her eyes off Hope and turned to the boy who was still lying on his back with his mother hovering over her.

A split second, barely enough time to register the dual streams of blood streaming from each of the kid's nostrils.

"Sorry, I don't have any tissues," she grumbled.

You shouldn't let your kid play on the swings by himself when he's two, dumbass.

When she turned back to the play set, she could no longer see Hope's head peeking out from atop the faux-wooden fence.

"Hope? Hope!"

This time, however, the little girl didn't pop up when she called.

Like MacKenzie a few moments ago, Arielle sprung to her feet. She bolted across the playground to the play structure, first peering between the wooden slats, then actually climbing onto the structure itself to get a better look.

Hope wasn't there.

Arielle's heart was racing, her body tingling with an adrenaline rush.

"Hope!" she screamed. Hey wide eyes scanned the entire park and playground. "Hoooope! Where are you? Hooooope!"

MacKenzie glanced up from her bleeding son who had thankfully stopped his wailing.

"Hope!"

Arielle could feel panic begin to well up inside of her, usurping the adrenaline dump.

MacKenzie helped her son to his feet, and then began to call for Hope along with Arielle. Together, they hollered.

When Arielle stopped yelling to catch her breath, she realized that MacKenzie had made her way atop the play set with her son in her arms.

"Maybe she left with her friends?" the woman asked.

Arielle turned to face the woman, her eyes burning, partly from fear and partly from dread.

"Friends? What friends? What are you talking about?"

MacKenzie recoiled and instinctively switched her son to the arm opposite Arielle.

"Her friends," she began hesitantly, her thin, dark eyebrows migrating up her pasty forehead. "You know, the ones she was playing with up here?"

Arielle's eyes narrowed.

Friends? What the fuck is this crazy bitch talking about?

Hope had been up here by herself, playing with the steering wheel. Climbing the stairs and going down the slide. Up and down. Up and down. Alone.

Without thinking, Arielle grabbed the woman's arm.

"What the fuck are you talking about?" she hissed. "Did she send you? Did *Mother* send you?"

MacKenzie looked more than frightened now, she looked terrified. Her lower lip began to tremble like little Petey's.

"Mother? I'm sorry, I don't—"

Arielle shook the other woman.

"Don't fuck with me," she hissed.

The boy broke into a cry again, and the woman tried to pull away, but Arielle's grip held fast.

"What friends?"

"The—the—the—"

All of a sudden, this woman who wanted to chat only a few minutes ago was at a loss for words.

"You're hurting me," she whimpered.

Arielle looked down at her hand and saw that her fingers were buried at least a half inch into the woman's soft flesh. Her eyes darted up and she stared at the woman—*really* stared at her—burrowing holes into her pin point pupils.

Her grip loosened. This woman knew nothing.

"I'm sorry," MacKenzie said, cowering, "I saw three blond girls... with braids. They were all up here playing, they..."

The words hit Arielle like a blow to the solar plexus and she staggered backward, finally releasing MacKenzie from her grip.

Three blond girls with braids.

The memory that followed was so powerful that she feared toppling over the side of play structure.

'You have to drink your milk. All of it. Mother is watching.'

'I don't want to. It's too sweet.'

She was being petulant, like a child. But she was also sleepy.

One of the blond girls, the oldest of the three, exchanged a look with the others, but Arielle was too tired to try to interpret it.

'You need to drink the milk, Arielle. Mother said so. We will wait here until you do.'

Arielle snapped back into reality like the crack of a whip.

"You saw three girls? Up here with my Hope?"

MacKenzie nodded. She was already halfway down the stairs, her eyes trained on Arielle, her son tucked so far on her hip that he was nearly behind her, like a piggy-back ride.

"Did you see where they went?" Arielle was nearly in tears now.

Her Hope, gone. Vanished.

'When the child turns four...'

"I'm sorry," MacKenzie stammered. "I don't know. Do you want me to call someone, or...?"

Arielle ignored the woman and turned her attention back to the park and the streets surrounding it.

"Hope!" she screamed at the top of her lungs. "Hooooope!"

Then she saw it; her drifting eyes fixed on the round object that lay abandoned in the sandbox.

Arielle started to weep.

There, lying in the sandbox, the sand around it undisturbed, pristine, was a bright orange Frisbee.

Chapter 37

Martin sat on the edge of the bleached church steps, his foot tapping impatiently on the hard ground.

He had been sitting for so long that his ass had started to go numb. Thankfully, like Friday, today was slightly overcast offering him a reprieve from the hot sun. Otherwise he would have been soaked in sweat.

It was Sunday, and he knew that she would be there.

She just had to be.

But despite his confidence, it was already nearly noon and the first service had already come and gone, while the second was trapped inside. Martin scanned every patron's face as they came and went, pretending that he was looking for someone that he knew.

And he supposed in a way he was.

Filia obcisor.

Maybe not someone he knew, *per se*, but someone that seemed to know Arielle, or in the very least something about her.

But now it seemed that maybe he was wrong. Maybe he had spooked her away when he had bumped into her on the street.

Maybe, like Arielle before her, she too had just vanished.

And maybe he should just let it all go.

The problem was, he *had* let it go, what with going for a date with Stacey, but then —

A church bell rang somewhere high above him, and his eyes darted up the steps. The large wooden doors to the church swung open, and a throng of people started migrating out, their faces a mixture of grimaces and smiles, the underlying personal reasons for each unknown.

Martin stood, once again trying to scan all of their faces for the angular features that had been etched in his brain ever since he had seen the woman through the taxi's passenger window.

People were coming fast and furious now, spilling out of the doors at a rate that made it almost impossible for Martin to check them all.

C'mon, c'mon, you have to be here.

There were so many people around him now, that Martin was getting dizzy trying to look at all their faces.

His heart sank, and he started to sweat despite the cool air.

But then he saw something: a figure, dressed all in black, moving not *away* from the church, but *toward* it.

A hunched, bony figure.

Martin immediately started to move, pushing his way through the crowd.

"Hey!" a man with a shaved head and dark sunglasses shouted at him.

Martin ignored him and continued to elbow toward the church.

He bumped into an elderly woman with a pearl necklace that seemed so large that it might be the sole cause of her stooped stature. Martin reached for her, grasping her arm before she fell into a man behind her.

"I'm sorry," he grumbled, helping her straighten as best the pearls would allow.

"Watch where you're going," a young man in a navy suit chirped at him.

Like the bald man, Martin ignored him and squeezed by the pair, trying to locate the dark figure again.

It was too late, he was trapped in the crowd and she was gone.

"Damn it," he swore, ignoring several people that stared at him with shocked expressions.

Eventually the crowd thinned, and Martin was able to make his way up the bleached steps and to the large wooden doors.

It was predictably dark inside, and he could make out very little in the poor lighting.

Where is she? He wondered, his eyes scanning the dim interior.

Martin took two steps inside the church and a sound from his right almost made his heart leap out of his chest.

"You don't belong here," a woman's gravelly voice told him.

Martin turned and squinted in the poor light.

It was the hunched woman, the woman with the angular face, the one with the beady eyes.

The *filia obcisor* woman.

Martin wasn't sure what to say now that he had finally found her.

"I—I—"

His right hand subconsciously made its way to his pocket, where his fingers began to fondle the small stone within.

"You don't belong here," the woman repeated.

Martin took a step back. Despite having two days to think about what he would say if he saw this woman again, he was unprepared.

Instead of speaking, he gaped.

"Where is your wife?" the woman whispered, her eyes peaking around and behind him.

The mention of Arielle's name snapped Martin out of his stupor.

"She's gone," he said, and when the woman's eyes went wide for the briefest of moments, he added, "She's missing."

Martin wasn't sure why he had chosen those words to utter, as the idea of Arielle being 'missing' after four years seemed ludicrous, but they just seemed *right*.

The woman's eyes, a moment ago big like large ball bearings, narrowed to slits as she inspected him.

"She's gone," Martin repeated, "disappeared. Can we talk?"

The woman reached out with surprising speed and grabbed his arm. Martin flinched and resisted the urge to pull away from her bony grasp.

"Not here… we can't talk here."

Then the woman leaned in close to Martin's ear and whispered an address and instructions. Her breath reeked of sour milk.

"Ten o'clock," she repeated, "don't be late."

Chapter 38

Arielle was a wreck by the time the police officer finally got her back to the station to provide a statement.

"Please, you need to help me," she repeated over and over again. Tears were streaming down her face, making her cheeks red and raw. "They took my baby!"

The officer didn't respond this time; instead, he got out of the car and helped Arielle out of the back.

"Are you listening? They took my baby!"

"Ma'am, my partner is already setting up a perimeter at the park. I just need to you to come inside and give an official statement. We'll have a search party up within the hour."

Those same words, repeated nearly as often as Arielle's pleas for help finding Hope.

Fucking asshole! Is that all you can say?

Arielle bit her tongue and nodded. A moment later, the officer ushered her into the building and she was quickly passed off to another—Officer Jenkins—who led her toward the back of the station.

The police station was small, not much more than a glorified coffee shop, with only three desks, one of which was reserved for a blue-haired receptionist. They immediately headed toward the desk at the back, ignoring the other officer seated at the first desk.

Even before she sat down, Jenkins began typing away on his computer. The police officer was tall, tall and lean, with short-cropped brown hair, and when he typed, he hunched over his keyboard. He was young-looking, and when he crouched like that over his keyboard, he looked like a child who was trying to hide what he was doing from a nosy parent.

"Please," Arielle pleaded, tugging on the officer's sleeve. "Please, you need to help me find her."

Office Jenkins turned to face her.

"Arielle, is it? Let's start by you giving me your full name and we can go from there."

My name? My name?

She shook her head.

"You need to help me find my daughter! We were at the park and—and—"

—and the woman, MacKenzie, that stupid fucking bitch, distracted me, and then they took her. The girls from Coverfeld Ave took her—

"—I was distracted and my daughter was taken, snatched up. I—oh God—I looked everywhere."

The officer leaned forward and placed his hand on her shoulder in an attempt at comforting her. It was awkward, what with her hand on his right sleeve, and his left hand on her shoulder as if he were inaugurating her into some sort of secret club. Clearly, this young boy, this Officer Jenkins, was new at this.

And this did not instill Arielle with confidence.

We have to stop this 'getting to know you' bullshit and get out there and look for Hope.

Arielle pulled her arm back and shrugged the officer's hand off of her shoulder.

Officer Jenkins cleared his throat.

"Okay, Arielle, tell me about your daughter—anything you can tell me will help. Do you have a picture? Do you know what she was wearing?"

Arielle quickly turned to the purse at her hip and began rummaging through it.

"I have a picture," she said.

At first, she tried to flip through the items in her purse, but when this proved fruitless, she just started pulling things out and tossing them haphazardly onto the officer's desk.

"She was wearing gray sweatpants; you know, the tight kind, like leggings?" Arielle told Jenkins as she searched for the photo. "And a green t-shirt. It was a plain t-shirt—a light green. Seafoam."

C'mon, where the fuck is the picture?

"That's good," the officer said. "Anything else you can tell me about her that might help? You said her name is 'Hope'?"

"Hope McLernon—she just turned four last week. She has long blond hair, almost white, that comes down halfway down her back."

Where is it?!

"Fuck," she swore, staring at the mess that she had made on the officer's desk. Almost every personal item she owned was on that table—everything from her credit cards to her foundation, her lipstick, and a prescription bottle full of pills that she hadn't seen in years. Everything but the photo of Hope.

Finally, only when her purse was completely empty, she found the photograph. It was pressed up flat against the inside of the purse.

"Okay," Arielle said with something that might have been construed as a sigh, "found it."

With the back of the photo to her, she reached over the desk and held it out to Officer Jenkins, who grabbed it and brought it close to his face. One of his light-colored eyebrows rose up his forehead.

"*This* is your daughter?"

"Yeah, that's her." Arielle nearly cried with frustration. What little patience she had was waning fast. "I've seen the shows, Officer; we have twenty-four hours to find her, and that's it. After that—" She swallowed hard. "After that, the chances are next to nothing. We have to do something now."

Why did I look away? Why did I listen to that fucking lady and her stupid kid?

"This"—the officer pointed at the photograph that only he could see—"*this* is your daughter?"

"Yes, yes! For Christ's sake, it's my daughter—Hope McLernon. What's the problem?"

The officer lowered the photograph and stared at her more intently.

"Is this a joke? Do you have a birth certificate for Hope?"

Birth certificate? Why does he need a birth certificate? What the fuck is going on?

"No, but there's the picture right there. Why are we just sitting here? We have to get out there and start looking."

"What about the girl's father, is he around?"

An image of Martin's handsome face flashed in her mind.

Birth certificate. Father. She hadn't expected all of these questions.

"No, no, he's not around. What's wrong? Why aren't you doing anything?"

"Well, Mrs. McLernon, it's just that this photo—"

"What is—?"

She reached out to grab the photograph, but the officer turned it around for her to see and her breath caught in her throat and her hand hung in mid-air.

What the fuck?

Arielle jumped to her feet, toppling the chair behind her.

"Is this a joke?"

A look of confusion crossed Officer Jenkins' face.

"Ma'am? You gave me this—"

"Did *she* put you up to this?"

The officer gaped.

"What the fuck is that? I've never—I've never—"

She couldn't get all of the words out. The photograph didn't show her daughter's smiling face; instead, it depicted a dark corpse... a blackened, burnt corpse.

"What the *fuck*?"

Is the girl's father around? Do you have a birth certificate? Why do you have a photograph of a fucking burnt corpse?

All these goddamn questions.

And where the fuck did that picture come from?

"Ma'am, you sure you're feeling all right? It's pretty hot out there, and people have been coming down with all sorts of sun stroke."

Arielle swallowed hard.

Too many questions that she couldn't answer to anyone's satisfaction, let alone the police.

Her heart sank. The police were not going to be able to help her. She knew that now.

"I... I do feel hot. I was out all day."

Arielle slowly started scooping her belongings from the officer's desk and jamming them back into her purse.

Slowly, don't raise concern.

Officer Jenkins nodded and then made a motion to someone behind him. It was clearly meant to be a subtle gesture, one that she wouldn't pick up on, but she caught it nonetheless.

"You should probably get looked at, have one of our EMTs take a peek to make sure you're okay. And what about the other lady at the park? MacKenzie? We haven't been able to find her, either."

Arielle shook her head.

"No, no, I'm feeling much better now. I think... I think I'll just stay inside and make sure to drink plenty of liquids. I'm sorry, I was just confused. I—I—" She could barely speak. "I don't have a daughter. I just get confused sometimes. I'm very sorry."

She offered a tight smile.

"I'm gonna insist, Arielle. No offense, but you really don't look that great. And, uh, we need to talk about *this*," he said, indicating the photograph that was still clutched in his hand.

'There is one condition: when your daughter turns four, you must bring her back to me.'

A life for a life.

Filius obcisor. Filia obcisor.

Arielle readied herself.

She was going to have to find Hope on her own. And she knew just where to look first.

"I'm fine," she insisted.

Before the officer could utter another word, she turned and started to run.

Officer Jenkins didn't even make it to his feet before Arielle was already racing through the station toward the front door.

"Hey, wait! You can't just leave! Hey!"

A few more strides, and the warm outside air hit her in the face like the blast from a hairdryer, Jenkins's shouts chasing her into the street.

Chapter 39

Martin waited outside the apartment building until the clock on the dashboard hit 9:55 PM.

Then he opened his car door and stepped into the night.

The day had remained overcast, but now that darkness had swallowed the sky it had become cool; frigid even. He wished he had worn more than just jeans and a t-shirt.

As promised, the front door of the apartment complex was held open by a brick, and Martin stepped inside.

The foyer smelled of weed and sweat, but this dissipated when he entered the stairwell, and was completely gone by the time he made it to the fourth floor. As he approached the door to apartment 441, another smell became apparent: burning incense.

After a deep breath through his nose, Martin knocked lightly on the worn wooden door, just as he had been instructed. A second later, the door opened a crack and Martin caught a glimpse of a dark eye peeking out from behind a chain.

No words were exchanged; just that eye peeking out, first looking at and then looking around Martin. A moment passed, and then the eye closed and the door followed suit. He heard the sound of the chain being unlatched before the door was opened again and he was ushered inside.

The smell of incense was so strong in the apartment that Martin instinctively scrunched his nose. The cloying scent tickled the hairs in his nose and throat, and it was all he could do to avoid sneezing or coughing.

Much like the hallway, the inside of the apartment was in rough shape: all peeling paint and rotting wood—what he could make out, anyway. The room was dark, with the only light being offered by a series of candles seemingly placed on every flat surface.

"Sit on the couch," the woman whispered. Her voice, so strong in the church all those years ago, was but a meek, pathetic whisper now.

Martin did as he was instructed, but he took his time, trying to better gauge his surroundings as he made his way to the couch.

Like the candles on the surfaces, there was a series of photographs that seemed to cover nearly every square inch of wall space. And they all depicted the same young girl with long, blond hair and a radiant smile. There were nearly a hundred photographs on the walls, Martin surmised, and a couple dozen more leaning on the mantle, coffee table, and kitchen counter. As he strained to get a better look, he realized that they weren't just all of the same girl, but that there were only three unique images, repeated over and over again: one was a professional portrait, one was of the girl on a swing, her head thrown back in laughter, while the third was a candid shot of her sitting on the floor opening a present.

"My daughter, Charlotte," the woman informed him, noting his gaze. "She went missing more than a decade ago."

Martin, unsure how to reply to this, kept his lips pressed tightly together. He didn't want to offend the woman by not commenting, but he didn't want to yank the scab off an old wound, either.

Thankfully, the woman seemed unfazed by his lack of response.

"Please, sit," she instructed again, and this time Martin obliged.

There weren't just pictures and candles strewn about the room, he realized, but there were crosses as well. Ornate wooden things, shiny metal ones, even some that seemed to be made out of some sort of fabric—religious crochet work.

Martin was beginning to think that coming here might not have been a good idea; that it was probably best to leave this strange, thin woman alone.

But then she spoke, and Martin figured what the hell. He was here; what could it hurt? And maybe, just maybe, she might know something about Arielle...

"Please, tell me what happened to your wife."

The words came more easily than Martin would have expected, and he found himself uncharacteristically opening up, recounting his story to this stranger. He started with his and Arielle's difficulties conceiving, to Arielle's blow-up, the mud tracks in the kitchen, her going missing, and then bumping into the woman across from him just a few days ago. The only thing he left out was he and Woodward breaking into the house, and the gardener nearly choking him to death.

The words came out in a rush, and while his openness was initially surprising, Martin came to the quick realization that it should have perhaps been expected, what with him being alone for so long, and being completely engrossed in his work.

After all, the only person that he had told this to was Woodward, and they hadn't spoken in years.

The woman, who was pale to begin with, went stark white as Martin recounted his tale.

After a moment of silence—of awkward, dead silence—the woman's lips started moving. There were sounds coming out of her mouth, Martin was sure of it, but they were too quiet for him to hear.

He leaned forward on the edge of the dusty couch, trying hard to make out what she was saying, but the words didn't seem to make any sense.

Martin was tempted to reach out to her, to ask her if she was alright, but her eyes rolled back in her head and her eyelids began to flutter, and he hesitated. When she brought an arthritic hand to her forehead and started crossing herself, the candles in the room flickered.

Or maybe they didn't. Martin couldn't be certain.

What was clear however, was that the woman was praying.

I'm going to leave. I'm going to get up and get the hell out of here right now.

But then the woman's eyes rolled forward and they appeared surprisingly lucid.

"Have you ever heard of *mater est, matrem omnium*?" she asked, her throat dry.

Martin shook his head. Now that the woman seemed to have regained her faculties, he relaxed a little and sat back down.

Five minutes; I'll give her five minutes, and if by then she hasn't revealed anything about Arielle's whereabouts, I'll leave. I'll leave and put this behind me, once and for all.

"It's Latin; it means *mother of one, mother of all*."

The woman slowly moved toward an adjacent room as she spoke.

"You know, there was a time when not being able to carry a child was more than something that derailed the quest for the perfect suburban family."

Martin waited as the woman flipped through a stack of papers.

Where is this going?

"Back in the sixteen-hundreds, people farmed for their food, and the more children you had, the more prosperous you were. Back then, people — *children* — got sick all the time — they *died* all the time. And if you only had two or three kids when dysentery struck, well, you were in serious trouble. Lose enough children to disease, and you would starve."

A history lesson. I came all the way here for a fucking history lesson. What the hell does this have to do with Arielle?

The woman cleared her throat and continued.

"Having kids was so important back then that even without a basic knowledge of medicine, so-called doctors — charlatans, really — were hocking conception aids, be they herbs or roots, tinctures or potions. But none of these ever worked. *Nothing* worked, until Anne LaForet — a young girl herself at only twelve years of age — gave birth to a beautiful baby girl with blond, almost white hair. You see, Anne was just a normal peasant girl — normal until she had her baby. *After* she had her baby, she found out that she had a special talent."

Martin made a face.

What the fuck is this woman talking about?

"No one knows for sure how Anne came to learn about her talent — some think that she ran out of cow's milk when guest came for tea and she substituted breast milk, while others have proposed more lewd theories — but it doesn't really matter *how*. What matters is that Anne's milk had a way of… of, well, helping women become *fertile.*"

She turned to face him then, and once again Martin was struck by the angularity of her face. The woman's gaunt features were so *obtrusive* that he had to look away, and instead he focused his attention on the blue notepad clutched between her thick and knotted fingers.

"And it worked... it worked so well, in fact, that little Anne wasn't able to keep her special milk a secret for long. And once word got out, women came from all over the South East to visit her and drink her milk. Which said something; keep in mind that travel back then was no trivial undertaking. Travel back then, even traveling only a few hundred miles, was a significant ordeal; it was a real *commitment*.

And these visiting women taxed Anne. You see, unlike most girls her age, she didn't have a husband, and it isn't clear—even to this day—who the father of her child was. As a peasant without a husband, Anne had no means to support herself. So she became an accidental business person, and eventually she started to encourage financial compensation in return for her services. For a time, rumor has it that it even became a very profitable business. Even her daughter, four now, got into the act and helped out; she would help take care of the visitors, keep them company in the swamp. Truthfully, it was probably one of the—or perhaps *the*—first fertility clinic ever.

For a while, things were going quite well for Anne, but she knew that this was not something she would be able to keep up forever. So when Jane Heath came to visit, Anne thought that this was it; help this woman, and she would be set for life."

She paused to clear her throat.

"You see, Jane wasn't one of her ordinary 'customers', if you will. Nope, Jane Heath was married to Benjamin Heath, one of the wealthiest men in all of the South East."

The woman looked at Martin as if he were supposed to react to this, as if he were supposed to know who the hell Benjamin Heath was.

He did not.

"Anyways, so it was no surprise that Anne canceled all of her other patients to tend to Jane. Jane was older than most of her visitors, but she wasn't the oldest—not by a long shot. But after only a few visits, Anne thought that there *was* something different about Jane—well, not about Jane directly, but her husband. You see, while Benjamin Heath was one of the richest men in the South East, he was definitely not one of the *nicest*. Now, you have to remember that smacking your wife around here and there was not horribly uncommon in those times. But Benjamin was different. Benjamin would beat Jane. He would beat her badly—*very* badly—and often she would make the long trek to visit Anne with broken ribs, black eyes, and horrible bruises marking her skin. And every month when Jane visited, the beatings got worse, and her need to conceive more desperate. It soon became clear to Anne that if Jane wasn't with child soon, Heath would beat his wife to death."

The woman paused and took a seat down on the chair opposite Martin, placing the blue folder flat on her lap. Her arthritic hands smoothed the cover once, twice, and then she continued speaking.

"Jane came every month to drink from Anne's breast, but no matter how often she came to visit in secrecy, she would return the following month without child. It's not clear how long this went on for—some say months, others the better part of a year—or even why what had worked for so many others failed to work for Jane, but eventually Benjamin grew suspicious of her monthly outings and—"

The woman swallowed hard, her throat parched. Martin opened his mouth to say something, to offer her some water, but the woman stayed him with a finger. It was clear that she was determined to finish.

"—and one time—one time Benjamin followed Jane. With his most trusted friend in tow, he followed Jane all the way from their luxurious estate to the dredges of the swamp—to

Anne's simple lodge. And then they sat and waited; waited for Jane to drink Anne's milk, and remained hidden in the swamp until she left again. And the whole time, Benjamin's fury grew; to him, what he had seen was not only disgusting, but it was also *offensive*. After all, people of his standing should not interact with, let alone *suck from the breast* of a peasant. He was incensed. So after Jane left, he slipped into Anne's home and tried the beloved nectar for himself. And then he raped her — while his favorite henchman, a despicable creature by the name of Jessie Radcliffe, kept watch outside, he *raped* her."

Jessie.

The name struck a chord with Martin, and his mind immediately flipped back to when he and Woodward were inside 8181 Coverfeld, to when the gardener's long fingers had gripped his throat.

Martin swallowed hard.

Coincidence. It was just a coincidence.

The old woman, misjudging his expression, quickly continued.

"And it wasn't enough for *just* Benjamin to rape Anne; no, when he was spent, he brought Jessie in to take part in the fun, even as her four-year-old daughter watched on. But Benjamin was so enraged that even this, this *desecration of her soul*, wasn't enough. When they had both finished, Benjamin told Jessie to go back to the caravan and grab his seal. Then he dragged Anne's naked body out onto the porch, and put that seal in the fire. Like everything about Benjamin, the seal was big, blocky, and ostentatious. A giant brass seal with his ugly initials: big, ugly, *B* and *H* letters. And when that seal got glowing hot, he flipped Anne over and drove into her soft skin."

She took a deep breath.

"He branded her, forever leaving his mark on her lower back, just above her hip. Finally satisfied, Benjamin and Jessie left, leaving the young mother bloodied and beaten, but thankfully alive."

Now it was Martin's turn to take a breath. He wasn't sure where this tale was going, or if it was even true, but the imagery was hard to shake.

A woman raped and then branded — Jesus.

"Anne never told anyone about the beating — doing so would probably mean certain death — but she couldn't bear to see Jane again after what her husband had done to her. So when Jane came to her on the first of the month to taste her milk, Anne hid under the bed. On the second month, she did the same. She felt bad for Jane, because no matter how horrible the acts that Benjamin had committed with her, it had only been one night.

Jane, on the other hand, had to live with the monster.

On the third month, something horrible happened: Anne realized that she was pregnant. And when Jane came, she hid again. But on the fourth month, her pregnancy had made her clumsy and she was unable to hide before Jane spotted her. Like her husband, or perhaps because of him, Jane had an angry streak in her, as well. Furious that she had being ignored, by this commoner no less, Jane broke into Anne's home and took her anger out on the girl, first berating her, then physically hitting her. And the beating only intensified when she saw that Anne was again with child. It made no sense that this *peasant* could have not one but *two* children, while she, the all-important Jane Heath, was destined to be infertile. Jane screamed at Anne, calling her a fraud, a charlatan, all the while punching and kicking the pregnant girl. And then things took a turn for the worst. At some point during the assault, Anne's shirt came up at the back and Jane saw it: her husband's iconic seal, those two block letters, *B* and *H*, on Anne's lower back."

The woman paused to hand the folder to Martin, but he didn't open it right away. Instead, he kept his eyes trained on the woman across from him, waiting for her to finish this horrific tale.

"And then, when Anne was convinced that she would be killed, Jane unexpectedly left. But while Anne was 'but a peasant', she wasn't stupid. She knew that the rage Jane had shown—rage like that—didn't suddenly disappear. She *knew* that Jane would come back. So Anne started to pack up, preparing and take her four-year-old daughter and leave. Only she was too slow. Before she could abandon her home, Jane returned. Only this time, she didn't come alone. You see, Jane, like her husband, had influence, and from the moment she left the swamp, she started to spread rumors about Anne, telling people that she was a whore, that she had tricked each and every one of them, that she had manipulated their husbands to have sex with Anne and that the babies they held were actually *hers*. Jane convinced them that Anne was a witch, that she had put a spell on her husband to have sex with her. You have to remember, this was the sixteen hundreds... and peasants were easily swayed by people in power. So this time when Jane came to the swamp, she wasn't alone. This time she had the townsfolk with her."

The woman paused, leaving Martin to his thoughts in the near darkness. After a few moments, Martin realized that the woman across from him was crying—soft, almost silent tears.

Should I go to her?

But the woman wiped her face and continued before he could make up his mind. Her voice had become deadpan.

"When Jane returned, she ripped the five month old fetus out of Anne with a pair of rusty pliers. *Pliers*, for Christ's sake."

Martin cringed.

"And then, with blood dripping down between her legs, Jane and the townsfolk paraded Anne around the swamp, all the while chanting *mater est, matrem omnium*—mother of one, mother of all—and *filia obcisor, filius obcisor*—daughter killer, son killer. They took turns punching her, spitting on her, pulling her hair. And when they were done parading her around the swamp, they tied poor Anne LaForet to an old tree behind her house and burned her alive. *Mater est, matrem omnium* they chanted as her skin bubbled and peeled and she turned black."

"Jesus," the word slipped out of Martin's mouth.

"That wasn't the worst part," the woman whispered, tears streaking her pale, hard cheeks. "The worst part was Anne's four-year-old daughter."

She cleared her throat, clearly having difficulty getting the words out.

"They burned her alive, too. They put a stake in the ground beside Anne's burning corpse, tied the four-year-old to it like a mangy dog, and set her alight."

Chapter 40

No one chased after Arielle as she'd expected them to. No cop tackled her, forced her into a small, poorly lit room, and made her confess that she had birthed a child in a horrible place and had taken the baby away even before her husband had seen her.

Maybe she half wanted them to do just that, if for nothing else but to get it off her chest, to tell someone.

Maybe.

Instead, she again found herself alone, as she had been for so many years, even while living with Martin. Alone and afraid.

And confused. Arielle's confusion was like a dark storm cloud that wouldn't clear even during the sunniest of days.

How did that horrible photograph get in my purse?

She tried to think back to the afternoon of the Woodwards's party, to when she first returned from 1818 Coverfeld Ave —

Did one of them plant it in there?

Arielle stopped cold, just twenty feet from the park where this horrible afternoon had started.

Feeling dizzy, she took a seat on the nearest bench.

Does it matter? Does it matter that someone had swapped out a picture of her daughter for some disgusting corpse?

It didn't, of course; none of that mattered. The only thing that mattered was finding Hope.

She pictured the officers — Jenkins and the one that had driven her to the station — at a bar after work, sucking down Budweisers and laughing at her expense. Calling her a crazy lady. A widow, perhaps. A crazy widow who was confused about having or not having a daughter, one that kept morbid pictures in her purse.

And maybe she really was crazy.

But Hope was real. Despite all the fucked-up things that had happened and the probably worse things that she couldn't remember, Hope was real. And she needed her mother.

The police clearly weren't going to be of any help. It was up to her—it was up to her and her alone to find Hope.

Her frustration came to a head.

"Fuck!" she screamed. "You can't have her!"

Her mind started racing, and something occurred to her. Maybe she didn't have to do this alone, maybe there was one other person she could call.

Arielle reached back into her purse and pulled out her cell phone so quickly that several sheets of paper and other personal items came out with it.

Arielle quickly scrolled through her contacts, taking a deep breath when she found the one name in there that she had wanted to call for all these years, but had promised herself that she wouldn't.

But now was different; now she needed help.

She hesitated.

Coverfeld Ave—she was going back there for the... third time?

It didn't matter how many times she had been there before. Nothing mattered now except for finding Hope.

Mother, or whoever the fuck you are, you messed with the wrong woman.

A sharp exhale, and she thumbed send. There was a brief pause before the phone started to ring. As she waited for someone to pick up, an image of Dr. Barnes's bruised face filled her mind.

No one fucks with Arielle Reigns.

Chapter 41

The room was suddenly warm, and Martin felt increasingly uncomfortable. A sheen of sweat had begun to form on his forehead, and the armpits of his t-shirt had gotten heavy with it.

As terrible as the tale that the woman across from him had already recounted, it appeared that she wasn't quite done yet.

"Even after both Anne LaForet and her daughter's bodies had been reduced to soot, it *still* wasn't enough for Jane Heath. After all the townsfolk had upped and left, Jane walked up to Anne's remains and spat on them, denouncing her as a witch whore. Unfortunately for Jane, even though she had burned Anne's body, her spirit was far from dead."

The woman looked up when she said these words as if to gauge Martin's reaction. But he offered none—his mind was lost in the woman's story, trying to wrap itself around the coincidences of the tale that all seemed to center around Arielle.

The blood dripping down between her legs, the photograph, the goddamn house in the swamp. Jessie.

"Anne came back," the woman continued in a hushed voice, "spitting on her grave was the final straw... Anne came back from whatever hell she had been banished, and she traveled from that pile of burnt bone and flesh and *up* Jane, *inside* her, filling her broken womb with a foul, evil spirit—like a demented child that Jane always wanted in life. And Anne, now possessing Jane's body, sought revenge against the townsfolk that had murdered her and her child—*both* of her children. She sought out all the children she had helped conceive and forced them back to her home where she intended to raise them as her own. A big *'fuck you'* to the people that had paraded her bruised and beaten body around the swamp, those that had listened to Jane's fucked up story about her sleeping with their husbands, tricking them into impregnating *her*. The town, a small, simple place, usually content with just *being*, suddenly became the focal point of something much greater. And the townsfolk were either too confused or too scared to act, to try and get their children back. Instead, they deferred to the two men who had started this whole mess: they went to Benjamin and Jessie. They knew nothing of what Jane had done, of course, and cared less about the town that she had destroyed. But, oddly, what Benjamin *did* care about was his punching bag of a wife. And she was missing. So, with Jessie once again in tow, they returned to the swamp. Only when they found her, they wished they hadn't. Jane cursed them both for what they had done to Anne; she cursed Jessie to stand watch, to burn any other man or woman that came looking for their children. And Benjamin, who had so much fun raping her? She cursed him to have sex with her over and over again, impregnating her each and every time — she cursed him to drink her milk, to fill her with his evil seed."

And with that, the woman let all the air out of her lungs in a whoosh. She looked as if she had aged a decade in the hour or so that Martin had been sitting on the dusty couch, listening to her story.

Everything had been so vivid, her conviction so absolute, that Martin *almost* believed her. But part of him, the rational part of his mind, refused to acknowledge the absurdity of her tale; there was no such thing as demons or possession. That was madness.

He cleared his throat and offered the only response that he felt comfortable with.

"How do you know so much? How do you know about this *Anne LaForet?*"

The woman squinted, her dark pupils receding into the shadows of her face.

"Because I was there. I went to see Mother Anne."

Martin nearly choked on his spit.

"You *what?*"

"I went to see Mother Anne; she still draws desperate women who—"

Martin shook his head.

"Wait? You went to *see* her? Where?"

The woman crossed herself again.

"Open the notepad," she instructed, ignoring his question.

Martin, incredulous, did as he was told.

Each page of the plain blue notepad had a newspaper article stapled to it. Every page, all fifty or so, had what seemed like a different article, starting from the late nineties.

Martin turned to the first one.

It was short, only maybe fifteen or twenty lines of text, about a woman named Jennifer Matlen, who had been released from the Creston police station after spending more than fifteen hours being assessed by a clinical psychiatrist.

"Jennifer was detained after reporting her four-year-old daughter missing. Police became suspicious when Jennifer was not able to produce any record of her daughter's birth, or any record of her being admitted to a hospital. The police investigated the house where Jennifer claimed to have given birth, a house in Stumphole swamp on a secluded dirt road named Coverfeld—"

Martin's eyes bulged.

He reread the street name again. And then a third time.

Coverfeld.

"It can't be," he murmured, forgetting that he wasn't alone in the room. "No fucking way."

The woman suddenly rocketed to her feet and quickly moved away from him. She wagged an arthritic finger accusingly.

"You've been there," she hissed. "You've been to the house!"

Martin looked up at her, the fear on her face giving him pause.

"Yeah," he began hesitantly, "I went there with a cop friend, but we—ugh—we didn't find anything. How—how can this be the same place? I mean, what are the odds?"

The woman backed as far away from him as possible, and in doing so she bumped against a small table that lined the back wall, sending the candles on top if it swaying dangerously.

"Did you see her?"

Martin tilted his head.

"Who? See who?"

"Her? Did you see *her*? Did you see *Mother Anne*?"

Martin frowned.

"The place was abandoned—there was only a gardener—"

"*Jessie*," the woman spat with venom.

Martin was starting to get dizzy. There were just too many coincidences at play. He began to ponder if maybe this woman had followed him, or maybe she had spoken with Arielle... or Woodward... or...

What the fuck is going on?

The woman, who he was now almost certain was the Jennifer Matlen described in the article in his hands, tried to lean back even farther, but with her back pressed up against the table, there was nowhere to go. As it was, her black dress dangled dangerously close to a lit candle.

"You need to leave!" she hissed at him, her voice raising an octave. "You need to leave now! She's seen you, she knows you! She knows who you *are*."

Martin stood, laying the blue notepad on the couch beside him.

"She will burn you, like she burned the others. She will make you pay! *Mater est, matrem omnium*! She will make *you burn!*"

Then he remembered the photograph from his bedside table, the one that he had once thought depicted Arielle as a child. He reached into his pocket and pulled it out, unfolding it and showing to Jennifer.

The woman's eyes focused, and then went wide.

"Is—"

—*this the place?* He intended to ask, but she cut him off.

"It's her!" Jennifer screamed, "*Mater est, matrem omnium!*"

Her outstretched finger recoiled, and she began to reach behind her, to feel her way into the next room without taking her eyes off Martin or the photograph.

Martin blinked, amazed at the strength of the voice coming from such a small woman. The candles bobbled again as her hands jostled the table edge.

"Careful, you're close to—"

"Get away!"

Martin reached for Jennifer then, his eyes fixed on the candle that was but a mere hair from the back of her dress.

"No! Don't touch me!" Jennifer screamed, forcing her body farther onto the table.

Martin wouldn't have believed that a fire could grow so big so quickly. The woman's dress only just brushed the tiny, almost infinitesimal flame, but it was enough. The dark fabric ignited like the wick of a Molotov cocktail.

Now it was Martin's turn to scream.

It only took two, maybe three seconds before he was on her, but during that short period of time, Jennifer's entire dress ignited and the woman began wailing at the top of her lungs. Still, despite the fire that licked at her flesh, she spun away, not wanting to be touched by him, all the while spreading the flames to the dry floor, the curtains, the old, peeling wallpaper.

Martin threw himself on top of the woman, her bony body collapsing beneath him like a small piece of tinder. He tried to smother the flames with his arms and chest, patting her, spinning with her, but no matter what he did, they continued to grow in size and intensity. He could feel the heat of the fire spilling from between his armpits and legs, but there was too much adrenaline flowing through him to feel his own burning flesh. He sat up and tried to roll the wailing woman with his hands.

It didn't matter what he did; the flames just wouldn't extinguish. Martin, still rolling the woman across the floor, looked up, trying to find something, anything, to put out the fire.

She will burn you like she did the others.

The wallpaper had caught and the photographs of Jennifer's daughter had started to melt, her pretty, girlish face popping and dripping like old wax.

He saw nothing—no blanket, no fire extinguisher, he couldn't even find the damn sink.

When he turned back to Jennifer, the woman was staring up at her, the skin on her face pink and riddled with blisters. Smoke was coming from somewhere on the back of her head. Seeing this, he was made aware of his own burning hands and he instinctively pulled them back.

"Don't let her have me—don't let Anne have me!"

The woman shrieked as her eyes rolled back and her body started to convulse.

The fire was all around them now, and Martin realized that the air had gotten so hot that it hurt to breath.

"No!" Martin shouted when she stopped screaming. "No!"

Jennifer's concave chest stopped rising and falling.

She was dead—the fire had turned her face black and crispy, like overcooked bacon. Her eyes had gone completely white and smoke spilled from her open mouth.

Martin began to cough, the acrid smell of smoke burning his throat and chest. He rolled off the woman, trying to get away from her burning body and to somewhere cooler. It was impossible; the fire had spread throughout the small apartment.

Somewhere amidst the crackling of the flames he heard the sound of a fire alarm going off; an incessant beeping that reminded him that if he didn't flee the burning apartment now, it would only be moments before he was rendered much the same as Jennifer, starting with his already blistering hands.

Martin, still crouched low, grabbed the blue notepad, which, unbelievably, seemed to be the only item untouched by the fire. Coughing hard now, he used the notepad to grasp the sizzling doorknob and fled into the hallway, the thick, black smoke following him like an obedient pet.

Several of the doors to other apartments were open now, concerned faces peeking out.

"Get out!" Martin yelled as he made his way to the stairwell. "Get out now! The whole place is going to burn!"

He waved his arms, gesturing madly for them to flee.

There was a scream, then a mother jumped out of her doorway with a toddler in her arms.

Martin followed the woman down the stairs, doing his best not to bowl her over, and together they made it out into the cool night.

When the cold air hit his throat, he inhaled deeply. Martin kept moving, stumbling by several people who had gathered and stared up at the building, which now had flames licking out of several fourth floor windows.

Firetruck sirens cut through the night.

He made his way to his car, throwing the door wide and tossing the blue notepad on the seat before collapsing.

A coughing fit hit him then, and he spasmed until his mouth filled with phlegm. Eyes burning, he spat onto the grass.

There was another sound, he realized, one that was slightly muted compared to the alarm from the building, the sirens from the approaching fire trucks, and the blood rushing in his ears. It took him a moment to place it: his phone.

It took three attempts to click the green icon with his burned fingers.

"Hello?" he croaked.

A female voice answered, and although it was one he hadn't heard in many years, he recognized it immediately.

"Martin—she took our baby girl, Martin. They kidnapped Hope," the woman said. Then she added, "Coverfeld Ave," and Martin's blood, nearly boiling from the burning apartment building, ran icy cold.

"Arielle?" he shouted into the phone, his throat raw, his head spinning. "Arielle?"

But Arielle had already hung up, once again leaving him in the dark.

Chapter 42

Arielle sped along the highway, her mind racing faster than her Audi. With the city lights fading into her rearview, she tried to recall the events that had preceded her first going out to Coverfeld Ave.

First, there was the girl, a girl that didn't look that much unlike Hope, now that she thought about it—a girl with long blond hair and a missing front tooth—playing Frisbee. Then she had found the poster and had dialed the number.

Could the girl have put the poster there? It was possible...

There was something else about the girl, too, something that she couldn't quite place. It was like trying to see out a frosted window; she knew things were there—shapes, shadows, colors—but when she tried to bring them into focus, they just blurred into unrecognizable forms.

Fuck, why can't I remember?

The temperature had cooled considerably from the warm afternoon. Still, despite the plunging temperatures, she had the window down, and the cool air whipped her in the face. It felt rough on her skin, like sandpaper assaulting her raw eyes and cheeks. But she let it burn; she was feeling tired again, and she couldn't afford to sleep. Not yet.

Hope needs me.

Arielle's foot pushed the gas pedal just a little harder and her Audi jumped forward, pealing down the nearly empty highway. At this rate, she would be back at Stumphole in less than two hours.

And then what?

Arielle wasn't sure.

I'll think of something. I'll think of a way to get my daughter back.

*   *   *

Arielle switched off the lights even before she turned onto Coverfeld Ave, despite the fact that the house — something that, oddly, she *could* remember — was still a couple of miles down the road.

It was better this way; quiet, stealthy. She needed any advantage she could get. Even though she had spent the better part of nine months in this fucking place, she had no recollection of what it was like inside or out.

The only things she remembered were the milk, the mice, and the gray — she remembered that everything about the place was a dull, monochromatic gray.

She cut the engine early, letting the car just coast closer to where the house lay in the swamp. Just before it finally came to a rest in the mud, the tires slipped into some old treads — tire treads that had been made a long time ago, ones that were deep in places, then shallower...

A vision suddenly hit her, a memory of —

A giant of a man, a tall, spindly beast telling her to get out of her car. To head inside.

"Shouldn't I park the car?"

The man shook his head.

"No, Mother needs to see you now."

"Well, what are you going to do with it? You can't just keep it here... and I doubt you can fit inside."

The man grunted.

"I'll push it," he said, and she made a face. *"I'll push it. Mother will see you now."*

Arielle shook her head, clearing the fog.

It still bothered her that she had found the house in the first place... after all, she had only the street name to go on. This should have tipped her off that something was up when she had come four, nearly five years ago. How could a person find a gray house on a mud road adjacent a foul swamp without ever having been there before? A house that was tucked away, hidden from sight. And all this based only on a *street* name.

The mailbox; she found the house again this time because she caught a glimpse of the mailbox poking out of the mud. The one with 1818 written crudely on the side.

Just like before.

Arielle sat in her car in the dark, trying to make out where exactly the house was through the maze of trees that dotted the lawn. Moonlight sent slivers of glinting steel through their trunks, but this was of little help; all it served to do was to give her the impression that she was looking into a smashed mirror.

Still, she knew the house was there, just sixty or so yards up the mud trail.

A toad belched from somewhere to her left, and she jumped.

Keep it together, Arielle, keep it together. Hope needs you.

She reached into her purse and grabbed her cell phone, and as she did, her eyes caught a small container, one that she had seen earlier in the day when she had been tossing things onto the police officer's desk.

Pills.

Arielle brought the bottle close to her face and inspected it. *Promethazine – 25 mg.*

The word was foreign to her, but the transparent orange container stirred a memory. They were the pills that Dr. Barnes had given her for her nausea back when she had first been pregnant. Which meant that they were more than four years old, and had probably lost some of their efficacy. Still, the bottle was full…

A part of her wanted to take one herself, right now, to help rid or at least alleviate the anxiety that twisted her intestines.

Arielle decided against taking one. She needed to be sharp… for whatever happened when she left the safe confines of her car and braved the mud. Despite her lack of memory, she had a feeling that Mother would not give Hope back easily.

Mother. Now that was someone she remembered clearly, what with her heavily painted eyelids and pale pink lips. The nicotine-stained fingers, the tendrils of gray and white hair.

A life for a life.

A shudder rattled the pills in the orange container.

She had made a deal with someone worse than the devil.

She had made a deal with *Mother.*

Even though she decided against taking one of the pills herself, that didn't mean that they might not be still be useful.

She rattled the pill container again.

The problem was, her sounding like a maraca was not going to facilitate a stealthy approach. Arielle pulled the cap off and stared at the pills.

Crush them, I can crush them and…

She reached over and rustled through her purse, her searching fingers finding another photograph. This time, however, it *was* the photo of Hope she had taken just a few months back. Hope, with her soft, blue eyes and long blond hair.

Where the fuck…?

Arielle shook her head, trying to focus.

…I can crush the pills and fold them into the photograph — that could work.

And then Arielle set about doing just that, somewhere in the back of her mind realizing that she must have seen this on a TV show a while back. She used her car keys to grind the white pills against the bottom of the container, extracting a modicum of satisfaction with every *crunch*. When the entire bottle had been reduced to a fine white powder, she bent it carefully and poured the powder into it. Then she folded it again, made sure that the powder wouldn't spill out, and tucked the small square into her bra.

A deep breath, a quick moment of silence with her eyes closed, and her hand fell to the door handle where it rested briefly.

A life for a life.

I will get my daughter back.

With that, Arielle opened the door and stepped into the cool, dark, and foul-smelling night, her hands unconsciously balling into fists.

Chapter 43

Martin tried calling the number again and again, but it always ended with the same robotic voice telling him that the mailbox of the person he was trying to reach was full.

He sped down the highway at breakneck speed, his mind full of images of burning flesh, be it the melting photographs of the smiling girl plastered around the apartment, Jennifer burning and dying beneath him, or the demon, Anne LaForet in the swamp, burned at the stake, her four-year-old daughter screaming in agony beside her.

"Fuck!" Martin swore, slamming his hands down on the steering wheel. He cried out in pain as the blisters that had formed there during the fire burst.

Please, Woodward, be ready.

His estranged friend had sounded confused on the phone, so utterly shocked that Martin had called him after so much time without speaking, that he had stammered through the conversation.

Please be ready, he pleaded again. And please have something for me...

When Martin pulled up to Woodward's house, sweat was dripping from his face. Three times he had to brush it away from his eyes from fear of it blinding him and causing him to veer off the road, and all three times his fingers had come back dark with soot.

He was too frightened to look at his reflection in the mirror.

Martin hadn't even put the car into park before the door to Woodward's ranch-style home swung open and a figure lumbered out.

A second later, the passenger door swung outward and Woodward heaved his large body into the car. Martin noticed that the man held a folder in one hand and he was wearing his service revolver in a holster on his hip.

Both of these were good signs.

With the door closed, Woodward finally turned to him and stared directly into his face.

"How nice of you to call," he said, his voice hushed, his small mouth and tight. "And you look like shit, by the way."

Martin put the car into drive and the vehicle shot forward.

*   *   *

They had been driving for a good ten minutes before Woodward finally broke the silence.

"Well? You gonna tell me what the fuck happened to you? You been drinking, Marty?"

The blisters on Martin's hands had started to throb, and the sensation was slowly creeping up his singed forearms.

He swallowed hard.

"Did you look for what I asked? Did you find anything?"

Woodward gently waved the folder in his hand.

"Read it to me," Martin demanded.

Woodward shook his head.

"No fucking way. You call me after what, three, almost four years? And you tell me that Arielle called... and that you have a *daughter*? What the fuck, Marty?"

Martin just stared straight ahead, jaw clenched. He knew that if he even tried to offer a retort, he would likely break into tears.

"Then you show up looking like you just fucked a fireplace, and you're giving *me* orders?"

Martin pushed the gas pedal just a little bit harder and his car shot down the dark highway.

"Nuh-uh. No way. You spill the beans, man. And you spill them right now."

Martin took a deep breath and then he started to speak, going way back to when he had bumped into the woman from the church after leaving the cafe, and ending with her burning to death beneath him.

By the end, he was crying. Just as he suspected.

For a while, Woodward didn't say anything. He just sat there in the passenger seat, breathing heavily, eyes trained on the increasingly darkening road.

"She died?"

Martin nodded.

"I tried... I tried to save her, Woods. Fuck—her fucking eyes were white, and there was smoke," his voice hitched, "there was smoke coming out of—"

Woodward hushed him.

"That's fucked up—really fucked up. And then Arielle? She called you? Told you that you have a daughter?"

Martin nodded and sniffed, wiping black snot from his face with the back of his hand.

Woodward didn't press anymore, at least not for the moment. The man was struggling to take it all in. In the end, he just left it alone, and changed subjects.

"I got what you asked," Woodward said after a brief pause, "Want me to read it?"

Martin nodded again, and Woodward started to read from the folder in his lap.

"Janice Dankins, four-years-old; missing in 1976. Emma Story, four-years-old; missing 1982. Fran Smith, five-years-old; missing 1986. Chelsea Pickett, four-years-old, 1990."

Woodward flipped through a few pages.

"Fifteen girls, Martin. Fifteen young girls, either four or five years of age in and around Stumphole have all gone missing over the last 30 or so years."

Martin felt his chest tighten.

Could it be true? Could what Jennifer told him about Anne LaForet be true?

"Never a clue, never a trace. None confirmed, either, mind you; no birth certificates for any of them. What the fuck, Martin? How could I not have heard about this?"

"Open the blue notebook," he instructed, ignoring the man's question, knowing that he wouldn't be able to provide an adequate answer. Woodward did as he was told.

"Old newspaper clippings," the police officer said, flipping through the pages, "Some about more missing children, something about a tree—some burnt tree by the swamp—another about—"

"—go back," Martin interrupted, "tell me about the tree."

Woodward flicked back to the page and started to read.

"Three vandals were arrested when they were caught defacing a tree out at Stumphole Swamp—at 8181 Coverfeld Ave. The three kids, all in their mid to late teens, were caught urinating on a tree that they claimed had once been the spot where Anne LaForet had been tied and burned to death... the teenagers said that—"

"Okay," Martin interrupted.

"—that they wanted to piss on the—"

" —okay, Woodward, that's enough. Stop reading."

Woodward obliged.

Another moment of silence ensued as his friend's words weighed on him. If nothing else, the article meant that Jennifer had not been completely bullshitting about the woman in the woods. It didn't mean that her story was true of course, but his mind kept wandering back to the man that they had seen when they had first made their way to the rundown house on Coverfeld.

The man that had gripped him by the throat.

The man named *Jessie*.

Filia obcisor.

Filius obcisor.

They drove in silence for a long while, but when Martin turned onto Coverfeld Ave, Woodward broke it.

"You don't believe any of this shit, do you?"

Martin took a deep breath and turned to face his friend. Woodward's eyes were wide, but his mouth was characteristically tight.

"I don't know," Martin replied honestly. He reached up and wiped more soot from his forehead. "I really don't know. I just want to find Arielle... and I want to find my daughter."

Chapter 44

Moonlight only penetrated the top layer of fog leaking off the swamp, coating it in an eerie blue glow. The rest of the woods were nearly completely dark, making it slow going for Arielle McLernon. This was compounded by the fact that with every step, her feet sank farther into the mud, and pulling them back out again was getting more and more difficult. To top it off, her feet felt heavy, as if the mud that coated her loafers was slowly solidifying into a block of concrete.

Arielle knew the house was back here somewhere, even if she couldn't see it yet. It was back here, and she just *knew* that Hope was somewhere inside. That was all that mattered.

This knowledge drove her forward.

The smell, which she recalled from her very first visit, a blast of rank, hot, sulfurous stench, didn't bother her as much this time, for reasons she didn't completely understand. She thought that maybe it was that she had just become accustomed to it, the way a fart only smelled offensive in the elevator for the first few floors. Or maybe it was because her mind was preoccupied.

The air around Arielle suddenly stirred, and a creaking sound reached her from somewhere no more than ten or fifteen paces directly ahead.

Her heart, already pounding in her chest, doubled or tripled in speed. It was the sound of the rusted chains holding the porch swing to the roof, and the creaking stirred a memory that had been buried deep inside.

She was sitting beside an old woman on the porch swing, spewing her guts about everything as the strange woman smoked silently beside her.

Why had she done that? Why had she shared so much with someone she'd only just met?

Arielle remembered the woman's pale pink lips twisting into a smile, telling her to come inside, that she had something that would calm her nerves, clear her head.

The milk.

Arielle's stomach did a backflip and she gagged. The sensation was accompanied by an image of a tall glass of milk that was so tangible that she could almost taste the sickly sweet substance. And the thickness... why had the milk been so thick, like a Plaster of Paris slurry? Milk, even whole milk, was never that thick...

She shuddered and was about to raise her heavy foot again, to inch toward the creaking porch swing, when another sound cut through the thick night.

It was the sound of a young girl laughing.

"Hope?" Arielle whispered. "Hope? Is that you?"

The only response was another giggle.

Arielle took an immediate left and headed toward this new sound, holding her hand out to one side to make sure she didn't bump into the porch that was somewhere just out of reach.

She was starting to sweat, partly because of the warmth of the night and partly due to the exertion required to raise her feet. Heart still racing, she crept closer to the house, and with two more labored steps, the peaked roof loomed overhead and blocked out all moonlight, shrouding Arielle in complete darkness. Even going just from poor lighting to zero visibility was disorienting, and Arielle had to pause to catch her bearings.

Eventually, fueled by another, more distant giggle, she mobilized again and carefully inched forward. Her outstretched fingers soon grazed the wooden porch railing, and she used this as a guide to make her way toward the side of the house.

"Mommy?"

The tiny voice seemed to come out of the darkness itself.

"Hope? I'm coming, baby, just stay still—don't move."

Arielle picked up her pace, grunting now as she raised her feet.

When she cleared the corner, the moonlight shone once again, and in that instant Arielle saw her.

Hope was standing twenty paces ahead of her, just in front of a door cut out of the side of the brick house.

"Hope!" Arielle cried.

The girl was standing completely still with her back to her, a long blond braid trailing halfway down her back.

"Hope?" Worry usurped Arielle's feelings of exultation.

Why is she standing so still? Why doesn't she turn and face me?

Arielle reached her daughter in only a few large strides, despite the mud's grasp. Cautiously, she lowered her hand on Hope's shoulder, relishing the feel of her warm body even through her green t-shirt. Upon contact, the girl turned, and Arielle's smile faded.

This wasn't her daughter.

Arielle took a step backward, nearly stumbling when her heels dug into the mud.

It wasn't her daughter, but another girl, one that looked just like Hope.

It was the girl with the Frisbee, the one that had met her in the park all those years ago back in Batesburg. The same girl who had served her milk during Arielle's months at this house.

Madison.

The name came to her in a flash.

'We'll stay here until you drink it. Mother won't be happy.'

The memory came smashing back to Arielle with such clarity that she fell backward, her ass immediately puckering into the mud.

It wasn't Hope; it was Madison.

"What did you do with Hope?" Arielle whispered.

But the girl didn't answer. Instead, she just lowered her gaze and her pretty lips turned downward.

"Why did you come back here?" the girl whispered. The words were strange, her voice distant, as if she were repeating words that someone had told her to say. "Mother is not happy."

Arielle scrambled to a kneeling posture, anger overwhelming her.

Mother? Mother?

"She took my Hope," Arielle hissed. "Kidnapped her."

She went to stand, but the mud grabbed her and pulled her back to her knees. Her hands were buried in the stuff halfway to her forearms. She was surprised at how warm the mud was—warm, like simmering soup.

Madison looked up, shaking her head back and forth, sending her braid whipping from side to side.

"You made a deal."

"Fuck the deal," Arielle said as she finally managed to rise to her feet.

"You made a deal," Madison repeated. She lifted her eyes, and Arielle saw that the girl was crying now.

Despite everything, Arielle felt sorry for this girl, as whatever her involvement was, at only seven or eight years old, she was not responsible. Still, if she was going to get in the way of her finding Hope...

"Fuck the deal. I will never give my child away. No one would… that's insane."

Arielle took a step forward, but then a sound from her right startled her.

It was the sound of a door opening, and as she turned, something struck her in the side of the head and she went down, her face cushioned by the mud like a molten pillow.

As her vision blurred and her mind began to swim, she felt large hands wrap around her shoulders and yank her to her feet. A second later, she was upside down, hoisted up over a man's shoulder, her head hanging down his back.

It could only be one man—there was only one man that she knew was large enough, *strong* enough, to lift her like a damp rag.

It could only be Jessie.

As her vision blurred, Arielle was spun around, and she caught a final glimpse of Madison staring at her, the wet tracks on her cheeks reflecting the pale moonlight.

"You made a deal," the girl whispered almost forlornly. Arielle didn't know if she heard the words, or if she only read Madison's lips. "Mother is not happy. *Filius obcisor. A life for a life.*"

Arielle's body went limp and her world faded to black.

Chapter 45

"There! You see that? It... it looks like a car."

Martin squinted hard, trying to make out the license plate. It was a Georgia plate, but still... it *could* be her car. After all, it was an Audi A4 and the swamp didn't strike Martin as a place where people drove Audis. Tractors, dirt bikes, maybe even alligators, but not Audis.

"You see it?" Woodward asked again.

Martin shut off the headlights.

"Yeah," he replied.

"You think it's hers?"

Martin shrugged.

She's here. She's definitely here.

"Yeah," he said again, slowing the car and then bringing it to a stop by the mailbox that was still buried in the mud; the mailbox with the numbers 8181 or 1818 or whatever the hell was written on the side of it. The mailbox that marked the lane to a house that Martin was beginning to think had a past far darker than he could have ever imagined.

Martin took a deep breath and reached for the door handle, but Woodward's voice stopped him short.

"Martin?"

"Yeah?"

"What's your daughter's name—I mean, if you really have a daughter and all that."

Martin hesitated, and he mulled the question over.

If. If Arielle has a daughter. If this daughter is mine. If I find her or them. If she's here in this godforsaken place. If. If. If.

"Hope," he replied at last. "Her name is Hope."

Woodward nodded.

"A beautiful name."

Martin would have said 'thank you', but his throat was suddenly too dry to produce any words. Instead he opened the door and gulped in the stinking, foul swamp air.

"If they're here, Woodward, let's find them. *If* they're here, let's find my wife and daughter."

*   *   *

"Take this and keep the beam low. Don't be shining it up into the windows. We'll scope out the outside first, then head indoors. Remember the lock on the floor in the kitchen I told you about?"

Martin took the flashlight from Woodward and shook his head. The only thing he remembered was being choked by some ogre—*Jessie*—before Woodward saved him.

"Well, there was a lock in the kitchen... on the floor."

Martin nodded.

"Stick to the outside first. Beam low."

Crouched, with the flashlight aimed low as instructed, Martin made his way up the muddy driveway. With every step, his shoes became increasingly covered with mud, restricting his pace to slow and methodical. Woodward seemed to have an even harder time, what with his immense weight pressing him deeper into the mud with each step.

The swamp was active, with bullfrogs, crickets, and other night insects singing their nocturnal theme song. Martin tried his best to force these noises into the background, and instead tried to pick up other sounds—*like giant men running through the mud at us*—like someone talking or crying out for help.

As they approached the porch, Martin realized that while there was no speaking to be heard, there *was* another sound that didn't quite fit in the swamp. Underlying the night noises was the sound of creaking metal.

The chain—the chain holding the porch swing to the roof.

Martin raised his foot to ascend the first porch step, but Woodward reached out and grabbed his arm.

"Outside first, you take the left and I'll—"

A loud creak from the porch interrupted Woodward, and Martin instinctively sprayed his flashlight up the porch.

There, sitting upright on the swing, was the blackened corpse of a woman.

"Oh fuck!" Martin shouted, as he tried to take a step backward. The mud grabbed his shoe and held him in place.

As he watched, the woman's head slowly turned to face him, her eyes a startling white against her crispy flesh.

"Please, not my child. Please don't burn her."

Her voice was calm, almost soothing.

This time when Martin tried to pull his foot from the mud, he started to fall backward, a scream stuck in his throat.

Woodward grabbed his arm and yanked him back to his feet. Martin's flashlight beam had strayed during his half-fall, and it fell on Woodward's face. The man's eyebrows were knitted, his lips pursed.

"What the fuck is wrong with you?"

Martin whipped the flashlight back to the porch.

The burned woman was gone.

"What the *fuck?*"

The bench was empty, save a burnt smear where the woman had been sitting.

"Lower the fucking flashlight!" Woodward hissed, bringing his hand down on top of Martin's, forcing the spray of light back to the mud.

"Did you see that?" Martin whispered.

His heart was racing and his entire body suddenly felt slick with sweat.

"See what? The fucking porch swing?"

Martin shook his head so violently that he felt momentarily dizzy.

"The woman... the burned woman on the swing."

Woodward's grip tightened on his arm.

"What the fuck are you talking about?"

Martin squeezed his eyes closed.

Get it together, Martin. You're freaked out because of the church woman—because of seeing Jennifer burning beneath you.

When he opened his eyes again, Woodward's big face was illuminated by the ambient glow from the dual flashlight beams aimed toward the mud at their feet.

"Get your fucking shit together, Marty. Now."

Martin swallowed hard and nodded.

"Good, now you take the left, and I'll head right. Go around the house, stick close to the wall and keep low. If you hear anything fucked up, you holler and I'll make it to you. And for God's sake Martin, keep the flashlight low."

Martin nodded in agreement, then glanced downward and realized that Woodward had drawn his revolver.

He wished his friend had brought two.

Without the comforting weight of a gun, he allowed his free hand fall to his pocket where his fingers met the turquoise stone therein. It wouldn't protect him from anything, of course—no amount of demon talk would convince him of the power of some benign talisman—but it offered him solace nonetheless.

Something to hold on to.

"Okay," he murmured.

Woodward squeezed his arm again as their gazes locked.

"Okay," Martin repeated more forcefully this time.

Woodward nodded.

"If you see or hear anything, just shout. Shout loud, and I'll get to you. Get it the *fuck* together, Marty."

With that, Woodward turned in the mud with a slurping, suckling sound coming from his shoes, and was gone.

And Martin was alone.

Chapter 46

When Arielle finally opened her eyes, she was surprised that she was somewhere inside. The left side of her face was stiff and caked, and when she finally managed to raise her hand to touch it, her fingers came back brown and red.

Her head hurt, but not as badly as she might have thought given the speed at which she had hit the ground. She had no idea what had struck her, but she vaguely recalled being picked up by someone strong, and staring into the face of a young girl —

Hope. I need to find Hope.

Arielle pulled herself to her feet, but did so too quickly and dizziness took over, forcing her back down. Hovering a few inches above the floor, she took this opportunity to catch her bearings. She was in a cell of some sort, a room made of cold, sweaty bricks that looked a dull gray in the light that shone from the bare bulb up above. There was a cot in the corner, a striped, uncovered, and veritably filthy mattress lying on top. A lone bucket sat in the corner, the purpose of which was plainly — and disgustingly — obvious.

Arielle was back here, after four years of being away.

She was back in her room.

"No," she moaned, slowly pulling herself onto her elbows, and then into a seated position.

"Welcome back, Arielle."

Arielle's head shot up.

There, outside a set of thick metal bars, was Jessie.

As usual, the man's head was high above her, making it difficult to clearly make out his features in the dim lighting. Even seated on the barren floor, the man was nearly as tall as she was when standing. Beside him was a tall glass of milk.

"No," she moaned again, her eyes focusing in on the milk. Fearing that she was going to be forced to drink it, Arielle shuffled away from the bars. Instead, Jessie brought the milk to his shadowed face and took a sip. The sight made her stomach flip.

"Yes, welcome back to your room," Jessie replied, misinterpreting her pleas.

Memories came flooding back in waves, and Arielle was brought back to the first time she had arrived at Coverfeld Ave.

'Do you want to see your room?' Mother asked as they shuffled through the dark hallway together.

Arielle nodded, taking another sip of the sour-tasting milk. It didn't really agree with her, but Mother insisted, and it had an addictive quality that was difficult to describe. It was kind of like trying not to grit your teeth after drinking something very sugary. You could do it, but it was much more satisfying to gnash your molars together.

The hallway that Mother took her down was old, with dated flower wallpaper, but it was nice enough, and her room, albeit plain and nondescript, was at least clean.

'Do I have to stay here?'

Mother nodded. The woman wasn't big on words, that much was clear, even though they had met only a few hours ago. Which was fine by Arielle; after all, the most important words had already been spoken.

'Drink, sweetie, drink your milk. You'd be surprised; the more you drink, the better this place looks.'

Arielle looked around at the filth that she had stayed in for the better part of a year. The fact that she had brought a baby into the world in a place like this made her stomach curdle, and the scar that ran the length of it itched like crazy.

"You want some milk, Arielle? You always drank your milk, even more than the other women," Jessie continued. Then he laughed—a horrible, grating sound.

Arielle shook her head as she tried desperately to figure out a way to get out of this cell that was, and had been, her room.

The cell door was locked, of course, and the only key dangled from Jessie's belt. The party line might have been that the tall, lanky man was the gardener, but the truth was Jessie was anything but—he was the jailer.

Arielle squinted and tried to clear her head.

She pushed her body with mud-caked hands to the back of the cell, and as she did, something dug into her breast. Her hand immediately went to the spot, thinking that maybe a piece of glass had lodged in her bra from her fall in the mud. But it wasn't glass; it was the sharp edge of a folded photograph.

Her eyes immediately darted to the glass of milk clutched in Jessie's massive hand.

Could I—?

Something scampered over her leg and a gasp escaped her.

It was a mouse—a fucking mouse had run over her leg.

Jessie laughed.

"You never liked the mice, Arielle. I don't mind them. Sometimes when I'm bored, I—"

But Jessie never finished his sentence. Instead, a muffled shout drew him to his feet. And then the man was on the move, his lanky frame lumbering quickly out of sight.

Again Arielle's eyes fell on the glass of warm milk, left unguarded on the cold, damp floor.

Chapter 47

Martin slowly made his way along the front porch, and then around the corner of the house.

His breathing was shallow and his heart continued to pound away in his chest. The only thing that kept him driving forward was a *conviction* that Arielle was here somewhere—and so was his daughter. Although peering into the parked Audi hadn't revealed much, save a car seat in the back and a fastidiously clean interior, he *knew* it was Arielle's car.

Please, don't burn my daughter.

A shudder racked through him.

If it weren't for them, he would have been long gone.

There were footprints around the side of the house—three pairs, by the looks of it. There were massive prints coming from somewhere behind Martin, somewhere from back in the woods. Large feet, impressions that seemed to lack a pattern, but appeared to be covered in something… a sock maybe? Was someone running around here in socks?

(Jessie)

The other set of footprints was from smaller feet—wearing shoes this time—while the third were smaller still; tiny, a child's.

Hope—these are Arielle's and Hope's footprints.

Martin followed the footprints, trying to reenact what might have happened here. He quickly made it to a spot where the footsteps converged. And then, suddenly, unexpectedly, there were only two: the large footprints and the child prints, both heading in opposite directions.

What the fuck? What happened to Arielle?

Despite Woodward's instructions to keep the flashlight low, Martin raised the beam and sprayed it around the muddy area adjacent the house, trying to pick up where Arielle's footprints began again.

Nothing.

The mud, aside from the footprints in front of him, was relatively undisturbed.

Nothing, except...

Martin pointed the flashlight away from the house, aiming it at the mud that he thought had previously been undisturbed. And now he saw more footprints.

But these were different. For one, the large sock prints and the child's—even Arielle's before they disappeared—seemed to flank the house. These didn't. These moved *away* from the house, toward the swamp in the distance.

And these were barefoot.

Small feet, like Arielle's, but clearly barefoot. Martin thought he could even make out the individual toes.

Drawn to these strange prints, he moved away from the house and took a step toward them. And then another, and another, thoughts of his wife and daughter momentarily displaced to the dark recesses of his mind.

Less than twenty paces later, Martin found himself at a spot where the footprints ended. He raised the flashlight slowly with a trembling hand, moving it up first the gnarled roots of the large tree before him, then up the trunk.

There was a woman tied to the tree, a woman with black, smoldering flesh. It was the woman from the porch swing. The burned woman with white eyes that bore into him.

As Martin watched in horror, her mouth started to open, hunks of crispy flesh peeling off and then falling to the muddy ground.

"You burned me and my baby—but you haven't killed me. I will never die... I will come baaaaack. I will come *baaaaaaaack*."

The word *back* drifted on and on until it, like the bullfrogs and insects before it, receded into a background cacophony.

"You killed my child, and now I will have yours!" Anne LaForet hissed.

Martin felt warmth spread on the front of his jeans.

And then the screaming started.

*   *   *

"Martin! *Martin!*"

Martin was staring into the woman's singed mouth as it opened and closed, shouting his name over and over again. He felt his legs go weak and his eyelids begin to flutter.

Anne LaForet was fading along with his consciousness.

Arielle—I need to find Arielle and Hope.

"Martin!"

Just as he felt his knees buckle, something gripped his arm and brought him back from the brink of whatever hell he was tumbling into.

"Martin!"

His eyes began to refocus, and he found himself staring not into the eyes of a burned corpse, but into Woodward's. The man's face was a deep scarlet and he was breathing heavily.

"Martin, what's wrong! What the fuck! Why are you screaming?"

Me? Screaming, there was screaming, but it wasn't me...

Martin collected himself and quickly whipped the flashlight around and aimed it back at the tree.

It was dark and dead, twisted knots of thick branches and roots wrapping around itself like a morbid embrace.

But there was no woman.

There was nothing.

His heart skipped a beat.

"Martin!"

He turned back to face Woodward.

"I'm fucking losing it, man," he stuttered, tears in his eyes. "I'm seeing things... I'm seeing the dead, man."

Woodward took a deep breath.

"We need to get you out of here Martin... you've been through shit today, and seeing a woman burn to death will fuck anyone up. We need to get you out of here and to go see someone. We need to report what happened, we—"

"—we need to find Arielle and Hope."

Woodward shook his head slowly.

"They're not here. I don't think *anyone* has been here in a very long time... maybe since we last came."

"What about the car? The footsteps? Look at the footprints."

Confusion crossed the man's broad face.

"Footprints?"

Martin gestured toward the ground behind them, where he had seen the barefoot prints, the ones that had led him to the tree.

"There," he said, but even as the words came out of his mouth they fell away.

There were no prints.

He raised the flashlight higher trying to locate the child's—*Hope's*—and the woman's—*Arielle's*—prints. He found that he had to raise the flashlight higher and higher—*Jesus Christ, how far did I wander from the house* — but the light died before he could find them.

"No prints," Woodward informed him.

Martin shook his head. There had been prints; he was sure of it.

Like the woman on the porch swing? Did you see them like you saw her? Or did you see them like the woman tied to the tree?

But then he *did* see a set of prints; huge, sock-like footprints.

"There!" he exclaimed, shaking the beam of light about ten paces from where they stood.

"I don't—ah, there *are* prints."

Martin, vindicated that he wasn't going *completely* insane, began following the prints with his flashlight. After only a few seconds, he realized that these weren't the same prints he had seen near the house. They were made by the same feet, surely, but they weren't the same *footprints* — those other ones had stayed close to the side of the house.

Instead, these seemed to be moving toward the tree, making a wide birth around it.

The beam of light made it to the tree — still no burned woman,   thank   God — and   then   the   footprints — or foot*smudges* — disappeared behind it.

"What the hell?"

Martin wasn't sure if it was he or Woodward who had said the words, but either way, they shared the sentiment.

The footprints reappeared on the other side of the tree.

Martin's hand started trembling again as he followed the tracks, realizing that they seemed to be coming straight toward them. The light bobbed up and down so rapidly that the foot*smudges* were blinking in and out like fireflies.

Woodward raised his own flashlight to the spot where Martin's stopped, and at first Martin thought that the prints ended at another set of trees.

But then Woodward moved the light upward ever so slightly, and Martin realized that what he was seeing weren't tree trucks.

Tree trunks didn't wear denim.

There was an audible grunt and Woodward cried out. Martin was momentarily blinded and deafened as his friend squeezed off three shots from his revolver in rapid succession.

Through his ringing ears, Martin heard two of those bullets ricochet throughout the swamp. The other bullet, the final shot, made a sickening, organic *thlurp* sound, but there was no exclamation of pain that Martin expected.

Instead, there was a massive slurping sound from the mud as Woodward's entire body was *lifted* out of it. One of the man's shoes got stuck, but it simply fell away like an overripe banana peel.

All three-hundred plus pounds of Tony Woodward lifted seemingly without effort.

What the fuck.

Martin somehow regained control of some of his faculties, and he raised his flashlight just high enough to see Woodard's feet running in mid-air while his hands clawed at the fingers that gripped his throat.

His friend was wheezing madly, and his face, purple from exertion before, now appeared nearly black. As soon as Martin directed the beam of light toward the other figure, toward *Jessie*, Woodward was thrown to the ground.

The force of Woodward's body hitting the mud in front of Martin was so great that it knocked him to the ground like a shock wave and sent the flashlight flying.

Martin cried out and tried to scramble for the flashlight, but his ass suctioned to the mud. Still, despite his futile efforts, he continued to reach for it, but to no avail.

It was then that he realized the light was pointed directly at Woodward's face, the beam shining into one open, unblinking eye. A line of blood dripped from his friend's nose and spilled into his half-open mouth.

Martin screamed and again tried to lift himself from the mud, not to get the flashlight anymore, but to get as far away from Jessie and this place as possible.

But this time, it wasn't the mud that grabbed him. This time, it was two powerful arms that grasped his shoulders and yanked him from the earth like a toy. And then they began to squeeze.

In less than a minute, Martin's world faded in a dull, black embrace.

Chapter 48

The screaming started almost immediately after Jessie left Arielle alone in her cell. At first it was just a dull moan, a low, undulating sound, but it soon transgressed into a wail. Not a pained cry so much as an angry scream—or perhaps a mocking one. The way the sound echoed down the dark corridor made it difficult to tell.

And then there were the gunshots. There were at least two, maybe three distinct barks coming from outside the house.

Could it be Martin? Could Martin have come here and tried to rescue me?

It was possible, after all, she had called him and told him the address. She had kept the conversation, simple, abrupt, *obtuse*, to avoid questions. But a gun? Martin didn't own a gun...

There was surprisingly little time for Arielle to mull this over, as shortly after what was to be the final gunshot, she heard a door open and the familiar sound of footsteps making their way down the long, damp hallway. There was something else accompanying the footsteps, too: a dragging sound.

Arielle pushed her way from the bars to the back of her cell, scuttling on her ass to near the piss bucket. Mice or not, she didn't want to be anywhere near Jessie when he made his way back. It was only then that her eyes first fell on a pile of papers on the filthy mattress. She reached up and grabbed the four inch stack, which was held together by a worn elastic.

A cursory glance and it was obvious that wasn't a stack of papers as she had first thought—it was a stack of *letters*.

Her letters.

Arielle's heart sank. The letters that she had written to Martin were still here and they had never been sent; they still had his address on the front in her hand, but there was no stamp affixed to the upper right-hand corner.

Her blood began to boil.

Mother promised —

It was irrational to be surprised by this after all she had seen. But she was; Arielle was surprised and infuriated.

Seething, she threw the envelopes back onto the mattress just as Jessie stepped into view.

The giant man appeared to be dragging something — something big. With one hand, Jessie threw the cell door wide, and then he reached back with two hands and grunted hard. With a thump, a figure was unceremoniously thrown into her cell, momentarily scattering any mice that might have collected with her presence.

Arielle didn't move at first, and was surprised that Jessie actually receded down the hallway again, leaving the cell door open. She pushed herself to a kneeling position and concentrated on Jessie's fading footsteps.

To her dismay, they didn't travel far enough to risk a dash for it. So, instead, she turned her attention to the figure on the floor of her cell, and she immediately gaped.

"Oh my God."

It was Woodward; even looking at only one side of his pale face as it lay flat on the damp floor, she knew it was him.

Arielle screamed. She hadn't meant to, but it just happened and once it escaped her, there was no stopping it.

She kept on screaming even when Jessie returned, throwing another limp figure on top of Woodard. The body bounced off the officer's very large and very dead stomach and landed on his back, face up.

Her scream caught in her throat.

The second body was her husband.

It was Martin.

Just as her mind started to wrap itself around this fact, Jessie slammed the door closed and locked it.

This was followed by more screaming, but it didn't come from Arielle this time. This time, it came from someone else, a woman somewhere down the abyss of a hellhole that she was trapped in. And now its purpose was patently obvious: it was a mocking cry.

A chill ran up her spine.

It was Mother.

Chapter 49

"Martin! Martin! Wake up, Martin!" Arielle was shaking her husband's shoulder, trying to force him to open his eyes, to confirm that he was still living. His slowly rising and falling chest was not enough proof for her.

Tears streamed down her cheeks.

"You bastard," she shouted at Jessie, who was now sitting with his back to the cell, sipping on his glass of milk. "You bastard! What did you do to him?"

Both Martin and Woodward's bodies were covered in mud, but they had no outward sign of injuries, save for the blood around Woodward's nose and mouth.

"You fucking bastard!" she screamed again, wiping snot from her nose with the back of her hand.

"Mother is very upset that you came back," Jessie said suddenly. His words were slurred, as if his tongue had started to swell from a bee sting. "You made a deal, Arielle."

Ariellllle.

"Fuck Mother! Tell that skinny bitch to show her face and I'll rip her tits off!"

No answer from Jessie this time, but from someone else.

Someone groaned, and Arielle scrambled away from the bars of her cell and back to her husband's body.

"Martin! Martin!"

But Martin's eyes were still closed, his breathing rhythmic, his lips twisted into a grimace.

A particularly long and loud scream came from somewhere down the hall, echoing off the dewy brick walls, giving her pause. When the reverberations finally ended, she turned back to Jessie.

"Mother is nawwwt happp—ppp—ppp—pp—eeee," the lanky figure outside her cell stuttered.

Arielle looked up just in time to see Jessie's body visibly slump against the cell.

"Fuck you," Arielle spat, her hands now cradling her husband's pale face. "Fuck you, you monster!"

She stared at Jessie's massive curled spine.

"You hear me?"

The man didn't respond.

"Jessie?"

And then something in her mind clicked. The appearance of Martin and Woodward had caused her to completely forget about the promethazine that she had stirred into Jessie's milk when he had been gone. Momentarily ignoring her husband and Woodward, Arielle scrambled to the front of the cell. To be safe, she poked the man's arm with a finger through the bars, prepared to scoot back toward the safety of her piss bucket should he awake.

He didn't.

Moving quickly, not knowing how long the effects of the promethazine overdose would last in someone of Jessie's stature, she snatched the keys from his belt and immediately set about opening the rusted lock on her cell door that looked like it had been stolen from the 1850s.

It took three tries, and once she almost dropped the keys, but Arielle eventually made it out of the cell. Hovering over Jessie, she hesitated, turning back to look at the litany of bodies strewn both inside and outside of her cell, her *room*.

Her eyes eventually fell on Martin's flaccid face.

"I'll come back for you," she promised. "After I save Hope, I'll save you, too."

After all the pain she had gone through to protect both Hope and Martin, her efforts had been a complete and utter failure.

But she *could* still save them.

Filius obcisor. Filia obcisor.

She could save her boy and her girl.

A moan fluttered down the hallway, and Arielle turned away from the cell and shuffled toward the sound.

I'll save you both. Nobody fucks with Arielle Reigns.

Chapter 50

Arielle stumbled down the hallway, careful to keep her fingers at least brushing against the dewy brick wall to maintain her bearings. As she moved through the damp space, memories started flooding back — twisted memories that were threatening to split her mind into two.

There was the time when she'd first arrived, before she had left to have sex with Martin. Back then, the house had been gray, but clean.

Normal.

But then there was the other time, toward the end of her nine-month stay, when whatever was in the milk had started to lose its potency, or when she had built up a tolerance. That was when things had started to change, and the veneer of fake reality that she had erected in her sick mind had started to peel and curl like wallpaper heated with a hair dryer. Desperate minds can conjure desperate images, shards of fake reality needed to keep one sane, to help facilitate the cognizant dissonance that was required when replying to an ad that promised a one hundred percent success rate.

And there had been no one more desperate than Arielle Reigns.

It was the latter reality that Arielle experienced now; a dim, dark dungeon of a hallway, wet and moist like the intestines of some rocky beast.

'Help me.'

She couldn't remember if it had been Jamie or Joan—JJ, as it were—who had said it, but they too had seen the cracks. And they'd wanted out.

'This is an evil place.' These were words spoken in hushed whispers, forever nervous that the ears sprouting on the damp walls would relay their conversation to Mother.

'Don't drink the milk!'

Arielle paused halfway down the hallway and shook her head, trying to force away the memories that she'd so desperately wanted to remember a few months ago. Now was not the time; now these recollections would only hinder her progress, her ability to find Hope. Her memories were something she would have to come to terms with later.

Just not now.

Not when Hope was still missing.

Turning back, she saw Jessie still slumped against the wall, the backs of his massive hands resting on his thigh, his open palms pointed upward in a gesture that could only be one of two things: a desperate man seeking salvation—*filius obcisor!*—or one that had lost all motor function.

Another scream echoed down the hallway, and Arielle realized that she wasn't far from the source.

Two more steps and a flash of light struck her from the cell on her left. The change in illumination was so extreme that it took several moments for her eyes to adjust.

And when they did, Arielle wished that the hallway had remained bathed in darkness.

"No," she moaned, bringing her hands to cover her mouth.

The first thing she saw in the cell was Melissa, the thick woman who had delivered a beautiful if tiny baby girl when Arielle had first arrived. Only she wasn't thick now, she was *enormous*. Flopped in a giant wheelchair, Melissa was completely nude, her giant body spilling over in rolls and rolls of excess skin and fat. Even though her face was partly obscured by a clear mask of some sort that was hooked up to two dull silver tanks behind her, Arielle knew this woman was Melissa. She could see the scar, identical to her own, making a line down her massive stomach, following the contours of her flabby gut like a twisted snake.

The woman's eyes were barely open, just a sliver of white peeking out from between thick lids. Her stomach rose and fell with every shallow breath, which was accompanied by a click and the sound of hissing air that temporarily fogged the mask.

Arielle realized that she was shaking her head back and forth like a petulant child, but she was helpless to stop. It wasn't even the sight of her obese friend, nude, hooked up to some sort of breathing apparatus—as horrible as that was—that sent her tumbling over the edge.

It was her breasts. Her giant, pale breasts, completely covered in a network of dark blue veins, rested on her distended gut like overfilled water balloons. Affixed to each nipple was a suction cup. And with every breath that Melissa took, the suction cups on her breasts contracted, pulling her dark, nearly purple nipples into the cone, filling the space, and a thick squirt of milk was drawn from each. Arielle watched in pure horror as the white liquid traveled the length of long, winding tubes to a vat just behind the wheelchair.

'Don't drink the milk.'

Arielle gagged and spat on the floor.

The milk; this was where they got the milk from. The milk— the milk that she'd been forced to drink each and every day, milk imbued with whatever drugs that Melissa was forced to inhale. Milk that had made her fat, had made them all fat. Milk that made her see things, that altered her reality.

Movement from the corner of her eye drew her attention from the horrible scene.

There was someone else in the cell with Melissa.

At first, she didn't even recognize that the figure was human, what with his long, spindly limbs and stooped neck.

Like Melissa, the tall man was completely nude, but that was where the similarities ended. The man was thin bordering on emaciated, all sinewy muscle fibers acting as bone coatings rather than having any functional purpose. His head was buried in the bright bare bulbs that lined the ceiling, causing her vision to halo, and nearly blinding her. Blinking repeatedly, her eyes traveled down his body, passing a thick patch of dark hair on his concave chest. When her eyes reached his penis, a thin, dark appendage that ended in a swollen, bulbous head just above his knee, Arielle gagged again and pulled herself even farther away from the cage.

Somewhere in the dark recesses of her mind she knew that she should flee this place, that she should just run and find Hope and then get the fuck out of here. But she couldn't; she was hypnotized by the tall figure's strange, ratcheting movements as he paced across the cell.

She watched as the stick figure made his way over to Melissa and then slowly bent down, something that must have been incredibly uncomfortable given his immense height. Arielle wasn't sure, but she thought this man might even be taller than Jessie.

As he bent, vertebrae jutted from the thin skin on his back like plates on some sort of pale, prehistoric dinosaur. And then he did the unbelievable: he pulled one of the suction cups off Melissa's nipple and leaned over and started to suckle.

Melissa's head tilted backward, and Arielle thought the woman moaned into her mask, the fog clinging to the clear plastic for just a few seconds longer than usual.

This time when Arielle gagged, bile filled her throat, and she could no longer keep it down. Like battery acid, fluid filled her cheeks and Arielle spat it to the wet ground at her feet, her eyes bulging with the force behind it. Then she puked again. And a third time. Her guts were contorting at the sight of the milk—the sickly sweet milk—at the man's horrible penis, and at him suckling on Melissa's purple nipple.

When her stomach was completely void of anything—food, water, bile—Arielle wiped her eyes and then her mouth with the back of her hand.

At some point when she'd been vomiting, the man had pulled away from Melissa's breast and was now staring at her, his lips but thin lines stretching the width of his face. He had sunken eyes and a huge, beak-like nose that cast shadows over the rest of his features.

A dribble of milk spilled from his bottom lip, and a thick, pointed tongue darted out, lapping it up before retracting into his mouth.

"You shouldn't have come here." The man's voice was a mere whisper, but it seemed to reverberate in her head, causing her molars to vibrate and her vision to bounce. "A deal is a deal. A life for a life. *Filius obcisor. Filia obcisor.*"

Arielle screamed again.

Chapter 51

When she finally stopped screaming, the sound carried on in an extended echo. After nearly a minute, Arielle realized that the sound she heard was no longer her own. The other person's screams from down the hall had also reached a crescendo.

Arielle stumbled away from Melissa and the thin man and continued down the tunnel, her stomach lurching. Her hand was firmly pressed against the wall now, her fingers making clear smudges in the sticky, wet substance that seemed to cover nearly everything in this dungeon.

Her legs were weak, her head light. It felt as if she hadn't eaten in months.

She wasn't sure how much more she could handle. As Arielle neared the next cell, she had to force herself to look.

Please be empty, please be empty.

But it wasn't.

There was a woman in the next cell, a thick woman who was asleep on her back, a soiled sheet only covering part of her naked body. It was cool in the basement passages of 8181 Coverfeld Ave, but the woman on the gurney appeared clammy and sweaty. One thing became clear as the woman's cheek twitched: this was not the source of the screams. This was just a woman, a woman like she had been: a desperate woman who wanted a child.

The screams were originating from somewhere farther along, and for some reason, Arielle knew that finding the source would also mean finding Hope.

She forced herself onward.

The next room was much larger than the others, and was much better stocked. Instead of a piss bucket and a soiled cot, there were several silver gurneys littered with glinting tools and kidney-shaped dishes.

It was an operating room. And in this room, Arielle finally found where the screams were coming from.

As expected, they were coming from Mother, but not for any reason that Arielle would have predicted.

The woman, all one hundred pounds of her, was propped atop a metal table at the back of the room, her feet jammed into bloody stirrups.

She was in labor.

Arielle blinked hard, trying to force what must be an illusion first from her eyes and then her mind.

Mother was old, *really* old; there was no way she could be giving birth.

But she was, and the baby was crowning before her eyes.

Arielle felt her stomach lurch again as she stared at the woman's naked, leathery legs hoisted up into the stirrups, and then the dark patch of blond hair atop the baby's head as it made its way out of the birth canal.

When Mother screamed again and her knotted, arthritic fingers grasped the handles on either side of the bed, Arielle looked away from the abomination between her legs and focused on the woman's face.

It wasn't the face she remembered; it was different somehow. With every moan or contraction or scream, Mother's face seemed to shimmer, like a serene pond disturbed by a wayward stone. With every bellow of pain, her features distorted — the heavy blue eye makeup, the pale pink lips, and the wisps of gray and white hair all faded, making them somehow less *real*.

Arielle stumbled backward until her tailbone jarred harshly against the wall.

The baby was coming—it was coming *now*.

And it was coming out of *Mother*.

That was when she first noticed the female figure, the one lying flat on her back, completely nude, not unlike the woman on the cot in the room adjacent.

Except this woman wasn't sweating—she was pale and dry. And there was an incision that ran the length of her abdomen, a thin line of dark red blood that stood out starkly on her pale, doughy flesh. Just seeing that incision made Arielle grab at her own stomach and scratch the network of fibrous tissue that sealed what had once been home to her daughter.

Hope.

Thoughts of her daughter and her blond hair, her long, swaying braid, brought her back to the present.

"Hope."

The word unexpectedly came out of her mouth, and Arielle immediately brought both hands up to cover her lips, to try to reel it back in.

It was too late.

Mother had heard, and her eyes shot up.

"Filius obcisor," the woman said, her lips returning to the soft pink that Arielle recognized.

Then Mother's face contorted into a scream as at that moment the baby unceremoniously fell out of her in a dark, slimy, and wriggling mass.

Mother groaned once, long and loud, and then she was racked by a momentous shudder, during which the woman's appearance flickered, shifting from the pale-lipped, blue-eyed old woman to something else. To something darker, something burnt.

Something unholy.

Then her image solidified and she grabbed the now crying baby and brought it to her face. When she opened her mouth, Arielle thought for a brief, horrible moment that the woman was going to bite down on the child and devour it.

She feared that the demon before her was going to consume the baby.

But Mother didn't; instead, she closed her lips on the baby's nose and sucked, drawing some horribly thick fluid into her mouth. Then Mother spat the wad onto the floor and the child immediately started to wail.

Arielle didn't want to watch anymore—she knew now that Mother was putting on a show for her—but she couldn't help herself. She needed to know.

Mother cut the umbilical cord next, even going as far as to tie it in a knot first. Then she hopped down off the metal bed as if she had just had her teeth whitened instead of giving birth.

With screaming baby in hand, she walked over to the anesthetized woman on the other hospital gurney and began driving her long, thin fingers into the line of blood on her stomach.

She can't—she can't be putting the baby in there?

But when the flaps of thick, fatty skin were pulled back, Arielle realized that that was exactly what Mother was doing.

Arielle Reigns collapsed to the floor.

Chapter 52

Melissa returned less than an hour later, slumped forward in a wheelchair, her damp, stringy hair covering most of her face.

Arielle could barely make out her eyes, but she saw enough to know that they were only partly open. She would have thought the woman dead, save for the shallow breaths that sent the tendrils of hair stirring in front of her mouth.

Jessie was pushing Melissa into the room, parading her about without shame. Showing off what was a massive baby bump.

Did she have that before? She'd always been big, but had she been that... pronounced?

Arielle couldn't remember. Even events of a few hours ago were cloudy.

But something wasn't quite right with this scene—something was off. A few seconds later, Arielle realized exactly what was wrong.

It was Melissa's gown: it wasn't naturally a dark crimson as she had first thought, but white—at least it had been white, originally.

"Mother said she is ready," Jessie said, a strange giddiness in his voice. "Almost ready for baby."

Arielle ignored the lumbering giant and instead focused on Melissa.

Was she okay? Where is this blood coming from?

The woman moaned then, startling Arielle out of her concentration.

The gown definitely had been white, which was obvious by the upper half, the frayed ends of the sleeves, the collar. But most of it was red now.

When Jessie turned the wheelchair, Arielle cried out.

Melissa was dripping; blood was pooling beside her on the over-sized wheelchair, and had just started spilling over. It was only a trickle at first, but it soon became a steady stream.

So much blood, Arielle thought, watching the wheelchair tires spin in the tacky substance, leaving a strange crisscross pattern.

"She's bleeding! Jessie, get her out of here!"

But Jessie didn't listen. Instead, he spun her around once more.

"Mother says she's ready," he repeated.

"She's bleeding!" Arielle screeched. She tried to bring herself to her feet, but her legs were tingling and numb.

And sleepy. She was so sleepy.

Why did I drink that damn milk again?

She tried to stand again, but her legs felt like cinderblocks. Instead, Arielle resigned herself to reaching out ineffectually for Melissa, whose entire body had started to shake.

Her hand missed and Arielle collapsed back down on the bed, her lids so heavy that she couldn't keep them open any longer.

As sleep took hold, she heard the sound of the rusty wheelchair leave her room, followed by Jessie's voice.

Or maybe it was Mother's.

Arielle didn't know.

"It'll be your turn soon, Arielle. Your turn to have a baby. A life for a life."

And then she heard the baby crying. It was a muffled sound, as if the baby were trapped beneath a blanket or maybe a wet washcloth.

Arielle smiled.

Baby; I'm going to have a baby soon.

Chapter 53

Arielle awoke to the sound of children giggling.

"Hope? Hope!"

She tried to sit up, but her limbs felt like dead weight and she couldn't move them.

"Hope?" Arielle opened her eyes wide, feeling her lids separate as some tacky substance slowly relinquished its hold.

Blood? Is it blood?

Then she remembered seeing Mother giving birth and the other—she cringed—the other woman... the one with the cut in her stomach.

Oh God.

Arielle managed to move her arms, and her hands found their way to her stomach where they probed the scar through her clothing.

No. It can't be. Not my Hope. She's mine, she came out of me.

"Hope?" She whispered the name this time, trying to shake the cobwebs from her head.

Arielle was in the operating room, but she was not alone. Mother was there, and someone had wheeled Melissa in to join her. The woman with the baby that had been transplanted inside her—*oh dear Jesus*—was gone.

"You," Arielle spat, her eyes burning a hole in Mother. The woman was slick with sweat, her gray hair sticking to her face and scalp. Thankfully, she had put on some clothes—a dark robe that covered her almost to her wrinkled knees.

"Me," Mother admitted. And then she tilted her heard back and laughed.

The reason for her awakening—children laughing—came back to her, and Arielle looked around the room, frantically trying to locate her daughter.

Eventually she found her.

Hope was in the operating room, as were the other girls, all standing in a row by the back wall, their heads bowed. They looked as if they could be quadruplets, even though Arielle knew that their ages spanned more than seven or eight years. And all their cute little blond heads of hair were pointed toward her.

"Hope?" Arielle said again, trying not to let fear creep into her voice. Her eyes focused on the girl at the end, the smallest of the group. That one was Hope; like any mother, she just knew it.

Upon hearing her name for the fourth or fifth time, Hope started to raise her head, but Mother let out a hiss/whistle sound, and the little girl quickly bowed her head again.

"Hope!" Arielle cried. She tried to swing her legs off the gurney, but they still felt too weak to actually support her. She turned to Mother. "What have you done to my daughter?"

Mother laughed again. It was a horrible sound, a grating noise that sent a chill up and down Arielle's spine.

"Your daughter? *Your* daughter? Oh, sweet child, these" — she made an expansive gesture in the girls' direction—"these are not your children. They are *my* children. *Mine.* You were only borrowing little Hope."

The woman laughed a third time, and all Arielle could do was stare at her in shock.

Mine. My children.

"Hope—what an ironic name."

Arielle shook her head.

No.

"Hope is mine," Arielle swore through gritted teeth.

Gathering all of her strength, she swung her legs over the side of the gurney.

It was then that she realized she was no longer wearing her clothes. Instead, someone had changed her into some sort of white gown.

What the fuck?

"No, sweetie, she isn't. She's mine. They are all mine. And she will stay with me—help me with my work. A life for a life, remember? *Filius obcisor.* This is a place of death and life, a facilitator of both ends of that spectrum. It has been called many things: the Burning House, and long before that *fons vitae;* the Fountain of Life. The name changes with the times, my sweets, but it is *always*—it is perpetual. Like me. Like Mother."

The woman smiled and Arielle balled her fists.

Fuck you. Hope is my daughter.

"What did you think by coming here? That you think you would just collect your daughter and leave? Do you not remember your agreement, my sweet, pretty thing? Hmm?"

"Fuck the deal, she's mine. And I'm gonna take her with me."

Mother made a *tsk, tsk, tsk* sound.

Arielle dangled her legs down over the gurney and was about to hop off when Mother made the whistle/hiss noise and she hesitated.

"Not so fast," the woman warned.

One of the larger girls stepped behind Hope and wrapped her arms around her in a tight bear hug. It was clear that this was no affectionate embrace even before another girl—Hanna, Arielle thought—reached up and grabbed a handful of Hope's blond hair and pulled it back, revealing the soft, pale skin of her throat.

Arielle gasped.

Then the third girl—the Frisbee girl, little Madison—walked over and grabbed a scalpel from a blood-soaked metal dish. Following a nod from Mother, Madison went back to Hope and held the blade against her throat. It was all so robotic, so *rehearsed* that Arielle felt as if she were watching some sort of demented play.

"You see, my pretty girl," Mother began, "none of these children are your daughter. They are all mine. And like good little girls, they listen to their *Mother*."

"Please," Arielle stammered, her eyes watering. "Don't hurt her."

Mother shook her head, her sweaty gray hair swaying slowly, collectively, like a school of fish.

"Oh, I don't want to hurt *any* of my children. But if you don't give me what I want, you will leave me with no choice."

What do you want? You have Hope... what else could you want?

"Ah, pretty girl, I see the confusion on your face." Mother chuckled. "You don't get it, do you? Look around."

She gestured toward Melissa. One of her painted eyebrows rose up her forehead.

"No? Still nothing?"

Arielle shook her head.

What is she talking about? She has Hope and the other girls... what else does she want?

A smirk passed over Mother's pale pink lips.

"It's not about the children, my pretty young woman, it's about you—it's about the mothers."

As if on cue, Melissa, her massive head still tilted backward in her chair as if her eyes were locked on to the ceiling, wheeled herself toward Arielle. It was such a disgusting sight, what with her massive, sweaty breasts and equally large stomach coming toward her, that Arielle nearly hopped off the gurney despite Mother's warning.

"Every mother also has a role to play in this circle of life, my sweets." She raised a thin hand, once again indicating Melissa, "And some are better suited for some things than others. You, pretty thing, are perfect for me. After all"—she tugged at the dark robe that clung to her wasted frame—"this *body* is almost drained."

Arielle started to sob, her mind near shattering.

Me? She wants me?

Mother slowly made her way over to Arielle, passing in front of the girls that still held the blade to Hope's exposed throat.

Arielle was helplessly torn; she knew that if she tried to rescue Hope or resist Mother, the girls would kill her daughter. But what Mother was suggesting was… well, she didn't quite know how to interpret that.

In the end, she made the only decision that she could.

She did nothing.

"I need your body," Mother whispered now, her voice almost seductive. She approached to within a few feet of Arielle, bringing with her a stink of rot and something akin to singed meat. "Your daughter will be freed, if you give me what I want."

Arielle felt Mother's cold, clammy fingers gently brush her forehead, and she slowly eased back into a lying position.

"And if you don't, Jessie will make you anyway."

That smile; that smile with the perfectly white teeth.

Arielle looked past her trembling daughter to the hulking, shadowy figure in the doorway of the bastardized operating room.

Jessie was back.

Arielle's eyes drifted back to poor Hope, her large blue eyes watering so much that she might have thought she was drowning.

"Now, sweet child, have some milk. Give in. Drink, sweetie, drink your milk. Driiiink."

Melissa wheeled even closer to her, and Mother began fiddling with the hose that was attached to her massively engorged breast. She pulled a mask from somewhere behind the woman's wheelchair and affixed it to the end of the tube that had once filled the vat. Then she slowly lowered the mask over Arielle's face.

She didn't want the milk—the sheer thought of it made her want to vomit—but Arielle she saw no other choice. Give this *demon* what she wanted and Hope would be set free. Give her—

Somewhere far away, she heard Melissa moan, and then milk started to slowly trickle down the sides of the mask and into her mouth.

"That's it," Mother whispered in her soothing voice, "drink up. It will all be over soon. A life for a life. All those years ago, you thought you could just get away with what you did, but I was there. I was watching." The woman's eyes rolled back and her voice suddenly changed; it became younger—spritely, even. "You can't have it! You need to get it out! A life for a life. You must never forget."

Arielle's vision blurred. In her mind, she was transported back to a bathtub, a bathtub full of rose-colored water, her mother using a sponge to clean her back.

The demon's voice switched back.

"And now I'm here to collect... only I don't want Hope, I want *you*."

The first few drops of the sickly sweet liquid stung like acid when they hit Arielle's throat.

Tired, so tired. It will all be over soon.

Arielle's eyes closed, and they seemed to take forever before opening again. When they did, everything was slightly out of focus, as if she was wearing reading glasses.

Mother was beside the gurney, her legs spread at an awkward angle as if she were giving birth again. She was trembling, too, wet hair flicking back and forth, speckling the metal table with her sweat. A foul-looking substance akin to smoke, only thicker, wafted from beneath the woman's dark robe and twisted upward, coming toward Arielle like an ethereal hand.

Mother moaned, a shuddering sound that might have been of pain or could have equally been of pleasure.

The dark cloud drifted upward, reaching the edge of the gurney before spilling—*crawling*—over it, coming dangerously close to Arielle's bare leg.

The effects of the milk started to overwhelm over. All she wanted to do was sleep, to just forget this entire mess and wake up beside Martin, tucked into his big arms, with Hope sleeping soundly in the next room. Back in Batesburg, dreaming of meeting up with the Woodwards and a play date with little Thomas.

Sleep didn't take her just yet. Instead, Arielle's eyes flicked open one last time, and she saw that Mother had once again changed.

The woman with the pink lips, leathery skin, and bright blue eyeshadow was gone.

In Mother's place was a blackened, hunched creature with large, white eyes and a red slit for a mouth that ran nearly from ear to ear. Strips of dead flesh flaked off of its body like rotting mummy wrappings with every trembling movement, and there were two holes in its face where its nose should have been. As Arielle watched, the burned creature crouched, its limbs akimbo. The only thing that remained of Mother were the turquoise stones that hung from its long, stretched earlobes — stones that took Arielle back to her time in the church — a lifetime ago.

Filius obcisor.

Arielle would have screamed, but the mask and the milk that dripped from it prevented any sound from coming out of her mouth.

Instead, she drank.

Chapter 54

Martin's eyes snapped open and he gasped for air. His whole world was spinning as if he were trapped on a carnival teacup ride that *just... wouldn't... stop.*

Where am I?

Somewhere far away he could feel his body, but it was an abstract notion, something separated not only by significant distance but also by time.

He squeezed his eyes closed again, trying his best to stop this nightmare. And it worked... sort of; the spinning slowed, but the nightmare remained. As his senses returned, the first thing he felt was something cold and clammy. It was his cheek—his cheek was pressed against something cool and wet.

Martin's eyelids fluttered involuntarily and he thought he might lose consciousness again. Thankfully, the tremor was transient and after only a few seconds his vision slowly began to focus.

As did his mind.

Woodward.

The image of his friend falling to the muddy ground, the beam of light from the flashlight reflecting off his open eye, blood dripping from his nose filled him.

With great effort and considerable pain, Martin manage to hoist himself to a seated position.

He was in a cell of some sort, some archaic cold, gray cell complete with a soiled cot that was pushed against the back wall. There was a stack of papers on top of the cot and a metal bucket lying beside it.

Jail? Am I in some sort of jail?

His eyes fell on Woodward's body next, and all other rational thought fled him.

"Woodward!" he hissed, scrambling across the damp floor to his friend who was lying on his back, his face turned away from him.

Martin reached his friend and gently turned his head toward him.

"No," he moaned.

Woodward's eyes were still rolled back in their sockets, revealing only the whites, and when he turned the man's head, the blood that had pooled in his mouth spilled out like vomit.

Martin didn't need to put his fingers on the man's pale neck to know that he was dead.

But he did it anyway.

And then he laid his head on the man's barrel chest and began to sob.

Fuck me. It's my fault... he shouldn't even be here.

Fuck me.

Martin pulled his head away from Woodward and sat up, wiping the tears from his eyes.

"I'm sorry," he whispered. "I'm so sorry."

Through watery eyes, Martin quickly scanned the rest of the room, noting that although the front of the cell was composed of metal bars, the door was open.

That was something.

He could leave. Unlike Woodward, he could leave.

Fuck.

Fury building inside him, Martin searched the rest of the room, looking for something—*anything*—he might be able to use as a weapon should Jessie return. His eyes drifted to the metal bucket, but it was cheap and flimsy and wouldn't serve to squish a cockroach, let alone brain a giant.

Then his eyes fell on the bed.

It was the simplest of cots, just four metal brackets arranged in a rectangle with a shit-stained mattress laid over top.

Martin scrambled over to the bed, wincing at the pain that radiated from his chest and shoulders. A cough overtook him, and he had to pause to collect himself. He was lucky to be alive—Jessie had nearly crushed him to death.

When the pain numbed, he continued to the bed, moving more slowly now, deliberately, trying to avoid the brunt of the pain in his chest. With a grunt, he yanked the mattress off the metal cot, gulping air with his mouth to avoid experiencing the brunt of the smell of human feces that wafted toward him.

Beneath the mattress was a series of metal coils pushed through holes in the frame. He easily pulled these out of one side, then set about unscrewing the long side of the bed closest him from the short head piece.

There were only two screws holding the pieces together, and only by two loose nuts. But it was hard going nonetheless, given the state of his burnt fingers; his fingertips were slick with burst blisters, and his ability for small manipulations had been lost.

But Martin eventually managed, and when he was done, he was left with half a bed, complete with the coils still attached, along with two freed pieces of metal. The one that had once made up the long end of the cot was too long to wield, but the other...

Martin picked up the four foot piece of metal and waved it back and forth with one hand. It fit well enough in his palm, but it was heavy. Still, with two hands he thought he might be able to swing it in a nasty arc. Or jab — he could jab with it like a spear.

Whether it would be sufficient to take out Jessie Radcliffe, he wasn't sure. But Woodward's gun was still in the mud outside by the — *burnt woman with the white eyes* — tree, and somewhere in this dungeon Arielle and Hope needed him.

It would have to do.

Metal bar in hand, Martin slowly made his way toward the open cell door, trying his best not to focus on his friend's flaccid body that lay in the center of the room. He would come back for him; if he got through this, he would come back for his friend's body.

The hallway outside the cell extended in both directions. On his left there was a door not ten paces from where he stood, an exterior door, while to his right he could make out more dimly lit cells.

A scream echoed up the corridor, drawing his gaze in that direction. It wasn't Arielle who had made that scream, but for some reason he knew that following that sound would lead him to her.

Moving slowly, gripping the piece of metal so tightly in his left hand that more blisters on his palm popped, Martin made his way toward the scream.

A tall, thin man paced nude in the second cell that Martin passed. The man was but a collection of spindle-like bones patched together with barely enough skin to cover them all. He was a hideous sight, one that churned Martin's stomach. Grimacing, he tried to avert his eyes, to sneak by without being noticed, but as he turned, the metal rod in his hand slipped.

No!

Somehow he managed to catch the metal piece before it fell completely, but he wasn't fast enough to stop the pointed end from clanking noisily off the hard ground.

The man in the cell turned toward the sound, and with two large, ungainly steps he was suddenly at the front of the cage. He wrapped his huge hands around the bars, squeezing them, twisting them with fingers that seemed too long, and then he finagled his way down to Martin's level, pressing his pointed face between them.

"Help me," the man moaned. "Please, help me… let me out of here."

His face was covered in sores, his cheeks and lips oozing either blood or pus or some other substance that Martin refused to consider.

Martin instinctively stepped away from the cage, retreating until he felt the cold wall against his back.

The index finger of the man's right hand unfurled from the cell bar, an impossibly long process, and he aimed it at the rusted wooden lock that hung from the latch.

"Do you have the key?" his voice was excited, almost giddy. A long, pointed tongue darted from between his thin lips and licked at them hungrily, sucking up some of the fluid from the burst sores. "Can you open it? Can you *open* it?"

Martin didn't answer the man right away. Instead, his mind was transported back to Jennifer's apartment before the fire started — back to her story of Anne LaForet.

A name came to him, and for some reason he felt compelled to utter it out loud.

"Benjamin," Martin said, his voice oddly detached. "Benjamin Heath."

The man's finger retracted as if it had been singed. Then his mouth, a horrible slit of a thing, broke into a smile, more of the sores cracking and oozing.

"She's gonna get you, Mother is gonna get you and make you like me... like *meeeeee*! She's gonna make you *burn*."

The sound was piercing, grating, and when the man started to shout—"He's here! He's here!"—Martin scrambled away from the cell and continued down the hallway, dragging the metal rod with him.

He passed another cell, then another, Benjamin Heath's words chasing him like a foul smell.

When Martin made it to the fourth cell, he saw her and stopped dead.

Arielle was lying on a metal gurney, her face covered in some sort of mask. Her hair was different—it was dark and cropped short—but he *knew* it was her; it had been more than four years since he had laid eyes on his wife, but he *knew* it was her. And his heart immediately filled with sadness, for her, for him, for the time they had lost.

Forcing these feelings away, Martin tried to get a better look at her body, to make sure she was okay, but there was someone blocking his line of sight. A tall figure, one not unlike the freak whose cell he had just run away from.

It was Jessie.

Martin took a step toward the open cell door, and then stopped cold.

As he passed out of Jessie's shadow, he came to the horrible realization that Arielle wasn't alone on top of the gurney.

There was something else with her—*on* her.

A figure was mounting her—a blackened, burnt figure.

And Martin immediately recognized what it was.

Its name was Anne LaForet or Jane Heath or... it didn't matter what you called it; it was one thing.

It was *Mother*.

And on *Mother's* back, just above where her hip bone was buried in that crispy, black flesh, were the letters *BH*, and they were glowing a deep, scarlet red.

It was the brand that Benjamin Heath had used to mark Anne LaForet after raping her all those centuries ago.

BH. A brand; a marking, something to let others know that he had filled this woman with his foul seed.

Chapter 55

There was too much blood—the entire bathtub was filled with it. The thick substance had started to coagulate, making it difficult for Arielle to even raise her arms. It clung to her swollen belly like taffy; it dripped from her breasts; it turned her hands a deep scarlet.

It was on her lips, nose, mouth, in her throat—it tasted like old, rusted pennies. Her eyelids stuck together.

So much blood, everywhere.

"You need to get it out!" she heard her mother's voice shout from somewhere behind her.

It.

Like the fetus inside her was a wine stain on a summer dress.

Get it out.

"Please," came a voice as Arielle felt her lips move, "please don't make me, Mommy."

But the deed had already been done, and she would have to live with the pain and anguish that came with it.

A life for a life.

Something buried in the blood bumped into her leg, something hard. She moved her hand through the thick fluid like a fly through amber.

The object was round, or at least mostly round.

What is it?

With great effort, Arielle brought the thing out of the blood. As tendrils of the red liquid dripped slowly off of the object, revealing its soft pink form, a scream caught in her throat.

It was a small baby, not much heavier than a pound, a baby that she could easily hold in both hands, and perhaps even one.

"No!" she screamed. "No!"

As the blood cleared from the baby's face, she felt a sharp, involuntary intake of air.

It was Hope, complete with patches of blond hair on her premature head. It had a face—it couldn't possibly have a face this well developed, but it did. It had a face, and it was Hope's face.

"No!"

Chapter 56

"No!"

Arielle tore the mask from her mouth, spraying milk all over her face and hair. She gagged and spat up the thick, offending substance that clogged her throat and windpipe, threatening to drown her.

Blinking the tacky liquid from her eyes, she was shocked to find that Mother had mounted her.

But it wasn't Mother anymore.

It was that *thing*, the thing with the white eyes, the one with the slit of a mouth with crispy hunks of flesh for lips that looked like singed hamburger.

So lost in whatever ecstasy it was experiencing, the beast didn't immediately notice that Arielle was awake.

But the girls did; the four of them with their blond braids had abandoned the knife and had all gathered around the metal gurney upon which she lay, their heads bowed, their eyes looking up at her.

They shouldn't witness this.

"Hope! Get out of here, Hope!"

The smallest girl's head popped up, and Arielle stared into her daughter's wet eyes for the first time in what felt like forever.

Hope. I don't care what this demon says, you are mine. You are my daughter and I am your mother.

It doesn't matter if she birthed you and put you inside me. I am still your mother. This beast—this beast is not your mother.

Arielle reached up and grabbed the creature by the throat. The thing gasped, and the white orbs that were its eyes lowered and focused on Arielle.

"You can't have her or me, you vile piece of shit!"

In one smooth motion, Arielle swept the thing over, surprised at how light it was in her arms. And then she was on top of it, her left hand still clutching its throat as tightly as she could manage.

Arielle felt a tingling sensation in her crotch, and glanced down just in time to see the black cloud exiting from beneath her gown and receding back up the demon's dark robe. The sight—the *thought*—of that foul substance inside of her only made Arielle tighten her grip.

The creature was gasping now, and Arielle realized that the milk-mask had wrapped itself around the side of the gurney. A quick glance over at Melissa and she realized that the fat woman's head had finally flopped forward and her wide eyes were staring at Arielle in fear, disgust, or both. The woman's sausage-like hands tried to wheel away from the gurney when their eyes met, but the mask was still attached to her breast and would not let go.

The girls, all four of them, were staring up at Arielle, the expression in their eyes matching that of Melissa's. They knew what she was going to do, but were helpless to prevent it.

Welcome to the club.

Arielle reached over and grabbed the mask with her left hand and unwrapped it from the gurney, all the while keeping the writhing creature pinned with her right. Then she reeled back, intent on smashing the mask into what had been Mother's face, when Hope spoke and she hesitated.

"Don't hurt her, Mommy." The girl's voice was light and airy, as if she were partly asleep.

Wait, what did she say?

It had sounded like, 'Don't hurt her, Mommy,' but when Hope repeated the words again, they were different.

"Don't hurt Mommy."

Arielle snarled.

"I am your mother," she spat, and then forced the mask down on the demon's face.

Milk immediately sprayed from the mask with such ferocity that even Melissa called out in pain.

"Drown, you fucking bitch!"

And indeed Mother was drowning in the thick, sweet liquid that flooded her slit of a mouth and pinprick nostrils. The thing gulped and writhed, but with Arielle mounting her, no matter how much the demon thrashed its head, it was unable to wriggle free of the mask.

Until, that is, Arielle felt two large hands grip her shoulders.

Jessie! I forgot about Jessie!

Arielle froze, unsure of what to do next.

This is it. This is how I die. And Hope is lost forever.

The creature beneath her finally wriggled free of the milk mask and sputtered and coughed.

And then it started to laugh.

It was fucking *laughing*.

Arielle tensed, but the grip on her shoulders matched her movement. They were so strong, those hands, so impossibly strong, that they seemed to force her shoulder blades together until they were nearly touching. Another ounce of pressure and she feared that her arms would snap out of their respective sockets.

Tears slipped out of her eyes and dripped onto the thing below her. One landed near its mouth, and its leathery, pointed tongue darted out to quickly lap it up.

"You can't kill me," the thing rasped. "You can't kill me be-cause I am your mother!" Then the laughing resumed.

The grip on Arielle began to tighten, like a ratchet or a vice slowly crushing her, causing pain to radiate from her shoulders all the way down to the ends of her ribs.

Her world was fading fast, and the last thing she was going to see was this maniacal demon beneath her, moments before it possessed her body.

No, this can't be the last thing I see.

She tried to turn her neck, to find Hope, but the grip tight-ened and a jolt of pain coursed through her entire body. But she wouldn't let this stop her. She kept turning her head, even as Jessie squeezed again and again, until she thought that with her arms folded behind her as they were, her ribcage would ex-plode out the front, showering the beast beneath her in blood and gore.

Good, she thought, *let this body be ruined... I will not let the demon have this vessel.*

She finally found Hope with the other girls, having at some point during the struggle receded to a corner of the room. The four of them looked different now; whereas before they had looked angry, now they were just scared. They looked like four normal young girls again, all falling between four and eight years of age, all with wide, wet eyes and long blond braids.

They all looked like they had seen a ghost.

As Arielle's world faded, a smile crossed her lips.

I love you, Hope. I love you.

A split second before Arielle succumbed to unconscious-ness, something happened.

Chapter 57

Martin watched frozen in horror as Arielle suddenly seemed to animate, and then in one fluid motion, his wife flipped the charbroiled corpse over and straddled *her*. His mind was a mess, trying to make sense of the shit he had seen over the past twelve hours. And it caused him to lock up, to not be able to move. It was as if his spinal cord had been severed, the signals screaming at his arms and legs—*Move! Move, goddamn it!*— never reaching their source.

But then the monster that was Jessie Radcliffe stepped forward, and his massive hands grasped Arielle by the shoulders. This act sent his mind into a panic, as twice now he had felt the strength of that grip—once around his throat and once around his shoulders. He didn't need to hear his wife gasp in pain to know that she was being crushed.

Move!

And this time he did.

Martin slid into the cell, stepping directly behind the towering figure, his eyes desperately searching Jessie's flannel shirt. Somewhere far away he could hear the demon sputtering on the table and Arielle wheezing, trying to take a deep breath, but he ignored it; he couldn't rush this.

His aim had to be perfect. Martin had one shot—missing would not only mean that Arielle be crushed, but that he would be next.

He let a breath out when his eyes fell on the spot he was looking for: a dot of blood just below Jessie's left shoulder blade where Woodward's bullet had passed through him.

Shuffling to one side, Martin gripped the bed frame in both hands, gritted his teeth and lunged.

The end of the four foot piece of metal slid directly into the bullet hole on Jessie's back. And this time, unlike when the bullet had struck and then passed through him, the hulking man made a noise, a grunt of sorts. But despite this outward expression of pain, he didn't let go of Arielle as Martin had hoped.

Instead, his grip seemed to tighten.

"No!" Martin screamed, knowing that it would only be moments before Arielle's chest exploded.

Keeping the section of bed frame firmly planted in the bullet hole, he moved to his left, twisting the other end so that the metal was aimed more towards the center of Jessie's body.

And then he took a step forward, driving the metal deeper into the man's chest cavity.

There was a popping sound, and from the side Martin saw Jessie's mouth go slack. Although this time the man's grip seemed to loosen, and he heard Arielle finally take that deep breath, Jessie didn't let go.

"Let her *go!*" Martin screamed.

He planted his back foot on the ground, and for once the mud that covered his shoes seemed a blessing as it helped root him in place. Exhausted, Martin prepared himself for one last heave.

"Let her go!"

And then he pushed, driving the metal deeper into Jessie's chest.

Where Jessie's heart was.

Should be—where his heart *should* be—if indeed he had one.

For a brief second, time seemed to freeze; even the demon on the gurney stopped thrashing and laughing.

And then there was a gaseous release as something inside Jessie gave way. Martin stumbled forward as the metal seemed to now nearly effortlessly slide through the rest of his body. It must have exited the other side as when Jessie finally hit the ground, a metal clang preceded the organic thump.

Martin's momentum kept him moving forward and he toppled on top of Jessie's body.

A thick black substance like warm oil, bubbled and then veritably poured from the hole in Jessie's back, coating Martin's hands and wrists. He instinctively yanked his arms away and rolled off to one side. And then he looked up, searching for his wife again, hoping that he had killed Jessie before she had literally been torn apart.

Relief washed over him when his eyes met Arielle's.

And his wife was smiling. Her lips were partly open, her breathing ragged, but she was *smiling*.

Chapter 58

The man that stared up at Arielle was older than she remembered, with deep lines around his eyes and mouth, and the familiar graying at his temples had spread to the top of his head.

It was Martin, and the sight of him after so long caused her to smile—she couldn't help it.

"No!" Someone screamed, and for once, Arielle was surprised that it wasn't her that uttered that fateful word.

This time, it was Mother.

Arielle turned back to the creature beneath her, her smirk immediately becoming a grimace. Her fingers reached for the thing's blackened throat and she raised the mask high above her head with her other hand.

"No! No, no, *no!*"

Mother's white eyes seemed to grow wider, until Arielle thought they might spill out, land on the floor and roll around like a child's toy.

A child.

Her child.

Hope.

Arielle pictured herself lying in the rosy pink bathwater all those years ago, and tears began to spill down her cheeks.

"A life for a life, you motherfucker!" Arielle screamed, and then she brought the mask down again, showering them both in a spray of sweet, tangy milk.

Chapter 59

When it was over, when the demon on the table stopped thrashing beneath Arielle, Martin felt all of his energy seep out of him like a thin liquid.

It felt as if it had been days since he had last slept.

But there was still one more thing he had to do—one more act before he would allow sleep to take him.

Grunting, Martin pushed himself to his feet, doing his best to wipe the black muck from his arms on his jeans as he stood.

Then he made his way to his wife, helping her off the gurney all the while trying not to look at the burnt creature on the table.

Arielle felt light in his arms despite his aching muscles.

He carefully lowered her to the ground, and then collapsed beside her.

On the floor of the cell beneath 8181 Coverfeld Ave, Martin wrapped his arms around his wife and hugged her tightly. Both of them were crying.

Death was everywhere in this place. On the gurney, the demon that Arielle had murdered, and on the floor, the demented monster of a man that Martin had skewered with the bed frame, and Woodward—*poor Woodward*—lying dead in another cell. The place reeked of death.

And it was quiet, which felt strange to Martin, given the screaming that had echoed throughout the humid dungeon mere moments ago.

But this silence was short lived—no more than thirty seconds later a voice cut through the gloom.

"Mommy?"

There was death here, but there was also life.

Arielle pulled her head out of her husband's shirt and looked up with rheumy eyes. Martin followed her gaze and his eyes fell on a cute girl with blond, almost white hair and big blue eyes who stepped out of the shadows.

Hope.

Arielle opened her arms and the girl's slow, hesitant pace changed; she started to run and then she buried herself in her mother's arms.

Martin reached around and hugged the two of them, tears streaming down his face now.

Hope.

He sniffed and wiped his tears away.

There were other girls in the room, Martin soon realized, three other young girls that looked exactly like Hope.

'...she sought out all the children she had helped conceive and forced them back to her home where she intended to raise them as her own.'

Arielle leaned back, gesturing for the other girls to join them. But then Hope whimpered, and she quickly embraced her daughter again. As she did, the back of her gown teased upward slightly, and Martin caught sight of something on her lower back.

What is that?

Martin squeezed around Hope to get a better look.

It was something red, like marker—some sort of design.

A tattoo, maybe? Did Arielle get a tattoo?

Squinting hard, he struggled to make out exactly what it was.

The closest girl reached them then, and Arielle leaned forward even farther, affording Martin a better view.

And his heart nearly stopped.

It wasn't a tattoo; it was too red and swollen to be that. And it wasn't a design either.

It was letters; two of them.

BH.

Benjamin Heath.

It was a brand.

Martin began to weep. As he sobbed, he subconsciously reached into his pocket and dug around, hoping that after everything that had happened it was still there.

The other three girls had squatted beside them now, and Arielle was struggling to embrace all of them—Hope, the three girls and Martin—at the same time.

Martin's blistered fingers finally wrapped around something small and hard. He pulled his hand out of his pocket and held his palm flat to Arielle.

For a second, a look of confusion crossed his wife's face, but then she smiled and reached out to grab the small, turquoise stone from Martin's open palm.

Filia obcisor, filius obcisor.

She brought the rock to eye level, letting the bright light above them reflect off its smooth, oblong surface.

Then she surprised him by pitching it over her shoulder, where it skittered across the hard floor before disappearing out of sight.

"I don't need that anymore," Arielle said, her smile growing.

Mater est, matrem omnium, Martin thought, tears streaming down his face. *Mother of one, mother of all.*

"I'm Mother, now."

Epilogue (Postpartum)

"This is stupid," Gerry said, leaning back in his seat like an obstinate child.

"You said that already. What are you even doing here, anyway? She said to come alone."

"Oh, yeah right, Cindy—I should listen to a crazy woman on the phone telling you to wander into Shitsville alone. Sounds just peachy to me." Gerry rolled his eyes and sank even farther into his seat.

"You shouldn't swear like that, Ger. I told you before, when we have kids, you can't swear like that."

"Well, we don't—we don't have kids." When Cindy's face twisted, Gerry softened his position. "Yet. We don't have them yet."

But the damage was done.

Gerry let the issue rest for a few minutes as they drove through the small, meandering swamp road. When Cindy slowed to a stop by a small, nearly hidden drive, he finally spoke again.

"I'm sorry, Cindy. I am. I'm just… confused as to why we are here. You heard the doctor. The chances are low for us—because, well, you know why. And he said the best thing we can do is just keep trying."

Cindy nodded, still clearly upset.

"So, I'm just confused. I didn't mean to be mean."

Cindy nodded again. Then she turned to face him, and he realized that her cheeks were wet.

Shit.

"So what's the harm, then, Gerry? What's the harm in coming here and giving it a shot?"

That was a can of worms that Gerry wanted to keep firmly closed. The last thing he wanted to do was upset his wife even more than he already had.

"Okay," he agreed. "Let's just take everything the woman says with a grain of salt. Okay?"

Cindy nodded and even attempted a smile.

A small smile.

A tiny smile.

"Grain of salt," she sniffed. "Promise."

They were barely out of the car when they saw her. A pretty woman in her mid- to late-fifties, with wavy blond hair billowing about her shoulders.

She was smiling, the corners of her pale pink lips lilting upward ever so slightly.

Not bad, Gerry thought with a nod, unable to help himself. He quickly glanced over to Cindy guiltily, but her attention was also rapt by the woman that approached. *Not bad at all. Maybe this wasn't the worst idea in the world.*

"Cindy, right?" the woman asked. Her voice was velvety smooth.

Cindy nodded.

"How did you know —?"

The woman shrugged this off.

"A mother just knows things. Come, come up onto my porch and sit for a minute."

Cindy smiled.

"Okay."

Gerry took a step forward, but the woman held up her hand, stopping him in his tracks.

"Not you, you stay here."

The smile stayed, but there was an authority in her voice that hadn't been there before. An authority that suggested that he should oblige.

Gerry sulked and wiped the sweat from his forehead.

Fucking too hot to be in the sun anyway.

"I'll be in the car, Cin. Holler if you need me. I'll be right here — very close — in the car."

He squinted at the woman, but she turned back to Cindy without acknowledging either his expression or his words.

Cindy didn't turn either. Instead, she allowed this stranger to hook arms with her and lead her toward the porch in the distance.

"What's your name?" Gerry heard Cindy ask as he pulled the car door open again. "What should we call you?"

Gerry sat in the car, but waited for a response before slamming the door closed.

"Oh, sweetie, you can just call me Mother."

END

Author's note

I hope you enjoyed 'MOTHER'. I had a blast writing it, and *some* of it is very pertinent to me as my wife and I are expecting our third in just a few short weeks. And, no, my wife is not allowed to read this book until after the birth.

Father, Book 2 in the *Family Values Trilogy* is out now! If you want to keep reading about the demon in the swamp, about *mater est, matrum omnium*, grab your copy today. Still need convincing? Check out the sneak peek right after this note. And keep your eyes peeled for Book 3, *Daughter*, out Spring 2017.

If you want to keep up to date about sales and new releases you can "like" me on Facebook (@authorpatricklogan) or, better still, sign-up to my newsletter at www.PTLBooks.com. I promise not to spam you.

As a final note, if you enjoyed this book, please make sure to leave a review where you bought it. **REVIEWS** are critically important for me to keep telling stories. Good, bad, or ugly, they all count.

Thank you for your support,

Patrick

Montreal, 2016

47358274R00182

Made in the USA
Middletown, DE
22 August 2017